DEAD AND BURIED

Daisy hoped Owen wasn't going to be blamed for whatever disaster had overtaken the azaleas and the irises. The poor boy was unhappy enough already.

Returning to the statue, she realized the sun was just right for the pose she wanted. "I'm going to fetch my camera," she said to the head gardener. "If Mr. Goodman comes, tell him I'll be back in a jiffy."

"Right, miss. What is it, lad?"

"There's something in the way, Mr. Bligh. 'Bout a foot and a half down. Like a mass of roots it feels."

"Try the fork, but go at it easy-like. Don't want to do any more damage."

Daisy left them to the new puzzle and sped back to the house. She had already put a fresh roll of film in the camera. Returning laden with equipment through the Long Hall, she met Ben Goodman on his way to rejoin her.

"You won't mind if I dash ahead?" she said. "I have to hurry to catch the light."

He nodded. "I'll follow at my own pace."

When she reached the Winter Garden, she was surprised to see that Owen had dug a trench right across the bare patch of soil. He and Mr. Bligh stood at one end, gazing down with fascinated revulsion.

"Go on, have a look," urged Mr. Bligh.

Owen knelt in the dirt. Reaching down, he moved something at the bottom of the trench.

"Oh, God! Oh, God!" He flung himself backwards onto his heels, his arms across his face. "It's her. It's my Grace!"

Daisy Dalrymple Mysteries by Carola Dunn

Published by Kensington Publishing Corporation

THE WINTER GARDEN MYSTERY

A Daisy Dalrymple Mystery

CAROLA DUNN

KENSINGTON BOOKS
Kensington Publishing Corp.
http://www.kensingtonbooks.com

KENSINGTON BOOKS are published by

Kensington Publishing Corp.
850 Third Avenue
New York, NY 10022

All Kensington titles, imprints and distributed lines are available at special quantity discounts for bulk purchases for sales promotion, premiums, fund-raising, educational, or institutional use.

Special book excerpts or customized printings can also be created to fit specific needs. For details, write or phone the office of the Kensington Special Sales Manager: Kensington Publishing Corp., 850 Third Avenue, New York, NY 10022. Attn. Special Sales Department. Phone: 1-800-221-2647.

Kensington and the K logo Reg. U.S. Pat. & TM Off.

ISBN-13: 978-0-7582-2733-1
ISBN-10: 0-7582-2733-1

First Mass Market Paperback Printing: March 2001
10 9 8 7 6 5 4

Printer in the United States of America

PROLOGUE

The night was mild for the time of year. The half-moon—shining at intervals between drifting clouds—provided all the light needed. The earth was friable, easily turned.

Nonetheless, the digger sighed with relief when the last spadeful was replaced. Smooth the footprints; out through the door in the wall and close it silently; latch it tight lest a ghost should follow.

Too late for regrets.

1

The elderly, silver-grey Swift two-seater clattered and coughed to a halt. For a moment, the Honourable Phillip Petrie sat at the wheel with his sleek fair head cocked in frowning concentration. Was that a new rattle he'd heard? His fingers itched to investigate under the bonnet, but Daisy had a train to catch.

He transferred his frown to the narrow, white-stuccoed house beyond the iron railing on the other side of the pavement. Whatever Daisy said, it bally well wasn't right for two girls to set up house together—especially in Bohemian Chelsea—and work for their livings when they both had homes and families to take them in. If only her brother had inherited Fairacres and the viscountcy instead of being blown to kingdom come at Ypres. . . .

But it was 1923; Gervaise was more than five years gone. No sense dwelling on past horrors. Phillip extricated his long legs from beneath the steering wheel, loped up the short garden path between leafless bushes and clumps of snowdrops and aconites, and rang the doorbell.

Lucy Fotheringay opened the door. Tall, with a fashionably boyish figure, dark, bobbed hair, and amber eyes, she regarded him as usual with an air of faint amusement. He found her rather daunting, though he'd have died sooner than admit it.

"Hullo, Phillip. Come in. Daisy's just putting on her coat.

These are her traps." Lucy waved at a pile of luggage stacked near the door.

"Right-oh, I'll start loading up the old bus."

"Careful with my camera." She went to the steep staircase at the back of the tiny hall and called up it, "Daisy, Phillip's here."

"Good egg! I'll be down in half a mo."

He stowed a shabby portmanteau and a heavy Gladstone bag in the boot and returned to the house as Daisy came down the stairs.

Above neat ankles in the latest flesh-coloured stockings, her dark green tweed coat failed to entirely subdue unfashionable curves. An emerald green cloche hat with a dashing bow over one ear crowned a cheerful, roundish face, with guileless, smiling blue eyes. Her mouth, no pursed Cupid's bow, was lipstick red; the freckles Phillip recalled from childhood were hidden by a dusting of face-powder; but she was still the same good old Daisy. Nothing daunting about *her*.

"What-ho, old dear."

"Hullo, Phil. It's topping of you to give me a lift." She picked up the camera in its leather case. "Will you grab the typewriter? It's supposed to be portable but it weighs a ton."

"Right-oh. And the tripod. Is that the lot?"

"That's it." She turned to Lucy, kissing the air beside her in the peculiar way women had—to avoid smudging their lipstick, Phillip supposed. "Toodle-oo, darling."

"Pip-pip, Daisy darling. I hope Occles Hall is worthy of your pen, but have a spiffing time anyway."

They went out to the street and he put the typewriter and tripod in the dickey. As he opened the door for Daisy, she said, "Don't buzz along too fast, now, Phil, or my hat will blow off. It doesn't pull down properly however low I knot my hair."

"I could put the hood up if you like."

"No, don't. It's too deliciously mild for February."

Sliding in behind the wheel, Phillip glanced at the rolls of honey brown hair on the nape of her neck. "Why don't you have it bobbed?"

"I should. Keeping it long is just a last-ditch attempt to try to please Mother," she admitted ruefully.

"Going to live with her at the Dower House would please her."

"And drive me potty! Don't let's quarrel about that again."

"Sorry, old bean." He pressed the self-starter, cocking an ear as the aging engine rattled to life. No new vibrations, he decided, half disappointed. Messing about with machinery was one of the joys of life. He let in the clutch and the Swift moved smoothly away from the kerb.

"How is business in the City?"

"Fair to middling." He hurriedly dismissed the disagreeable subject. "Tell me about this place you're going to write about."

"Occles Hall, in Cheshire. It's one of those Tudor black and white manors, frightfully picturesque."

"Who lives there?"

"I wangled an invitation from a girl I was at school with, Bobbie Parslow, one of those hearty hockey girls. Her father's a baronet and her mother's Lord Delamare's sister."

"Not Lady Valeria Parslow!"

"Yes, do you know her?"

"Not personally, but my mother had a bit of a set-to with her on the Riviera a couple of winters ago—some rot about bookings for a suite with a balcony—and you know what a peaceable sort the mater is. If I'm not mistaken, Lady Valeria won."

"Probably. I've heard she's a bit of a battle-axe. Tommy and Madge Pearson met her in Cannes last year. Her son was with her, a rather spectacularly beautiful young man, Madge said, but they didn't mingle much. She kept him on a short leash, and Tommy thought she was afraid of him finding himself a wife and escaping her clutches."

"It sounds like a pretty ghastly household. Do you really have to go, old bean?" Phillip asked plaintively.

"I do. My editor at *Town and Country* is panting for another article. The Wentwater Court one was quite a hit, you know, even though I couldn't write about all the exciting things that happened there."

He groaned. "Don't remind me! And now you're off to stay with another bunch of queer birds."

"Only for a few days," said Daisy, with her usual blithe optimism. But her voice was tinged with regret as she added, "Don't worry, old thing, lightning never strikes twice in the same place."

Arriving at Euston Station, Phillip bagged a porter and they plunged into the grimy, bustling cavern. He stood with Daisy in the line at the ticket window and was aghast to hear her requesting a second-class ticket.

"Here, I say, dash it," he protested, pulling out his wallet, "you can't go second-class." And despite her objections, he paid the difference for a first-class ticket. He'd have to lunch at a Lyons Corner House instead of the Piccadilly Grill, but Gervaise would have expected it of him. Let her travel second and there was no knowing what sort of queer fish she'd end up talking to. Daisy had no proper sense of her own position.

The porter bringing up the rear, they headed for her platform.

"Miss Dalrymple!"

At the sound of her name, Daisy's face brightened. She swung round, smiling. "Mr. Fletcher! Phillip, you remember Detective Chief Inspector Fletcher."

Phillip scowled. He recalled the policeman all too well, recalled being interrogated at Wentwater and the baleful black brows over grey eyes that could pierce a fellow through and through, however innocent. *And* make one feel like a callow fool. What the deuce was the blighter doing here now?

Admittedly he looked quite gentlemanly, in a dark lounge suit, overcoat, and soft felt hat not unlike Phillip's own. But after all, the fellow was nothing more than a glorified copper in mufti. He had no business making up to the Honourable Daisy Dalrymple, nor she to be so pleased to see him. That was what came of letting respectable females mess about with writing and such tommy rot!

He nodded coldly.

The detective's mouth took on a sardonic twist and he turned back to Daisy. "I'm glad I caught you. I have to dash, but I've brought you this for the journey." He handed over a modest box of chocolates.

"Alec . . . Mr. Fletcher, how too sweet of you! I shall make a pig of myself and they'll all be gone long before I change at Crewe."

Alec, indeed! In stern silence Phillip marched Daisy to her train, refusing to dignify the bounder's infernal cheek by any remonstrance.

"Buck up," said Daisy with a sunny smile, leaning out of the window. "On that subject Lucy would agree with you, but you must admit it might come in handy one day to have a policeman on one's side. Thanks for the lift, old dear. Cheerio!"

"Cheerio," Phillip echoed glumly.

Perched beside the weatherbeaten driver on the box of the station fly, Daisy could see over the bare hedges to the greening meadows of the Cheshire plain on either side of the lane. Fat, contented cows grazed on the new grass. Here and there in the distance, the towers of village churches stuck up from clumps of trees. Despite the grey sky, the air had a springlike softness, and celandines gleamed gold along the hedgerows.

The placid nag clopped onwards without much attention from its owner. Ted Roper, as he had introduced himself, was fully occupied in telling her all about his family. He was particularly proud of his eldest grandson, who had learned to drive "one o' they motor-lorries" and regularly hauled goods from Manchester to London.

Daisy was not surprised to find herself the recipient of a stranger's confidences. For some reason she had yet to fathom, people had a tendency to tell her all about themselves. While dispensing the appropriate murmurs of admiration or sympathy, she stored up details in her mind against the day when she'd find time to sit down and write a novel.

All, she felt, was grist to a novelist's mill.

The lane curled around a leafless spinney and suddenly a village street stretched before them.

"Occleswich," said Ted Roper. "See them chimblypots sticking up, up the top o' the hill? 'Tis Occles Hall."

The hill was a gentle slope, the most this part of Cheshire could provide. On either side of the rising street, identical white picket fences surrounded identical lawns and flowerbeds in front of identical half-timbered cottages, in pairs. All was neat: snowdrops in bloom and daffodil spikes protruding through the weed-free soil; black-painted beams unfaded against the white walls; sparkling diamond-paned windows; slate roofs without a hint of moss or lichen. Even the chimneys, as if well trained, all emitted the same straight plume of blue-grey smoke into the still air.

"Oh, please stop, Mr. Roper," Daisy cried. "Would you mind waiting for just a few minutes while I take some photographs? This will make a perfect picture and who knows, it may rain the rest of my time here."

"Whoa, Hotspur!" His inaccurately named nag obligingly halted. "Take as long as you like, miss. This here's what they calls a model village," he informed her. "Hundred, hundred and fifty years past, the lord o' the manor had the owld village pulled down and this un built in its place."

"Yes, I've seen one like it in Dorset," Daisy said, climbing down and reaching for camera and tripod, "but this is even prettier. So well kept!"

"Good job you didn't see Occleswich afore Lady Valeria come to the Hall. 'Twere she brung money to the Parslows. Proper run-down they was, Hall and village both, and family, too, come to think on." Ted Roper laughed heartily, then sobered. "Not that I've a word to say 'gainst Sir Reginald, mind. A proper gentleman, he is, though hen-pecked something fierce. It's her ladyship wears the trousers."

"And it was Lady Valeria set the Hall and the village to rights?" Daisy enquired as she fixed the camera to the tripod. The pinkish sandstone church halfway up would make a good focal point for the picture, she decided, shifting her apparatus to the other side of the street.

"Aye, set 'em to rights, she did. They's her la'ship's pride and joy, after young Master Sebastian, that is, and she makes sure the tenants keep the place just the way she likes it. Nary a cabbage nor a Brussels sprout dares show its head in the front gardens. There's nobbut one man in the village'll cross her, any more'n her family do."

"Who is that?"

"You'll see when we get there, miss," said Ted Roper cryptically. "Can't miss it, you can't."

Daisy took several shots of the scene. After the Wentwater Court photos had turned out so admirably she was more confident of her ability, but it was just as well to be sure. Satisfied, she stowed the things in the trap and nimbly mounted to the box once more. The horse set off again without waiting for Ted Roper's lazy flick of the reins.

Just beyond the church, on the opposite side of the street, stood a building in the same style as the cottages but somewhat larger. A sign above the door announced it to be "The Cheshire Cheese Inn." Daisy laughed at the painting, which depicted a large, orange cheese with a mouse peeking from a hole in its side at a grinning cat.

"Fred Chiver, the innkeeper, wanted to change the name to Cheshire Cat," her driver revealed, "but her la'ship put her foot down, Cheese being the historical name, seemingly. That there picture's near as he could get. Painted by a Welsh artist chap as stayed a few days a while back."

"I like it." Daisy noticed an old man drowsing on a bench

by the door, an equally somnolent dog at his feet, and she realized he was the first person she had seen in Occleswich. "Where is everyone?" she asked.

"Over to Whitbury, miss. 'Tis market day. Most o' the women take the early bus in to do their shopping. And the childer's in school, over yon behind St. Dunstan's, next the vicarage." As he gestured, he glanced back at the church clock. "They'll be out any minute, and the motor-bus from Whitbury's about due. Me and Hotspur's out of date, and that's a fact," he added sadly. " 'Tis her la'ship keeps us going, for she don't like to see any motors in Occleswich saving her own. Spoils the view. The bus has to stop down bottom."

"It certainly sounds as if Lady Valeria is accustomed to having her own way!" Daisy exclaimed.

"Oh, aye, that she be," agreed Ted Roper.

Beyond the Cheshire Cheese, the street curved to the right. Curlicued lettering over one cottage's door proclaimed: *"Village Store & Post Office,"* and a sign in the next-door window: "POLICE" Between them a fingerpost pointed along a gravel path to the Village Hall behind, hidden by a hedge. That appeared to be the entire extent of the commercial and social centre of Occleswich.

A hundred yards farther on, the street ended in a T-junction. On the far side of the crossroad, a high wall of the same pinkish stone as the church barred the way ahead. As Hotspur plodded patiently up the slope, Daisy saw a white wicket-gate in the wall.

"Where is the main gate?"

"Turn right and another quarter mile or thereabouts."

She glanced to the right—and gasped in astonishment. "My sainted aunt, what a simply frightful eyesore!"

The last cottage in the street was the village smithy, with living quarters beside and above the forge. Instead of a front lawn and flowerbeds, it had a paved yard. And the yard overflowed with heaps of rusting metal. Bent horseshoes and ploughshares, broken bedsteads, old-fashioned kitchen stoves and boilers, and countless bits of the bodies and innards of deceased motor-cars were precariously stacked higher than the sills of the grimy windows.

"Stan Moss, the blacksmith, he wanted to put in a petrol pump," said Ted Roper, grinning. "Her la'ship wouldn't hear of it, acourse. Spoil the pictureskew charicter o' the village, it would. Well, Stan do hold a powerful grudge. 'Tis a mite tidier round back, where he works. Nobbut a mite, mind."

"I'd have thought Lady Valeria would have forty fits. She lets him get away with that mess?"

"Not for want o' trying. Two year, now, they been battling. She brung in outsiders to clear it, but he chased 'em off. So she brung 'em back, and a couple o' coppers, too, when he was away to Nantwich. Well, blow me down if he didn't come back wi' a new load o' scrap, just like as if he guessed what she'd be up to."

"Irresistible force and immovable object," Daisy observed.

"No one don't move Stan," Ted Roper agreed. "Always was a cantankersome bloke, and young Gracie running off ain't sweetened his temper so's you'd notice. He lost her pay and his housekeeper all in one."

"Gracie?"

"His daughter. Went off wi' one o' they commercial travelers, couple o' months past. Mind you, there's not many as blames her. A pretty girl as liked a bit o' fun, and her drudging for Stan on her day off from parlour-maiding up the Hall, and him taking every penny o' her wages off of her. Oh lor', here come her la'ship. We best be on our way."

As he urged Hotspur to a trot, turning the corner, Daisy looked back to see a commanding figure emerging through the wicket-gate, followed by a liver and white pointer. Dressed in brown tweeds and a mannish slouch hat with a pheasant feather, Lady Valeria carried a hefty blackthorn walking-stick, brass-knobbed.

Glancing neither to left nor right, she marched across the

road, picked her way between Stanley Moss's scrapheaps, and beat a thunderous tattoo on the door with her stick.

Trees hid the forge from Daisy, but above the sound of Hotspur's hooves she heard two irate voices raised in furious altercation.

"At it again," grunted Ted.

Her first glimpse of Lady Valeria was not promising. When, a few minutes later, the lodgekeeper swung open the wrought-iron gates of Occles Hall, Daisy passed between them with considerable misgiving.

2

The east front of Occles Hall was utterly spiffing. The black-painted timbering was laid out in chevrons, hexagons, lozenges, rosettes, scallops—surely more decorative than structural. Each of the three storeys protruded a little above the one below. In the centre, a two-storey gatehouse stood out from the façade, its ground floor an open archway topped by a massive beam, warped with age. A flat stone bridge led to it over the remains of the old moat, a placid sheet of water in which the whole edifice was spectacularly reflected.

Daisy decided with regret that the late afternoon light was too poor for photography. In fact, a few stray drops of rain were just beginning to dimple the moat, so that the reflection wavered. However difficult Lady Valeria proved, she was jolly well going to stay on until she got some really good shots.

Ted Roper drove over the bridge and under the archway. With what sounded very like a sigh of relief, Hotspur came to a halt in the middle of a tunnel dimly lit from either end by rapidly fading daylight.

Peering about, Daisy saw a massive, iron-studded double door in the nearest wall. Lucy's precious camera slung over her shoulder, she clambered down and went over to the door. She was faced by an old-fashioned bellpull and a heavy iron knocker in the form of a snarling mastiff's head. Experience had taught her that old-fashioned bellpulls not infrequently attempted to pull one's arm out of its socket. She dared the mastiff and beat a resounding *rat-tat.*

She powdered her nose while Ted unloaded her bags into a neat pile beside her. Still no sign of life from the house. She paid him and was about to ask him to try the bell for her when at last the door opened, with a positively Gothic groan.

The butler was a gaunt, stoop-shouldered individual with lank, thinning grey hair, who looked as if he had just put his last half-crown on a non-starter at Goodwood. "Miss Dalrymple?" he enquired in a despairing voice.

"Yes, I'm Miss Dalrymple," said Daisy firmly, and stepped across the threshold into a small, paneled room lit by gas.

"I'm Moody, miss. Please to come this way."

Following him at a grave pace through a series of similar rooms, she hoped he had good moods as well as bad ones.

They emerged into yet another paneled room, but this one was long, though low-ceilinged, with a row of windows all along the opposite wall. What with rain, dusk, and the tiny diamond panes, Daisy could not see out. She looked around instead. The other three walls had numerous doors and the beginnings of at least three staircases, with portraits in elaborate gilt frames hanging in between. The only furniture consisted of several ancient chairs with backs so elaborately carved they must be excruciating to sit on.

"The Long Hall, miss," said Moody gloomily, "and this is Mrs. Twitchell, who will show you to your room."

The housekeeper, a cheerful middle-aged woman in a grey dress with white collar and cuffs, was a pleasant change from the regrettable butler. She chatted as she led Daisy up one of the narrow staircases, enclosed in the ubiquitous paneling.

"Miss Roberta'll be that sorry not to be here to welcome you, Miss Dalrymple. She went out riding after lunch and likely went farther than she meant to. It's getting dark, though, besides the rain. Not that rain ever stopped Miss Roberta, but she'll be back for her tea."

They continued round corners, up steps and down, through galleries and endless chains of rooms small and large, some paneled, some whitewashed. The Tudor builders appeared never to have heard of corridors, and to have made their ceilings whatever height they fancied without regard to the resultant varying levels of the floor above. There was even a step up to the door of Daisy's room when they reached it at last.

"I'll never find my way back!"

"You'll soon get the hang of it, miss. Here's Gregg, her ladyship's maid, to give you a hand. She'll show you to the Yellow Parlour for tea when you're ready."

Gregg, a sturdy, stolid countrywoman, had already un-packed Daisy's portmanteau, which had been in some magical fashion spirited up to her room ahead of her. She offered to iron Daisy's best evening gown, of rose pink charmeuse. Under the influence of Daisy's particular magic, she even roused herself to remark that it would be a pleasure.

"Being as her ladyship don't care about fashion and what I mostly do for Miss Roberta is get the mud off of her riding breeches and golfing stockings," she explained.

Remembering Bobbie at school, Daisy was not surprised.

She washed the railway grime from face and hands at the china bowl on the washstand in the corner of the small room, then renewed powder and lipstick. Tidying her hair, she pushed the hairpins in more firmly. Perhaps she *would* get a bob, or even go straight for the new shingle-cut, she mused. Lucy was always ragging her about it, and Mother already had so many causes for complaint, one more would not hurt her.

Her pale blue jersey jumper suit was presentable if not precisely elegant, a bit short for the latest near ankle-length hemlines. But after all, she wanted to appear professional, not glamorous. She announced herself ready to be escorted to the Yellow Parlour.

Two gentlemen rose to their feet when Daisy entered the room. She had eyes only for one. Madge's description of Sebastian Parslow as a beautiful young man had not prepared her for the reality.

In his early twenties, he was tall, broad of shoulder, slim of hip, and long of leg. He had thick, wavy hair of the purest corn gold. His eyes were cobalt blue with miraculously dark lashes; his nose and mouth were chiselled perfection; his chin was square and very slightly cleft. An English Adonis!

Daisy wished she'd changed into her amber chiffon tea-gown.

"Miss Dalrymple? How do you do. I'm Sebastian Parslow." His voice was a resonant baritone, and he moved with an athlete's light grace as he crossed the room to meet her, apparently oblivious of her stunned admiration. "I'm sorry the rest of the family is not here to greet you. This is Ben Goodman."

"Sir Reginald's secretary." The voice was light and dry. "How do you do, Miss Dalrymple."

Daisy wrenched her gaze from Adonis to the slight, dark gentleman beyond him. She appreciated both Mr. Parslow's delicacy in not announcing Ben Goodman's subservient position and his own in making it plain. He looked to be in his mid-forties. His thin, pale face was the sort that in a woman might be called *jolie laide,* plain to the point of ugliness, yet with a curious appeal.

"How do you do, Mr. Goodman." She offered her hand.

He limped as he came forward to shake it. She immediately knocked ten years off his probable age and inserted a war wound in his curriculum vitae. His warm smile confirmed his attractiveness, crinkling the corners of his eyes and deepening the lines by his mouth.

"I expect you're ready for your tea after that endless journey," he said. "I told Moody to bring it as soon as you came down."

"I could do with a cup, though the trek wasn't really too frightful." Thanks to a first-class ticket and a box of chocolates. "At least I didn't have to change at Birmingham, only at Crewe. I enjoyed the drive from the station. Ted Roper told me all about Occleswich."

A shadow of embarrassment crossed Mr. Parslow's faultless features. "The Daimler should have been sent to meet you," he said apologetically, "or at least the Morris, but. . . ."

"Daisy!" Bobbie Parslow burst into the room and slung a hard hat onto the nearest chair. She was dressed in a damp hacking-jacket and breeches, and her boots left muddy tracks as she strode across the carpet. "It's simply topping to see you." She wrung Daisy's hand.

Miss Roberta Parslow was obviously Sebastian's sister, but in her case nothing was quite right. The height and broad shoulders so impressive in a man were out of place in a woman, and her figure was robust, in contrast to his elegance. Her hair, straw to his gold, was cut in a very short bob as straight as a horse's tail. Her square face was a blurred copy of his, as if a painter had laid a portrait wrong side down before it dried, and her eyes were pale blue, with invisible lashes.

But she was undoubtedly delighted to see Daisy.

"I'm frightfully sorry to be so late," she said. "I was heading for the station, so as to ride home beside the trap, but Ranee cast a shoe. Have you met Mummy yet?"

"Not yet," Daisy told her, "though I saw. . . ." She stopped as a parlourmaid brought in the tea.

"Oh good!" Bobbie exclaimed. "Will you pour, Ben? I'm ravenous and I always spill the beastly stuff anyway. Have a sandwich." She offered Daisy the plate, helped herself to a handful of the tiny, crustless triangles, and dropped into a chair.

Mr. Goodman enquired as to Daisy's preference for milk or lemon, sugar or none, and Sebastian handed her her tea.

"The mater went down to the village to tell Mr. Lake what was wrong with yesterday's sermon," he told his sister. "You know she can never pass the smithy without ticking off Stan Moss, otherwise she'd be back by now. They'll come to blows one of these days. I'm surprised they haven't yet.

"Blast! He'll be in no mood to shoe Ranee for me tomorrow."

"You take your horses to the blacksmith in the village?" Daisy asked.

"Yes. The place is a filthy mess and Moss has a filthy temper, but he's still the best smith around, as well as a genius with machinery. I just wish Mummy hadn't chosen this afternoon to upset him. All the same, I'm glad she's still out," said Bobbie frankly, between mouthfuls of paté sandwich. "I was afraid I wouldn't get home in time to warn you, Daisy."

"Warn me?" Daisy asked with a sinking feeling.

"About Mummy. I say, Ben, is that a Victoria sponge? Cut me a nice big piece, there's a good chap. You see, Daisy, I'm afraid she wasn't frightfully keen on your coming to stay."

"Oh dear, I wish you had let me know. I can't write about Occles Hall without her permission."

"You needn't worry about that," Ben Goodman said with a reassuring smile. "Lady Valeria is delighted that the Hall will receive the public recognition it deserves."

"Then what . . . ?"

"Bobbie made a hash of it." Sebastian pulled a wry face. "She invited you without asking the mater's permission, a cardinal sin."

"Your letter came when Mummy and Sebastian were in Antibes," Bobbie excused herself with an absurdly guilty air. "Writing persuasive letters simply isn't my forte, and I didn't want to ask Ben to do it because he was feeling jolly seedy at the time. It was that beastly damp, cold spell, remember, Ben? You were coughing your lungs out."

Mr. Goodman flushed. "Mustard gas," he explained to Daisy. "I wouldn't want you to think you've been landed in a house with a consumptive."

Daisy nodded, putting as much sympathy into her glance as she could. There was nothing to be said. Since the War, England was full of young men with corroded lungs. Whether they were luckier than those buried in Flanders, like Gervaise and Michael, was a moot point.

"The mater wouldn't take Ben to the Riviera with us," said Sebastian. His lips tightened as if with remembered anger, then he shrugged. "It's useless arguing once she's made up her mind."

"Utterly useless," Bobbie agreed. "That's why I asked Daddy about inviting Daisy rather than risk a flat-out no from Mummy. Daddy thought it was a spiffing idea. Where is he?"

"Sir Reginald hasn't come back from the dairy yet," Mr. Goodman said.

"Poor Daddy. I suppose he's expecting another row now that Daisy's actually arrived."

"I don't want to be a bone of contention." Thoroughly uncomfortable, Daisy wondered if she'd be able to find another house to write about at short notice. If all else failed, she could always appeal to Cousin Edgar and Geraldine. Her old home, Fairacres, was nowhere near as picturesque as Occles Hall, but any port in a storm. Abandoning professionalism, she hurriedly suggested, "Perhaps I'd better leave in the morning."

"No!" All three voices were equally vehement.

"Please stay," Bobbie begged her. "Now Mummy's got her hopes up about seeing the Hall in *Town and Country,* she won't be fit to live with if it doesn't come off. To tell the truth, the real trouble is that she disapproves of girls having jobs—our sort of girls, that is. She thinks you'll give me ideas. But when she sees that one can still be a lady even if one works, perhaps she'll relent and let me do something useful. After all, you're a dashed sight more ladylike than I ever was or will be. Pass the biscuits, Bastie."

Her brother obliged. "Do stay, Miss Dalrymple," he urged. "We have too few visitors."

Uneasily Daisy recalled Tommy Pearson's notion that Lady Valeria was afraid of her son's escaping her apron-strings by marrying. Was that another, unspoken, reason why she objected to Daisy's presence?

Not that Sebastian showed any sign of admiring her, and not that she intended to encourage him if he did, even though he was twice as handsome as Rudolph Valentino, the new American film idol. The wife of Adonis, she suspected, would not lead an easy life, especially with his mother as an enemy.

"Well. . . ."

"I do hope you will stay," said Mr. Goodman with his engaging smile. "I have been delving into the history of Occles Hall for your sake."

"A great concession," Sebastian informed her. "Ben is a Greek scholar to whom English history is all bunkum."

"Hardly!" He laughed. "But I might not have gone so far had Lady Valeria not advised me that she considers enlightening you a part of my duties."

Daisy chuckled. "I can't possibly be responsible for your wasting your time on bunkum for nothing. Besides, I must admit I'd be hard put to it to find another subject for my February article at this late date. I'll stay."

"Good-oh," said Bobbie. "Have another biscuit."

"No thanks. Mr. Goodman, will you give me a potted version of the history now, so I can begin to plan my article?"

"By all means. I can't say the story is precisely enthralling, alas. The Hall was built after the Wars of the Roses, so it missed that excitement. The lords of the manor were always quiet, home-loving, law-abiding squires just sufficiently careful of their tenants' and neighbours' interests not to arouse rural troublemakers. They were far enough from London to avoid political factionalism, far enough from the Border to avoid marauding Scots, even far enough from industrial areas to avoid Luddite rebellions."

"A deuced dull lot," observed Sebastian.

"For the most part," Mr. Goodman agreed. "A moment of glory, if such it can be called, occurred in the Civil War. The squire was a Royalist. Cromwell had more important matters to attend to elsewhere, but a detachment of local Parliamentarians besieged the house. Since the only defenses were the moat and a few muskets, one small cannon quickly put the fear of God—or at least of Roundheads—into the defenders. They wisely surrendered after half a dozen shots."

"A sort of Cavalier equivalent of a 'village-Hampden,' " said Daisy.

Sebastian laughed. "So much for my 'mute, inglorious' ancestors."

Bobbie looked blank. How had she managed to get through her school years without meeting Gray's Elegy, that perennial favourite of English teachers?

"Don't laugh," Mr. Goodman advised Sebastian. "That brief defiance was good for a baronetcy at the Restoration. If they had held out a little longer you might be heir to a barony. More tea, Bobbie?"

"Yes, please. Do stop hogging the cake, Bastie."

Neither Lady Valeria nor Sir Reginald had put in an appearance by the time Bobbie's appetite was satisfied. She heaved herself out of her chair with a sigh of repletion.

"I suppose I'd better change. Come up to my room, Daisy, and we can have a proper confab."

Daisy was amused, though not surprised, to find the walls of Bobbie's bedroom dedicated to sports. Olympic champions such as Constance Jeans, Kitty McKane, and Phyllis Johnson mingled with Bobbie on horseback and in countless team photographs. Bobbie had been in every team at school—golf, tennis, cricket, rowing, swimming—and had captained most of them. Daisy, who had scraped in as twelfth man in the second cricket team in her last year, recalled admiring her enormously.

Noting on the bedside table the issue of *Town and Country* with the Wentwater article, she hoped she had turned the tables somewhat.

She wandered around the room, picking out well-remembered faces in the photos, while Bobbie dismissed the maid and disappeared into the bathroom next door, leaving the door open. Between whale-like splashings, her hopeful voice came to Daisy.

"I know you'll like Daddy. He's a good egg. He'll want to show you his model dairy but he won't be offended if you say no."

"It sounds like an interesting addition to my article. Sir Reginald is personally involved in running it, is he?"

"He spends half his time down there. Three quarters. It's all done frightfully scientifically and he keeps experimenting with new methods. His Cheshire cheeses win prizes at all the shows."

"I must certainly put something in." The poor fish probably used his dairy as a refuge from his wife. From what Daisy had heard, he was as much beneath the cat's paw as his children.

"I think it's fearfully clever of you to write. And you actually get paid for it?" Bobbie sounded full of envy.

"Isn't it marvellous? I tried stenography for a while and hated it, but I positively enjoy writing. Between these articles and a few other bits and pieces, and helping Lucy in her photo studio now and then, I manage to scrape along. I have a little money left me by an aunt, which helps no end. You said you'd like to find a job?"

"Awfully, but I'm no good at anything but horses and games. And I haven't a penny of my own." There came a gurgling splosh and a moment later Bobbie appeared dripping in the doorway, draped in a vast pink towel. "And if I once escaped and something went wrong, I simply couldn't bear to crawl back begging to be taken in."

"I know what you mean. Mother would never let me forget it if I had to go and live with her at the Dower House."

"Your brother died in the War, didn't he?" Bobbie asked gruffly, retreating into the bathroom again.

"Yes, and Father in the 'flu epidemic. My cousin inherited the title and Fairacres. To do him justice, he and Geraldine would gladly give me a home, but they are both fearfully stuffy. Or I could go and live with my sister Violet and her husband, who are dears, and be a useful aunt. I prefer independence, even if it's a bit of a struggle."

Bobbie reappeared, clad this time in pink flannel combinations, her damp hair sticking out in all directions like a haycock. Though large, she was not at all fat. In fact, many a weedy man might have envied her muscular frame. She made Daisy feel fragile and feminine.

"I'm most frightfully glad you came." As she spoke, she pulled on a crêpe-de-Chine petticoat over her more prosaic undies. "I know Sebastian is, too. I could tell he liked you, because he was actually talking. The poor lamb is usually desperately shy with girls."

The gorgeous Sebastian must have been warned against feminine wiles by his mother so often that he was gun-shy, Daisy guessed. "I expect your brother is much pursued," she said tactfully.

"He's pretty stunning, isn't he? I wish I had half his looks." Bobbie stuck her head into the folds of a ghastly olive green silk dress, heavily beaded, and wriggled until it fell into place. It hung on her like a sack. "I expect he would be chased if Mummy ever let him go anywhere."

"I gather he goes to the Riviera."

"In leading-strings. I think she feels she has to take him out and air him every now and then in case people think he's feeble-minded or something. He'd be as bored there as here if it wasn't for the swimming. He swims like a fish. And there's some sort of Roman ruins she lets him potter about."

"Mr. Parslow is interested in Roman ruins?" Daisy asked, startled.

"Well, when he was a schoolboy, he got frightfully enthusiastic about a bit of Roman mosaic that was found in one of Daddy's best hayfields. Mummy insisted on letting him dig up the whole field and he found a couple of coins, though I sometimes wonder if she didn't buy them and plant them for him. They were in awfully good condition.

"Would she do something like that?"

"Oh yes, anything to keep him happy—except letting him go," Bobbie said bitterly. "Anyway, he never found much else, but he never lost interest. Then Ben came to work for Daddy and got Bastie keen on the Greeks."

"Mr. Goodman really is a Greek scholar, then."

"First at Oxford, and he'd be a don if the War hadn't come along and upset things. Of course, he's keener on books and philosophy and all that rot, but he's terribly sweet about humouring Bastie and teaching him about pots and stuff. Mummy bought him a frightfully ancient and expensive amphi-something—amphora?—but he says it's not the same as digging it up yourself."

"I suppose it's impossible to earn a living as an archaeologist," Daisy mused. "The people who go into it all seem to be rich to start with, like Lord Carnarvon, who dug up King Tutankhamun's tomb last year."

"Oh, Sebastian has a goodish pile. Enough to live on, anyway. He inherited from an aunt, like you—she didn't leave me a bean, worse luck."

"And he hasn't buzzed off to Greece?" In her astonishment, Daisy forgot tact.

Bobbie flushed. "You can't blame him for not standing up to Mummy," she said defensively. "Wait till you meet her and you'll understand."

3

"So you're Maud Dalrymple's daughter." Lady Valeria's tone did not suggest she found any cause to congratulate the Dowager Viscountess on her offspring.

Under the critical gaze, Daisy wished she had put on her grey frock with its high neckline and left off her lipstick and face-powder. She wasn't sure the basilisk stare did not penetrate straight through to the frivolous artificial silk cami-knickers she had donned in place of her practical combies.

At least she should have made sure someone else had come down before joining Lady Valeria in the drawing room.

She was a professional woman, not a dependent, she reminded herself sternly, taking a seat on one of the fringed, tasselled, antimacassared Victorian chairs. She had no reason to wither beneath that withering eye. No mere imperious presence swathed in imperial purple could cow her unless she allowed it to. Even a voice horribly reminiscent of her headmistress's was insufficient to reduce Daisy to an erring schoolgirl.

"You know my mother, Lady Valeria?" she asked politely.

"She and I were presented in the same year, though we lost touch long ago. In those days young ladies were properly brought up. Emancipation! We did not know the word. I am shocked that Maud should permit her daughter to seek employment."

"Mother does not control my actions."

"Well, she ought to. Still, Maud never did have any back-bone."

Daisy held on to her temper with an effort. Her mother might be a querulous grumbler with a permanent sense of grievance, but it was not for Lady Valeria to criticize her.

"Mother is quite well," she said through gritted teeth, "considering her circumstances. I shall tell her you enquired after her. I must thank you for inviting me to write about Occles Hall." There, let her stick that in her pipe and smoke it. "Both the house and the village are charming."

Smugness chased censure from Lady Valeria's heavy, high-coloured features. "Everything was in a shocking state when I married Sir Reginald, but I flatter myself you will seldom find another estate so perfectly restored and maintained."

Revenge was irresistible. "Except for the smithy."

Lady Valeria scowled. "You will not write about the smithy," she commanded harshly.

"No, it's not the sort of thing *Town and Country* subscribers want to read about," said Daisy with regret. "I'm sure I'll find heaps to say without it."

"I have ordered Sir Reginald's secretary to give you every assistance. I suppose it will not take you more than a day, two at most, to gather material for your article. Naturally you may ring Mr. Goodman up on the telephone after you return to town, should you have any further questions."

Neatly dished, Daisy had to admit. She had been jolly well and truly given the raspberry. On the other hand, she had abso-bally-lutely no desire to accept Lady Valeria's reluctant hospitality any longer than she needed.

She smiled at her hostess and murmured, "Too kind."

Lady Valeria looked disconcerted. Honours even, thought Daisy, and awaited the next thrust with interest.

She was rescued from the fray, at least temporarily, by the arrival of a small, chubby gentleman in an old-fashioned crimson velvet smoking-jacket.

"Oh, there you are, Reggie," said Lady Valeria. "Why on earth aren't you wearing a dinner-jacket?"

Sir Reginald looked down at himself in vague surprise. "Your pardon, my dear. I was thinking about clover and quite forgot we have a guest." He smiled at Daisy. "Won't you . . . ?"

"What do I pay your valet for?" thundered his wife.

"He has a bad cold," said the baronet placidly. "I sent him back to bed this morning and told him to stay there until he feels better. Won't you . . . ?"

"I have told you before, Reginald, that nothing good ever came of cosseting the servants."

"I'm sure you are right, my dear, but I didn't want to catch his cold and perhaps give it to young Goodman. Now, won't you introduce me to our guest?"

"Miss Dalrymple, my husband, Sir Reginald. Miss Dalrymple is a magazine writer."

"Welcome to Occles Hall, Miss Dalrymple. May I pour you a glass of sherry?" His eyes, as blue as Sebastian's, twinkled mischievously. "I'm afraid we haven't got the ingredients for these American cocktails you modern young ladies favour."

"Thank you, Sir Reginald, I shall be perfectly happy with sherry."

"I should hope so," snorted Lady Valeria, not quite sotto voce.

He poured three glasses of sherry. As he handed Daisy hers, he said, "You are Edward Dalrymple's daughter? I regret to say I didn't know your father well, but he once gave me some sound advice about Holsteins. Very sound. A sad loss to agriculture. You were at school with Bobbie, were you not?"

"Yes, but she's two years older and frightfully good at games. I'm a hopeless duffer so I was utterly in awe of her."

"Ah, but I gather the positions are reversed now that you are an independent woman, earning your own way by your pen. I am delighted that you have chosen Occles Hall to write about. May I hope you will spare a sentence or two for my dairy?"

"What piffle, Reggie. Miss Dalrymple's article will be about the Hall and the village."

"I shouldn't dream of leaving out the dairy, Sir Reginald. I consider it a patriotic duty to support British agriculture. You will be kind enough to show me around yourself, won't you?"

Lady Valeria turned as purple as her frock and choked on a sip of sherry.

Bobbie and Ben Goodman came in together. Lady Valeria glanced with obvious dissatisfaction from her daughter to Daisy and back. Daisy was sorry she had worn the rose charmeuse, which made Bobbie's olive sack look drabber and less becoming than ever.

On the other hand, she was glad to see that Mr. Goodman dined with the family. She wouldn't be the only outsider among the Parslows, and besides, from what she had seen of him, she liked him.

"Mr. Goodman!" Lady Valeria summoned the secretary to her side and started complaining about some letter he had written for her earlier.

Bobbie joined Daisy and Sir Reginald. She kissed her father with obvious affection, then turned to Daisy. "Did Mummy rag you terribly?"

"Oh no," Daisy nobly lied, racking her brain for something good to report. "Apparently she and my mother made their curtsies to Queen Victoria the same year. It was kind of her to arrange for Mr. Goodman to tell me the history of Occles Hall, and she even suggested I should telephone him if I have more questions after I go back to town."

"I hope you will stay until all your questions are answered," said Sir Reginald with quiet firmness. "Bobbie, Miss Dalrymple has kindly promised to squeeze a few words about the dairy into her article."

"Good-oh!"

They chatted for a few minutes about Daisy's writing, until the butler, Moody, came in.

He looked around the room and his dismal expression became downright lugubrious. "Dinner is *ready,* my lady," he announced.

"Mr. Sebastian is not down yet," said Lady Valeria sharply. "We shall wait."

"Very well, my lady."

Sebastian breezed in five minutes later. Daisy caught her breath at the sight of him in evening clothes. In the hours since she last saw him, she had managed to persuade herself he could not possibly be as handsome as she remembered, but he was.

"Sorry I'm late, Mater," he said. "Thomkins couldn't find the cuff-links I wanted."

"My dear boy," Lady Valeria's voice was a mixture of indulgence and exasperation, "if you will insist on not sacking the fellow despite his carelessness. . . ."

"Oh, Thomkins suits me well enough. Sorry to keep you from your soup, Miss Dalrymple." When he smiled at Daisy, it was easy to see why his mother doted on him—and feared to turn him loose among the ladies.

Moody reappeared, walking as if his feet hurt. "Dinner is *served,* my lady."

Dinner was served by the butler and a parlourmaid; since the War only the grandest houses had footmen. Daisy recognized the girl who had brought the tea earlier, a plump brunette who moved awkwardly, with frequent whispered directions from Moody. Every dish she handed around seemed about to slip from her nervous grasp, but all went well until the end of the main course. Then Lady Valeria snapped at her for removing the plates from the wrong side.

The plate she had just collected crashed to the floor, knife and fork flying. With a wail of despair, she ran from the room.

"Really," said Lady Valeria angrily, "if she's still incapable of doing the job properly after three weeks, she will have to go. Moody, I can't imagine why you and Twitchell find it impossible to hire and train an adequate parlourmaid. You will have to do better than that."

"Yes, my lady," gloomed Moody. "Very well, my lady."

Dessert was consumed in fraught silence, except by Daisy and Sir Reginald, who struggled to carry on a conversation about cheese. At least she was able to congratulate him sincerely on the Cheshire cheese that closed the meal.

Lady Valeria rose to lead the ladies out. "The vicar and Mrs. Lake will be joining us in the drawing room," she announced, adding in a tone of surprised displeasure, "He was not at home when I called at the vicarage to reprimand him about his sermon. All equal in the sight of God indeed! Anarchist piffle."

"Bolshie piffle, Mater," Sebastian drawled. "The Anarchists are passé—in fact, quite exploded."

Daisy, Sir Reginald, and Ben Goodman laughed. Bobbie looked so puzzled Daisy wondered whether she'd ever heard of Bolsheviks or Anarchists.

"Very clever, Sebastian," his mother said with a thin smile. "Don't linger over the port, now, Reggie."

"No, Valeria," murmured the baronet.

The Reverend and Mrs. Lake were already waiting in the drawing room. They were very alike, both thin, spectacled, and anxious-looking. However, the look Mrs. Lake cast at Lady Valeria when her ladyship began to dress down her husband was one of loathing. And Daisy was surprised to overhear the vicar arguing his side of the question. The Lakes were not such meek rabbits as they appeared, then.

Bobbie explained when the gentlemen came in and relieved them of the responsibility for entertaining Mrs. Lake. "They are absolutely dying to leave St. Dunstan's, so Mr. Lake often preaches sermons he knows Mummy will disapprove of, hoping she'll persuade the Bishop to replace him.

It'll work, too. We've never had a vicar for longer than two years since old Mr. Peascod, who practically asked permission to breathe."

"It doesn't sound as if your parlourmaids last long, either."

"We've had three in two months," Bobbie said with a grimace. "They're promoted from housemaid and then reduced to the ranks again when Mummy gets fed up with their incompetence. There are two more housemaids to go, and then I suppose it'll be the kitchen maid."

"But they don't get the sack?"

"Gosh, no. It's far too difficult to find anyone willing to work in the house."

"Everyone seems to have trouble with servants since the War," said Daisy, who could not afford a maid if she could find one. She and Lucy made do with a treasure of a woman who came in daily. "The girls are used to more freedom and higher wages than they can get in service."

"And jolly good for them, I say."

Moody shuffled in with coffee. Daisy accepted a cup but only drank half of it before making her excuses and retiring to bed. She was tired after the journey; more important, she had a lot of work to accomplish and, unless by some miracle Sir Reginald prevailed, she had only two days to do it in.

Daisy was wakened in the morning by a flood of sunshine pouring in through the pink-check gingham curtains. In the rosy light, she couldn't think for a moment where she was. Then remembrance returned. She bounced out of bed.

The house faced east. This was the ideal time of day to photograph it, and for once the weather was cooperating. Any moment clouds might roll in. She flung on a pullover and skirt and her coat, grabbed camera and tripod, and set off.

She only lost her way twice. The first time a housemaid bearing a coal-scuttle directed her. The second time, she found a door opening into a sort of cloister in the courtyard around which the house was built, so she went out that way. Hoping the sun would rise high enough later to allow photography within the courtyard, she hurried across to the tunnel under the east block and a moment later emerged, blinking, by the moat.

Conditions were perfect. The February sun rose far enough south to make for interesting shadows. The frosty air was diamond-clear and so still the water reflected every detail of the intricate black and white façade. Daisy shot a whole roll of film before deciding that the next important item on her agenda was breakfast.

Bobbie and Ben Goodman, already in the breakfast-room, bade her a cheerful good morning.

"Help yourself," said Bobbie, waving at the sideboard. *The Times* lay beside her plate, unopened. "Isn't it a simply spiffing day?"

"Top-hole." Investigating the covered dishes, Daisy avoided the eggs, on which she existed at home, and served herself with smoked haddock, hot rolls, and tea. "I've already been out taking pictures," she said, sitting down at the table.

"Good-oh. Do you play golf? I have to take Ranee to the smithy first, but I thought we might pop over to the links and bash a ball around a few holes later."

"I can't," said Daisy, glad of an excuse. "I must get to work. Your mother made it rather plain my welcome is limited to two days."

"Two days? Bosh! I don't believe she meant it. Ben, what do you think?"

"I think I had better not offer an opinion," he replied with the smile that transformed his plain face. "I'm at your service any time, Miss Dalrymple."

"I'd like to see a bit of the gardens while it's fine."

"Certainly, though there's not much to see at this time of year, of course, except in the Winter Garden."

"There's a winter garden? Spiffing." She was about to ask

him to explain how to find it, not wanting to drag him around at her side with his gammy leg, when Sebastian came in.

He looked sleepy. Pouring himself a cup of coffee, he sat down as his sister said in surprise, "You're up early, Bastie."

"Beautiful day, and we have a beautiful guest." He grinned at Daisy and her heart fluttered. "Do you ride, Miss Dalrymple? I'll show you a bit of the countryside."

"Thank you, but. . . ."

Bobbie interrupted, "Bastie, Daisy says Mummy told her she can only stay two days."

"Not in so many words," Daisy put in hastily.

"Do you think she meant it?"

Stirring his coffee, Sebastian pondered. "Who knows? Stay longer and we'll find out."

"Don't be a hopeless ass! Daddy invited her to stay as long as she likes."

"A fat lot that has to say to anything," he said cynically.

"And Mummy knew Daisy's mother back in prehistoric times."

"Oh well, then, I should think you're safe, Miss Dalrymple, unless they had a frightful set-to?"

"Lady Valeria didn't mention one."

"She would have. Will you ride with me?"

"Thanks, but all the same I think I'd better see the gardens while it's fine, in case we get sleet tomorrow."

He nodded and did not press her, nor offer to tour the gardens with her.

"I expect I can find my way about without your aid, Mr. Goodman," Daisy suggested, "if you have work to do indoors."

"I'm glad of an excuse to be outside on such a glorious day," he assured her.

"It's bally cold out," said Sebastian abruptly, getting up and going to the sideboard. "I saw frost on the lawn. For heaven's sake, don't get chilled."

"I've already been out with my camera. It is a bit nippy."

Daisy had a feeling his admonition was addressed more to
Ben Goodman than to herself. She liked him the better for
his concern for the secretary's dicky health.

"We'll wrap up well," Mr. Goodman promised.

When they set off together, he had on a knit balaclava
helmet under his hat, covering his mouth and nose, and a
heavy Army greatcoat with the shoulder-straps removed.

"A sight to scare the crows," he said, a smile in his voice.
"I hope you don't mind."

"I'm not a crow. The cold air hurts your lungs?"

"If I breathe too deeply. But the sun feels warm already.
I'll take the balaclava off in a few minutes."

He took her first out onto a terrace on the south side. From
there wide stone steps led down to an Elizabethan knot garden. Within the elaborate pattern of low box hedges, the beds
were bare, but Daisy decided it would make a good photograph later in the day. She hadn't brought her equipment,
not wanting to lug it around unnecessarily.

They went on along a gravel walk with a high yew hedge
on one side, an ivy-grown wall on the other, till they came
to a door in the wall. Pausing to take off the balaclava, Mr.
Goodman pointed along the walk. "This turns into a footpath
across the park, a shortcut to the village. I don't know if
you'd care to walk down to the Cheshire Cheese with me for
a nip before lunch?"

"I'd love to, but ought you to walk so far?"

"A certain amount of exercise is good for my leg, otherwise it stiffens. You lost a brother in the War, I gather?"

"My only brother . . . and my fiancé."

"I'm sorry. It was a beastly show. Both Army?"

"Gervaise was." She didn't usually talk about Michael,
but a depth of compassion she sensed in him made her go
on, defiantly. "My fiancé was a driver in a Friends' Ambulance Unit."

"A conchie?" The way he said the hateful epithet was quite
different from Phillip's—most people's—absolute, unhesitat-

ing contempt. "It was one of those units pulled me out. Brave men, going into Hell with no weapon to defend themselves."

Tears pricked behind Daisy's eyelids. The need to bottle up her feelings unless she was prepared to defend him had kept the wound of Michael's loss raw and painful. Ben Goodman's understanding quickened the healing process recently begun by another rare, sympathetic soul.

He had turned away to open the door. As it swung open, the sound of running footsteps, boots on gravel, made them both turn. A dark, wiry lad in gardening clothes dashed up.

"Mr. Gootman, sir, a telephone call for you there is," he announced in the musical accents of Wales. "A trunk call."

"Blast. Still, never mind. Miss Dalrymple, this is Owen Morgan, who is undoubtedly much better able to show you the Winter Garden than am I, but I'll be back as soon as I can. Excuse me." He limped hurriedly away.

Daisy smiled at the blushing youth. "Good, an expert guide."

"But I don't know all the Latin names yet, miss," he blurted out. "Mr. Bligh, the head gardener, he knows."

"To tell the truth, I'd much rather have the common names. Come on, Owen." She preceded him through the door, and stepped into instant spring.

The garden was protected from cold winds by walls on all four sides. In the middle, in the centre of a paved square, stood a classical statue, a winged figure of a burly, dishevelled man with a conch shell held to his lips: *Boreas, the North Wind* according to the pedestal. And surrounding the paving, along the walls, was a wide raised border ablaze with colour.

There were evergreens—Daisy recognized laurel and variegated holly—and plants with grey-green foliage. Flowering vines and shrubs hid the walls, yellow cascades of winter jasmine, white honeysuckle and wintersweet scenting the air, the coral blooms of Japanese quince. In front, vying with snowdrops and aconites, grew scylla and irises, crocuses, violets, multi-hued primroses, purple-blue anemones, lilac periwinkles, crimson cyclamen.

"It's beautiful!" cried Daisy. "How I wish someone would invent an efficient way to take colour photographs. Even if I learn the name of every plant, words will never do it justice."

The young gardener led her around, pointing out delicate Christmas and Lenten roses, daphne, orange Chinese lanterns, and fluffy yellow hazel catkins. She enjoyed his voice as much as the flower names.

"Which part of Wales are you from?" she asked.

"Glamorgan, miss. Merthyr Tydfil."

"That's in the south. You're a long way from home."

"Oh yes, miss, and it's dreatfully I miss it."

"You have left your family there?"

His story came pouring out. "My pa wass killed down the pit—the coal mine. Mam wouldn't let us boys be miners. Fife brothers we are, scattered all ofer. Two's in the Nafy; one's a gentleman's personal serfant in London. Rhys iss a schoolteacher," he said with shy pride, "and so's one of my sisters. Married the other two are, at home in Merthyr."

"I expect you're lonely here, being used to a big family."

"I wass walking out with a young woman." His face crumpled in misery. "Nearly engaged we wass, look you, but she ran off to London."

"Then she didn't deserve you," said Daisy firmly as they turned the last corner, coming to the bed to the right of the entrance. Owen looked less than comforted. "Are these daffodils here, just coming up between the snowdrops?" she asked to distract him, though she recognized the green shoots perfectly well.

He blinked hard, sniffed, and answered, "Yes, miss, and narcissus. They come out here earlier than anywheres."

"And that bush?" She gestured at an unhappy-looking shrub in the middle of a bare patch of ground. "What's that?"

"Azalea, miss." He frowned, puzzled. "They bloom early in here, too, but. . . ."

"What's wrong?"

"It's terrible it looks. And where's the irises around it? Myself I planted them, the kind that's flowering now, and hardly any hass come up." He stepped over the low kerb and picked his way carefully to the small bush. Most of its few remaining leaves were brown, except for one bronze-green sprig.

Daisy saw that the dark soil of the bare patch was broken by a few scattered iris shoots. "Perhaps a dog got in and dug them up and buried them again too deep," she proposed, though there was no sign of the earthworks usually left by an excavating canine.

"The azalea iss dying." Owen Morgan turned, panic-stricken. "All the buds are dead. What'll her ladyship say? Please, miss, I must find Mr. Bligh."

"Of course, Owen. I'll just wait here until Mr. Goodman comes back."

She wandered around, trying to work out whether it was worth taking photos when all the marvellous colours would be lost. The knot garden, however dull in fact, would turn out better on film, but Boreas deserved a picture, she decided.

Presumably he was supposed to be exhaling a gale from his conch, though hair, beard, and tunic were all streaming in the opposite direction and he actually faced north-east. Moving from side to side, she tried to work out the best angle for a shot. She was wondering whether to go and fetch her camera or wait for Mr. Goodman when Owen returned.

He brought with him a wheelbarrow, spade, and fork, and a bent, weatherbeaten ancient. Mr. Bligh wore a drooping tweed deerstalker of an indeterminate colour, breeches tied at the knees with string, and woolly gaiters in startling pink and blue stripes. He tipped his hat to Daisy, revealing a hairless scalp as weatherbeaten as his face, and brown eyes as bright and knowing as a sparrow's.

"Fine marnin', miss," he remarked, and went to examine the patient.

Owen followed him, looking anxious. Daisy hoped he wasn't going to be blamed for whatever disaster had overtaken the azalea and the irises. The poor boy was unhappy enough already.

"She's dead," said Mr. Bligh. "Dig 'er out, lad, an' we s'll find summat else to put in afore her la'ship takes a fancy to come by. I s'll take kindly, miss," he added unexpectedly to Daisy, "if 'ee'll not tell her la'ship, being she don't foller as you can't lay down the law to plants like you can to people."

"I shan't say a word," Daisy promised as Owen took the spade and started digging, watched by the old man propped against the wheelbarrow. Returning to the statue, she realized the sun was just right for the pose she wanted. "I'm going to fetch my camera," she said to the head gardener. "If Mr. Goodman comes, tell him I'll be back in a jiffy."

"Right, miss. What is it, lad?"

"There's something in the way, Mr. Bligh. 'Bout a foot and a half down. Like a mass of roots it feels."

"Try the fork, but go at it easy like. Don't want to do any more damage."

Daisy left them to the new puzzle and sped back to the house. She had already put a fresh roll of film in the camera. Returning laden with equipment through the Long Hall, she met Ben Goodman on his way to rejoin her.

"You won't mind if I dash ahead?" she said. "I have to hurry to catch the light."

He nodded. "I'll follow at my own pace."

When she reached the Winter Garden, she was surprised to see that Owen had dug a trench right across the bare patch of soil. He and Mr. Bligh stood at one end, gazing down with fascinated revulsion.

"Go on, have a look," urged Mr. Bligh.

Owen knelt in the dirt. Reaching down, he moved something at the bottom of the trench.

"Oh God! Oh God!" He flung himself backwards onto his heels, his arms across his face. "It's her. It's my Grace."

4

The young Welshman's racking sobs shuddered through the sunny garden. Daisy froze in the doorway.

"What's the matter?" Ben Goodman came up behind her.

"I think. . . ." Her voice shook. She moistened her lips. "I think they've found a body."

"A *what?*"

Of course he was incredulous. But Daisy had a horrid sense of history repeating itself. She turned to him, heart-sick.

"She can't still be alive if she was buried, can she?"

"She? My dear Miss Dalrymple, what on earth are you talking about?"

"Grace. Owen says it's Grace."

"Good Lord!" With a hand on her arm he gently moved her aside, limped past her, and stood staring. "They've found Grace Moss buried in the flowerbed? The poor child."

Something in his tone caught Daisy's attention. Behind the sincere pity, did she hear the merest hint of relief? No, she had imagined it. His face was sober, compassionate, as he took in the sight and sound of Owen Morgan's grief.

She had placed Grace Moss now. The gardener's dead sweetheart was the blacksmith's missing daughter, the pretty, fun-loving parlourmaid Ted Roper had told her about. Missing how long? Daisy's brain began to work again. Buried when? By whom? Why?

Murdered?

Ben Goodman recovered from his shock and took charge. Making his halting way around the corner of the bed, he called, "Bligh, is it true? You've found a body?"

The old man started. His mesmerized gaze fixed on the trench beneath his feet, he seemed to have shrunk. "Aye, sir. A corpus it is, sure as eggs is eggs. Dead as a doornail, poor creetur."

The secretary bit his lip. "Miss Dalrymple, please go and telephone the police. The 'phone is in a closet off the Long Hall. And not a word to Lady Valeria until the authorities have been informed. Not a word to anyone, in fact, if you can help it, unless you can get hold of Sir Reginald."

Daisy quite saw the point of not enlightening Lady Valeria before it became absolutely necessary. "All right, but I'd better take some photographs first. I was mixed up in a police investigation just a little while ago, and they really appreciated my pictures."

By that time Mr. Goodman had reached the trench. He glanced down. His already pale cheeks whitened and he shook his head. "No. Leave the camera and I'll take a few snaps."

She didn't argue. The previous occasion had not exactly been a pleasure, and a young girl who had been buried, perhaps for weeks, must be much worse. Setting the camera and tripod on the North Wind's pedestal, she once more hurried to the house.

The temptation to ring up Alec was almost irresistible, but she had learned enough of police procedures to know Scotland Yard could not intervene unless called in by the county's Chief Constable. Not the village bobby, she decided, even if he had a telephone. Anyway, he'd very likely be out on his bicycle making his rounds. Chester was probably the nearest sizable police station.

She found the Long Hall without difficulty, and the fourth door she opened was the telephone cubby-hole. The narrow, confined space, inevitably paneled, held only a Windsor chair, a small table, and the apparatus. Daisy wondered what on earth it had been used for before the telephone was invented.

Closing the door, she was plunged into a sepulchral darkness. Hastily she opened it again. Grace *was* dead before she was buried, wasn't she?

She forced the thought from her mind. There was a gaslight fixture high on the wall and a box of matches in a drawer in the table, along with a pad of paper, a pencil, and a directory listing local subscribers. She lit the gas, adjusted the flame, and closed the door again. Either there was some invisible source of ventilation, or sooner or later someone with a desire for privacy was going to be found asphyxiated. Asphyxiated. Buried. Dark and airless . . . Her breath came in frantic gasps.

Sternly she stopped her involuntary movement towards the door handle. Lifting the receiver, she jiggled the hook.

"Hullo, operator! Please get me the main police station in Chester."

"Yes, madam. I'll ring you back when your call is through."

"No, it's urgent. I'll hold the line."

A sharply indrawn breath warned her that the girl was going to listen in. She'd recognize the Parslows' number, and an urgent call from Occles Hall to the police was too good to miss. Well, Grace's death couldn't be kept secret for long. Circumstances at Wentwater Court had been entirely different.

Buzz, click, fizzle, hum. "Hullo, Chester exchange. Police station, please." Click-click, ring. Ring once; ring twice.

A bored voice: "Chester police."

"Go ahead, please, caller."

"Officer, I'm ringing from Occleswich." Daisy admired the steadiness of her own voice. "I want to report a"—a murder? a body in the flowerbed?—"an unexplained death."

"Unexplained death?" The voice sat up and took notice. "I'll put you through to Inspector Dunnett, ma'am."

A moment later she repeated her report.

"Unexplained death?" Inspector Dunnett queried, then, suspiciously, "Who is speaking?"

"This is the Honourable Miss Dalrymple, ringing from Occles Hall. I'm a guest here. The owner hasn't yet been informed about it."

"About this here 'unexplained death,' miss?"

Daisy was beginning to hate the phrase and to wish she had never used it. "About the dead body in the Winter Garden," she said flatly. "I thought it was more important to telephone you at once than to waste time hunting for Sir Reginald or Lady Valeria."

"Lady Valeria!" the inspector exclaimed in alarm. Her ladyship's reputation stretched as far as Chester, it seemed. "That'll be Lady Valeria Parslow? You won't mind, miss, if I just confirm where you're phoning from. We do get these young people playing their little jokes."

Fuming, she waited while he checked back through the Chester operator to the local operator. When he spoke to her again, he had become deferential.

"Beg pardon, miss, but we can't be too careful these days. It don't do to disturb Lady . . . the gentry for nothing. The Honourable, did you say, miss? Dalrymple—that's D, A, L. . . ."

She spelled her name for him.

"And you haven't told Lady . . . Sir Reginald yet?"

"I was in the garden with his secretary when the gardeners discovered the body. I came straight in to phone you." And how she wished she had made Ben Goodman do the phoning while she took photographs. "I can't really tell you any more. Are you coming to investigate or not?"

"Yes, we're coming, miss." Inspector Dunnett sounded injured now. "We'll be there inside the hour. I . . . er . . . it'd be a good idea if Lady Valeria was to be informed before we arrive. And Sir Reginald, of course."

"I'll see that *he's* told," she snapped, and hung up. The coward, expecting her to do his dirty work for him! She'd be dashed if she was going to be the one to break the news to Lady Valeria.

The coffinlike walls of the cubicle closed in on her again. In her annoyance with the policeman, she had almost forgotten the horror of the poor girl lying out there in her makeshift grave. With a shiver, she opened the door, but she stayed seated there in thought.

Sir Reginald was probably at his dairy, wherever that was. She understood he usually went to supervise the early milking, returned to the house for breakfast, and then retreated to his refuge for the rest of the day. Taking the pad and pencil from the drawer, she wrote him a brief note saying no more than she had told Inspector Dunnett.

As she folded it, she had a sense of someone watching her. She looked up. Moody stood there regarding her with despondent disapproval.

"There's writing paper in the library, miss. *And* a writing desk. Also in the Red Saloon, the. . . ."

"Thank you, I have all I need. Is Sir Reginald at the dairy? Have someone take this to him, please."

He took the sheet of paper from her as gingerly as if it were a small creature of uncertain but probably distressing habits. "With your permission, miss, I shall enclose your communication in an envelope. Unfortunately the lower servants all learn to read these days."

"Do what you want," Daisy said impatiently, "only see that Sir Reginald gets it within the next twenty minutes. If he asks for me, I shall be in the gardens." She was dying to escape from the house before Lady Valeria crossed her path.

She ought to go back to the Winter Garden to tell Mr. Goodman the police were on their way. In any case, she had left Lucy's precious camera there.

* * *

Ben Goodman was alone, perched uncomfortably at Boreas' feet. He stepped down and came to meet her, tripod in hand, the camera slung around his neck.

She glanced at the trench, which looked just as before. "You didn't let them do any more digging?"

He gave her a wry grin. "I've read enough detective novels to know one mustn't move or even touch anything. Poor Owen was in a bad way anyway, in no fit state to dig even if I'd been hard-hearted enough to make him excavate his girl."

"It really is Grace Moss?"

"Oh yes, quite recognizable. She was wrapped in a sheet. It gave old Bligh rather a shock, too, for a man his age. I sent them off to his cottage to have a bracer."

"I hope he has something stronger than beer."

"Whisky—strictly for medicinal purposes, naturally."

Daisy managed to smile. "I hope they don't get squiffy. I'm afraid the police will insist on talking to both of them."

"They're coming?"

"An Inspector Dunnett from Chester. I thought I'd better bypass the village constable, but I must say the Inspector sounded like a bit of a blister on the telephone. He's petrified of Lady Valeria."

"A not uncommon condition," said Mr. Goodman dryly, "and not unreasonable. Her ladyship is not going to be pleased. I take it you didn't tell her or she'd be here by now."

"No. I sent a note to Sir Reginald."

"Sebastian?"

She sensed an odd tension in him, which relaxed at her answer. "I didn't see either him or Bobbie."

But all he said was, "Just as well." He handed her the camera. "Here. I took half a dozen shots of . . . the hole in the ground. I wasn't sure what it was you were hurrying to photograph while the light was right."

"Boreas." She frowned at the statue. "Too late for the

best, but I'll take a couple in case it rains tomorrow. I hope you don't think I'm frightfully unfeeling."

"Those of us who work for our livings can't afford to be oversensitive."

"Then I'll go and do the knot garden, if you don't mind being left alone on guard?"

"No. But it's in this sort of situation I'd kill for a cigarette, if a cigarette wouldn't kill me."

"Jolly hard luck," she sympathized, though smoking, like bobbing her hair, was a facet of emancipation in which she had not yet indulged. She disliked the smell of cigarette smoke, and cigars were even worse.

Yet Alec's pipe wasn't bad, she mused as she returned to the knot garden. How she wished it was he who was on his way, not the Dunnett blister.

Grace's death was banished to the back of her mind by the complications of photographing the knot garden. In order to look down on it from a sufficient height, she climbed onto the stone balustrade of the terrace and set up the tripod in one of the huge stone urns flanking the steps. Then, to see through the viewfinder, she had to clamber up beside it. There she balanced with her feet on the rim, trying not to step on the bare soil within in case some as yet invisible plant was growing just beneath the surface.

She took several shots she hoped had a fair chance of turning out well. Time to get down. That was when she remembered that, in her tree-climbing youth, descending from trees had always been much more difficult than ascending them in the first place. The ground looked an awfully long way away.

"Allow me to assist you, Miss Dalrymple."

Cautiously she turned her head. Sir Reginald stood there, in tweed knickerbockers and a disreputable shooting-jacket, gazing up at her with grave kindliness. Beyond, Moody stared in outrage.

"Thank you, Sir Reginald." She gave him a grateful smile. "If I may pass you the equipment, I think I can manage."

A moment later her feet were safe on the crazy-paving of the terrace.

"I must admit," he said, "I had not allowed for the spirit of the modern young woman. I expected to find you prostrate on a sofa, not scaling the heights."

"You had my note? Oh dear, you must think me horribly callous."

"Miss Dalrymple!" Lady Valeria burst forth from the house. "I saw you from a window. I could not believe my eyes! How am I to explain it to your mother if you break your neck indulging in childish tricks while staying at Occles Hall?"

"My dear, I'm afraid we have far worse trouble to worry about. Perhaps you ought to come and sit down. . . ."

"Sit down? Nonsense, Reggie. What on earth are you blethering about now?"

"Miss Dalrymple informs me. . . ."

"Then she had better inform me too."

Daisy sighed. So much for her efforts to avoid being the one to break the bad news. She had no high opinion of Lady Valeria's sensibility, but she couldn't bring herself to just blurt out the worst.

"One of your gardeners was showing me the Winter Garden," she began. "I noticed a dying bush. . . ."

"Disgraceful. I shall speak to Bligh about it. But hardly worth all this fuss, Reginald."

"Lady Valeria, listen, please! Mr. Bligh had his assistant dig up the plant and they found a body underneath. The body of Grace Moss."

"Grace Moss!" Lady Valeria's choleric face paled. Then, as Daisy had half expected, she turned on the messenger. "This is all your fault! Coming here where you're not wanted, poking and prying, interfering. . . ."

"My dear!" For once Sir Reginald interrupted his wife. "You can't blame. . . ."

"I'll blame whomever I please. This is what comes of your issuing invitations without consulting me!"

"Inspector Dunnett, my lady," announced Moody's ominous tones.

Lady Valeria swung round. "Police! I suppose I can guess whom I have to thank for this," she added with a venomous glance at Daisy.

Cap in hand, the officer in his blue police uniform stood beside Moody in his butler's black. They could have been brothers. Inspector Dunnett's long, craggy face gazed out at the malevolent world with an identical jaundiced expression; his shoulders slumped in the same defeated way. He looked perhaps ten years younger, about fifty, but the chief difference, Daisy thought, was that Moody had long ago ceased to let Lady Valeria's outbursts increase his general pessimism.

Inspector Dunnett appeared to regard her ladyship with misgivings amounting to dread.

She glared at him. "This matter is nothing to do with me, Doublet," she proclaimed, "nor with my family. Miss Dalrymple seems to know all about it. You may deal with her. Come, Reginald."

Not waiting for an answer, she swept past the policeman into the house. To Daisy's relief, Sir Reginald didn't follow her. As a support he might prove more reed than oaken staff, but she was glad to have him beside her anyway.

"In just a moment, Valeria," he called after his wife. He patted Daisy's arm. "I shan't desert you, my dear. Inspector, I am Sir Reginald Parslow. I'm sorry such an unpleasant occurrence has brought you to Occles Hall."

"I do my duty, sir," he said stolidly. "With your permission, sir, I'll have the doctor examine the deceased and my men search the scene. They're waiting at the front of the house."

"Yes, of course. But I don't actually know. . . ." He looked an appeal at Daisy and she remembered her note to him had not specified the place.

"The Winter Garden. I'm Daisy Dalrymple, Inspector."

"Ah, Miss Dalrymple. You found the deceased." His tone was accusing.

"I reported the discovery," she corrected him. "The gardeners did the finding."

"Yes, miss. All the same, I'll need a statement from you."

"I'll take you there and tell you what happened on the way."

"I'd better come along too, my dear," Sir Reginald said anxiously. "Moody, direct the Inspector's men to the Winter Garden."

"And put my camera somewhere safe, please."

"Very good, sir." The butler accepted his master's order with his usual gloom. A body in the Winter Garden was no more than one might expect, his demeanour said. "Very good, miss."

As they started down the terrace steps, Daisy began. "One of the under-gardeners was showing me around the Winter Garden."

"Just a minute, please, miss. An under-gardener? You're a guest here?"

"As a matter of fact, I'm writing an article about Occles Hall."

"A reporter!" Inspector Dunnett clearly considered reporters among the lowest forms of life.

"A guest," said Sir Reginald. "A welcome guest."

"A magazine writer," Daisy affirmed.

"A magazine writer? The *Honourable* Miss Dalrymple?" asked the policeman skeptically. "That's what you claimed, wasn't it?"

Once again Sir Reginald came to the rescue. "Daughter of the late Viscount Dalrymple of Fairacres."

"If you say so, sir. Go on, miss. Please."

Her employment had obviously reduced to vanishing point

whatever status her title had given her in Dunnett's eyes. She remembered how Alec had dismissed her views while he thought her a mere society butterfly, but taken her seriously when he found out she was a working woman. She sighed.

"I noticed a dead bush," she said tersely. "The head gardener told Owen to dig it up. I went back to the house to fetch my camera and when I returned they had found the body."

"So you left these gardeners to guard the deceased and returned to the house to telephone?"

"No, by that time Mr. Goodman, Sir Reginald's secretary, had joined us. He asked me to telephone. The gardeners were naturally distressed at finding Grace Moss dead, so he sent them away and stayed himself."

Inspector Dunnett pounced. "Grace Moss? You knew the deceased?"

"I didn't even see the body," Daisy snapped. "I've never been here before and I wouldn't know her from Adam. Eve, rather."

He gave her a wary look as if he suspected she was mocking him. "Then who identified the deceased? Who was Grace Moss?"

"Grace was our parlourmaid," said Sir Reginald sadly. "A pretty, cheerful child."

"Mr. Goodman, Bligh, and Owen Morgan all knew her. They told me."

"So your evidence is nothing but hearsay," Dunnett reproached her. "In that case, I've no need of you at present. My sergeant'll take a formal statement later, miss. Ah, here's Dr. Sedgwick and my men."

He strode off to meet an approaching group of uniformed police led by a plump civilian with a black bag. Dismissed and ignored, Daisy tramped disconsolately back to the house.

Sir Reginald and Ben Goodman soon joined her. Sir Reginald enquired after his wife. He breathed a sigh of relief when Moody told him she had gone off in the Daimler to preside over a session of the Mothers' Meetings county committee.

"Then, if you'll excuse me, my dear," he said to Daisy, "I'll be getting back to the dairy."

Mr. Goodman offered to begin the historical tour of the Hall. "We can't do anything for poor Grace. We might as well have a look at the outside while it's fine. You can still see the marks of the Roundheads' cannonballs."

So Daisy fetched her notebook and was soon scribbling away in her own idiosyncratic version of Pitman's shorthand. They reached the stables, now partly converted to garages, just as Sebastian rode in.

If possible, he looked even more stunning on the back of his roan gelding. The position lent him an air of strength, of masterful vigour, absent from his ordinary demeanour and belied by his subservience to his mother. He smiled down at Daisy and Ben Goodman, and Daisy beamed back.

"Let me tell him," the secretary said softly to her, and with a shock she remembered Grace Moss.

"All right. I'll go and start transcribing my notes. Thanks for all the stuff."

He nodded with a faint smile, but his face was troubled as he turned to Sebastian.

Slightly puzzled, Daisy headed for her room and her portable typewriter. She wondered if Ben was afraid Sebastian would go to pieces when he heard about the corpse. Was he trying to prevent such a revelation of weakness before a stranger? He was no relation of Sebastian's, but Daisy had cause to appreciate his sympathetic nature.

Bobbie had defended her brother against Daisy's implied criticism of his failure to escape his mother, and Lady Valeria guarded him against husband-hunting harpies. He seemed to bring out a protective instinct, which suggested an essential weakness of character. The news of Grace's demise might well shock him into an unbecoming emotional display.

No, that was hardly fair, Daisy chided herself. Ben Goodman, who had seen all the horrors of the Great War, had been shaken by the death of the innocent young girl. Sebastian was too young to have fought in the War—only natural for him to be shattered by the murder of a girl he knew.

And there it was again, the word she'd been avoiding. *Murder.* Those who died a natural death, those who succumbed to an accident, did not end up under eighteen inches of earth in a flowerbed.

Grace Moss had been murdered.

5

Daisy deciphered the last curlicue of shorthand, typed the last word, and stacked her papers neatly. The seventeenth-century siege of Occles Hall was a bit of a wash-out. She couldn't blame the inhabitants for their rapid surrender to Oliver Cromwell's men. The moat, though it had then surrounded the house, was no protection against a cannon; had they fought on, there'd be nothing left today for her to write about. Still, she needed lots more to make her article interesting.

Unfortunately, *Town and Country* was not the sort of publication to revel in murdered parlourmaids.

She went downstairs. No one was about. From her window she had watched the solemn procession of police bearing the covered stretcher out to their motor-van, then driving away. Presumably the sergeant had been left behind to take statements, but there was no sign of him.

She went out to the terrace, and thence her steps inevitably turned towards the Winter Garden. Not that she expected to find any clues. Even a police search would be lucky to turn anything up after so long.

At least, she assumed Grace had been there since her disappearance. Long enough, anyway, for the bush to expire after its mistreatment. Daisy thought she recalled Ted Roper saying the blacksmith's daughter ran off two months ago, and Bobbie had certainly mentioned three unsatisfactory parlourmaids in two months.

The murderer had had plenty of time to miss a lost glove or scarf and return for it. In that time, even in that sheltered spot, rain and snow, frost and wind would obliterate signs of a struggle, wash away footprints and blood. . . . Ugh!

All the same, it was odd no one had noticed the dying bush and missing irises sooner. The gardeners might have had no reason to go to the Winter Garden, since thoroughly weeded beds would not put out a significant new crop of weeds in January. But the garden was in full bloom. Had none of the family bothered to go and look at it?

Reaching the door in the wall, she opened it and glanced around. Amidst such a profusion of colour, she conceded, a deficiency in that particular corner might be overlooked by anyone who didn't walk around closely studying the plants. She herself hadn't noticed it until she and Owen reached the spot. Inclement weather, everyone busy elsewhere; no, it wasn't really so surprising.

So for two months everyone thought Grace ran away, when all the time she was dead and the evidence leading to her murderer. . . .

Heavy footsteps crunched on the gravel behind Daisy.

Her heart thudding, she swung round. "Oh, Bobbie, it's you!"

"Yes. I . . . er . . . I came back through the village." Bobbie sounded oddly evasive and her face was even pinker than her usual healthy colour. She was dressed in a golfing costume but she didn't have her clubs with her. "Isn't Ben with you? I didn't mean to hop it and leave you alone."

"I almost wish I had gone to play golf with you. I'm afraid something dreadful has happened."

"To Ben?" Bobbie asked anxiously. "Sebastian?"

"No. The gardeners found a body in the Winter Garden. Your parlourmaid, Grace Moss."

Bobbie turned white as a sheet. "Grace Moss?" she faltered in a faint voice.

"Here, come and sit down." Daisy pulled her towards the old mounting block that stood beside the door. "Put your head down between your knees. That's it. I'm frightfully sorry, Bobbie. It was absolutely asinine to tell you so suddenly."

"No, I'm all right. Honestly. I . . . It was just a bit of a shock. So Grace came back."

"She wasn't just lying there, she was buried. It seems to me she probably never went away, but I don't know what the police think."

"Police! Oh hell! I must talk to Bastie." She jumped up, apparently quite recovered. Nonetheless, Daisy went with her, almost trotting to keep up with her swift stride. "That must be what the police were doing at the smithy when I passed—telling her father. The way he was carrying on, I thought Mummy had sent them round again. I must say he sounded livid with rage, not grief, but that's the way Stan Moss reacts to everything."

As they came to the end of the walk and were about to turn right into the knot garden, a policeman appeared from the left, around the corner of the Winter Garden wall.

All three stopped abruptly. Bobbie clutched Daisy's arm.

Saluting, the policeman looked interrogatively from one to the other. "Miss Dalrymple?"

"I'm Miss Dalrymple. This is Miss Parslow, who lives here. You must be the sergeant Inspector Dunnett said would take my statement?"

"That's it, miss. Sergeant Shaw. I've been taking statements from the gardeners. If I might 'ave a word with you now, miss, and I'll be needing to see the secretary gentleman."

"I'll find him for you. Daisy, tell Moody to show you to the Red Saloon." With that, Bobbie hurried on towards the house.

Daisy and the sergeant followed more slowly. He was a heavyset man, though not as stout as Alec's sergeant, Tring, but Tom Tring walked as soft-footed as a cat whereas Sergeant Shaw lumbered along at Daisy's side like a hippopotamus. On the other hand, Shaw's uniform was a definite improvement over Tring's deplorable taste in loud checks.

Daisy liked Tom Tring, and she was prepared to like Sergeant Shaw, despite his charmless superior. At least he began on a more amiable note than Inspector Dunnett.

"Nasty business, this, miss. Murder's bad enough, but murdering young girls is what I don't 'old with."

"It was murder, then?"

"Looks like it, miss. Dr. Sedgwick says she were 'it on the 'ead with a blunt instrument. 'It from be'ind 'ard enough to crush 'er skull."

Daisy shuddered, feeling sick. "She would have died at once?"

"Died instant, miss. Never knew a thing."

"I'm glad." At least not buried alive, thank heaven. One nightmare receded.

"It's that young furriner I'm sorry for, miss."

"Foreigner?"

"The gardener, Owen Morgan. It's knocked 'im for six all right. Seems 'e was walking out with 'er." Sergeant Shaw puffed up the steps to the terrace. " 'Course, it could be they 'as a tiff and 'e up and biffs 'er one."

"Surely not!" Her heart sank. From the first she had felt a deep sympathy for the unhappy Welshman. "He was fearfully upset when he found her."

"Well, 'e would be, miss, wouldn't 'e, 'aving to dig 'er up and all. Stands to reason. There's more murders is done for love nor money, mark my words, miss."

Moody awaited them, and directed them to the Red Saloon with an air of such reproachful despair that Daisy actually felt guilty. By now all the servants must know what had happened. Moody, like Lady Valeria, seemed to hold her responsible. She hoped the rest of the staff were more reasonable.

As a change from paneling, the small room was papered in a dark red, with a thin gold stripe that did nothing to lessen the oppressive feel. Over the mantelpiece hung a grim Victorian painting of a battle scene dripping with gore. Daisy hurriedly turned her back on it.

Bobbie must have chosen the room because of the convenience for the policeman of the elegant antique writing-table under the window—if, indeed, she had been *compos mentis* enough at that moment for a logical choice, which Daisy wasn't at all sure of.

Suddenly weary, she sank onto the chair Sergeant Shaw placed by the desk for her.

"You won't mind if I takes the weight off me feet, miss? It's easier for writing." Sitting down with a sigh of relief, he took his notebook from his jacket pocket. His tone became fatherly. "Now, not to worry, miss. It's all a matter of routine. Just tell me what you told the Inspector. I'll write it down; summun at the station'll type it up; then you'll be asked to sign that we got it down right what you said. If you'd spell your name for me first, please, miss."

Laboriously he wrote it down. Daisy repeated her brief story, pausing between phrases as the sergeant's pencil crawled over the paper. Mr. Goodman had told Owen to show her the garden; she had noticed the dead bush; Bligh had told Owen to dig it up; she had returned from the house just as Owen uncovered the girl's face and identified her as Grace Moss.

"And 'e was upset, would you say, this Owen Morgan?"

"Dreadfully." She didn't want to recall the young gardener's terrible grief. "Mr. Goodman arrived then and asked me to telephone the police, so I came away. After I spoke to Inspector Dunnett, I sent a note to Sir Reginald. . . ."

"Mr. Dunnett says there's no cause to trouble the family,"

said Sergeant Shaw hastily. "This 'ere Mr. Goodman can tell us all we need 'bout the deceased. Right, miss, that's it."

"Will I have to give evidence at the inquest?"

"Prob'ly not, miss, seeing you didn't know the deceased and there's other witnesses saw the same as what you did. And 'ere's the last of 'em now," he added as Ben Goodman opened the door and looked in. "Come on in, sir. Thank you, miss, that'll be all."

Dismissed again, Daisy departed. Holding the door for her, Mr. Goodman smiled, but he looked grey with fatigue. She hoped her tour of the outside of the house had not made him ill.

She hesitated outside the room, not sure what to do next. Though she shied away from thinking about the gruesome murder, curiosity gnawed at her. She didn't want to believe Owen Morgan had killed the girl he loved, but who else could it have been?

Money as a motive made no sense at all, parlourmaids not being noted for affluence. Nor did Grace sound like the sort of girl to make people hate her. Ted Roper, who surely had no axe to grind, had described Grace as fun-loving, and Sir Reginald had called her a cheerful child. Daisy wondered what her fellow-servants had thought of her.

Perhaps among them Owen had had a rival for Grace's affections.

If Daisy were investigating, she'd start by talking to the servants. Inspector Dunnett didn't appear to have any intention of doing so. No doubt he was afraid of calling down Lady Valeria's wrath on his head.

If Daisy were investigating. . . . Alec's voice sounded inside her head: "Stay out of it, Daisy."

The warning voice was drowned by her rumbling stomach. She had missed morning coffee and she was ravenous. It must be nearly lunchtime. She'd go up to her room to wash her hands, and if she just happened to meet the ladies' maid,

Gregg—well, it would be unfriendly not to have a word with her about the sad end of Grace Moss.

A few minutes later she sat at the dressing-table in her bedroom brushing, re-coiling, and pinning up her hair. She had noticed it loosening when she climbed down from the urn on the terrace, but then she'd forgotten about it and it must have been drooping ever since. No wonder Inspector Dunnett had looked at her askance. Perhaps she really would have it bobbed when she went back to town. Short hair was much more practical, especially for a photographer.

She hadn't bothered with powder or lipstick this morning and she decided not to now. Bobbie hadn't for dinner last night. Quite likely she didn't even own any. The trouble was, Daisy thought, wrinkling her nose at herself in the glass, those freckles made her look so frightfully *young*. And there was the tiny mole by her mouth, but then powder never covered that properly anyway.

"Miss?" Gregg came in. "Is there anything I can do for you?" The maid's eyes were red and her face blotchy.

"Not at present, thanks. You've heard about Grace Moss, I take it? I'm so sorry. You must have known her well."

"Yes, miss, she was at school with my sister, and then working here at the Hall. A merry creature, she was, always looking on the bright side of things. There wasn't an ounce of harm in Gracie, for all Mr. Moody says she was a flighty piece and he wasn't surprised when she run off."

"Flighty? I know she was walking out with Owen Morgan, but she didn't run off after all."

"To think she was lying dead all this time!" Gregg sniffed and wiped her eyes.

"So you can't very well call her flighty."

"Well, it's true she had an eye to the young master. I'm not saying there was anything in it, mind."

"A girl would have to be blind not to have an eye to Mr. Sebastian," said Daisy uneasily. Did Owen have still another

rival? Had Sebastian been a passive object of admiration, or
had he played a more active part?

"He's handsomer than any film actor, isn't he, miss? And
him going to be Sir Sebastian one day. No wonder if poor
Gracie had her head turned. Oh, there's the lunch gong, miss.
Shall I show you the way?"

"I think I can find it now, thank you, Gregg." As the distant
vibrations died away, Daisy gave her hair a last pat, smoothed
her skirt, and set out for the dining room with a hollow feeling inside that was not entirely hunger.

Lady Valeria had returned. Her husband, her children, her
husband's secretary, and her unwanted guest were all subdued by the tragedy, but Lady Valeria was angry.

"I met a reporter at the gates," she announced, as Moody
ladled Scotch broth and the tiptoeing maid handed it round.
"A man from the local paper. I sent him off with his tail
between his legs but doubtless others will follow."

"My dear," said Sir Reginald mildly, "would it not be
better to make a brief statement? They may invent stories to
amuse the public if they don't know the truth."

"Truth! Those troublemakers don't know the meaning of
the word. Give it them and they'll only twist it. I have already
told Moody that any servant who speaks to them will be
instantly dismissed. Naturally none of us here will pander to
their nosiness, except. . . ." She scowled at Daisy. "Of
course I can't stop you tattling to your colleagues, Miss Dalrymple."

"They aren't my colleagues, Lady Valeria," Daisy said
coldly. "I'm not a reporter. I write for a magazine, a most
respectable magazine, not a newspaper or scandal sheet. Nor
am I in the habit of tattling to anyone. You may be sure that
as a guest at Occles Hall I shan't discuss your affairs with
the Press."

Lady Valeria's sour look assured Daisy her words had hit
their mark. "As a guest" she'd shun the Press, so her hostess
was not likely to continue to press her to cut short her visit.

She found something else to fume about instead. "Our affairs? The fact that it was on our property the silly girl died does not make it any affair of ours."

From the corner of her eye, Daisy thought she saw Sebastian's hand move in what might be a gesture of protest, but when she glanced at him, he was languidly eating his soup. He seemed apathetic, as if in the aftermath of an emotional storm, though she had no way of knowing if that was the case.

What had his relationship been with the dead girl?

"I have spoken to that little man from the police," Lady Valeria went on, "Inspector Rennet or whatever his name is. He quite understands that the family have nothing to contribute to his investigation. I see no need for any of us to attend the inquest, though unfortunately Mr. Goodman and two of the gardeners are required to give evidence."

"I was told I may be called," Daisy said, interpreting the sergeant's "Prob'ly not" the way she chose.

"A distressing prospect for any *lady*." Cheered by this dig, Lady Valeria changed the subject. The steak-and-kidney pie and the apple charlotte which followed were enlivened by a blow-by-blow account of her triumph over her incompetent fellow committee-members.

The rest spoke scarcely a word.

After lunch, Ben Goodman offered to show Daisy over the interior of the house. She thought he still looked tired, and as the sun still shone she wanted to photograph the courtyard and the back of the house, so she declined.

"Tomorrow morning?" she proposed.

His lips quirked. "No hurry, since you've persuaded Lady Valeria to let you stay indefinitely."

Daisy managed to take her pictures without climbing on any more urns. Last of all, as the sun sank in the west, she returned to the Winter Garden and shot a few more snaps of Boreas. Not ideal conditions but not too bad, she hoped. Even the most respectable magazine in the world might be glad to print a photo of a most respectable statue which happened to stand in a garden where a brutal murder had occurred.

She kept her back to the trench.

When she went in for afternoon tea, only Bobbie was there. They talked about photography. Daisy had the impression that Bobbie was on tenterhooks. Once or twice she seemed on the brink of confiding whatever it was that disturbed her, but she drew back at the last moment.

Daisy suspected she was giving the same impression. She was dying to talk about Grace, but her chief interest was in Sebastian's dealings with the dead girl. It wasn't the sort of subject one could put to a protective sister.

After tea, Bobbie said she had some letters to write. Daisy decided she ought to write to her mother, her sister, and Lucy in case they were worried by the reports that were bound to be in the newspapers tomorrow. She finished just in time to change for dinner.

When she went down to the drawing room, Ben Goodman was alone there. "I've been notified that the inquest will be tomorrow afternoon," he told her, "in the Village Hall."

"They didn't inform me, so I suppose Inspector Dunnett doesn't want my evidence, but I shall go anyway."

"I'll be glad to escort you, Miss Dalrymple."

"Daisy, please. Thanks, I'd like to go with you. I've never been to an inquest. It'll be interesting, though I must say I'd have liked to give evidence."

"What an unusual young lady you are, Daisy!"

"Young woman. I have it on the best authority that any *lady* must find such a prospect distressing."

Ben smiled. "It's good to see someone who isn't cowed by Lady Valeria."

"I don't have to live with her," Daisy said diplomatically.

Now she was on Christian-name terms with him, she considered asking him about Sebastian and Grace. After all, he was an employee, not a member of the family. But Lady Valeria came in just then and the moment passed.

As far as Lady Valeria was concerned, the subject of Grace Moss was closed. Her name was not mentioned once.

By the morning Daisy had changed her mind about consulting Ben. It would be unfair to ask him to be disloyal to his employer's family. Also, his anxiety about Sebastian's reaction to Grace's death suggested he was as concerned as Bobbie was to shield her brother—which, in turn, suggested there was a reason to shield him.

Somehow she'd find out, Daisy vowed, since Inspector Dunnett had cravenly relinquished his duty to investigate. Not that she suspected Sebastian of murder, but so brutal a crime must not go unpunished and no clue could safely be neglected.

She neglected the whole affair that morning, however. Ben had dug up enough anecdotes to make the unexciting history of the house entertaining, and she wrote reams of notes. Then after lunch they set off together to walk down to the inquest.

As they passed the smithy, two men hung with equipment were photographing the piles of scrap metal. The Press had arrived. When she saw the crowd around the entrance to the Village Hall, Daisy was glad of Ben's company, but no one took any notice of them. The centre of attention was a burly man, not tall but brawny, in oil-stained mechanic's dungarees. Waving his arms, he was ranting about titled bloodsuckers who robbed a man of his livelihood and his children.

"Stan Moss," murmured Ben.

The blacksmith was surrounded by eager reporters. Village people stood about watching and listening, some scandalized, some nodding agreement, and not a few both. In one group Daisy saw Ted Roper.

Ben and Daisy slipped past and entered the barnlike wooden building with a stage at the far end. The village bobby, P.C. Rudge, directed Ben to the front row and pointed

out the public benches to Daisy. She went with Ben anyway
and sat beside him on a hard chair not designed for human
anatomy. Bligh and Owen Morgan were already there, at the
far end of the row. The old man looked stolidly ruminative,
Owen forlorn, his face drawn and unhappy. Daisy's heart
went out to him. She would have gone to speak to him if it
weren't for Sergeant Shaw planted in the middle of the row,
his bulk blocking the way.

At a table on the left side of the stage sat a small, grey
man in a grey suit, presumably the coroner. He was talking
to Inspector Dunnett and a plump gentleman Daisy recognized as Dr. Sedgwick. On the right side of the stage, the
jury benches began to fill with a solemn array of villagers,
farmers, and tradesmen.

The crowd from outside had been drifting into the gloomy,
draughty room. Daisy glanced back and saw the "gentlemen" of the Press rush in to squeeze into the back two rows
set aside for them. Stan Moss came down the aisle as the
doctor and Inspector Dunnett descended from the stage, and
all three found places at the front. The coroner rapped on
the table. The room quieted.

The first witness called was Stan Moss. He identified the
deceased as his daughter Grace and admitted he hadn't seen
her since the second week in December. No, he hadn't reported her missing.

"Thought she'd gone orf to make 'er forchin in London,
din't I," he justified himself. "Never satisfied, the young uns
these days, allus grumbling. Good luck to 'er, says I.
Getchaself out from under them as thinks acos they calls
themselves gentry they can. . . ."

"Thank you, Mr. Moss, that will be all," said the coroner
sharply. The blacksmith sat down, his sullen face resentful.
Daisy couldn't blame the coroner for preventing a tirade, yet
she wondered if he was as anxious as the police to avoid
involving the Parslows. For all she knew, he was their solicitor.

"Arthur Bligh." He picked up a sheet of paper. "I have here your statement to the police," he said as the old man rose, shoulders hunched, his hat clutched in rheumatic hands. "You are head gardener at Occles Hall? You ordered your assistant, Owen Morgan, to dig up a border in the Winter Garden? And you were present while he dug and when he unearthed the deceased?"

"Aye, that I wor, your honour, Mr. Crowner, sir. But if your honour pleases, I want for to say. . . ."

"Thank you, Mr. Bligh." The coroner was kindly but firm. "Unless you have any specific and hitherto undisclosed evidence to present to the court, or you wish to draw attention to an explicit inaccuracy in your statement, that will be all for now."

Bligh hesitated, but perplexed by words he didn't understand he made a helpless gesture and sat down.

"Owen Morgan."

A murmur rose from the public benches as Owen stood. Daisy heard someone behind her mutter, "Furriner," and a scornful whisper, "Taffy." A lonely outsider in the close-knit Cheshire community, Owen had good reason to miss his home and family.

"Mr. Morgan, you were ordered by your superior, Arthur Bligh, to dig up the Winter Garden flowerbed?"

"Yes, sir," Owen responded in a low voice, listlessly.

"You immediately recognized the deceased as Grace Moss?"

"Yes, sir."

"I understand you were . . . er . . . keeping company with the deceased before her disappearance?"

"Yes, sir." Almost inaudible.

"How did you account for her sudden absence?"

"I thought she'd run off to London, look you!" His quiet answer was a cry of pain. "Dull she found it here and the bright lights she wanted. Those there were. . . ."

"Thank you, Mr. Morgan," pronounced the inexorable

coroner. Owen slumped into his seat and buried his face in his hands.

Something nagged at Daisy's mind. Something Ted Roper had said? It faded as the coroner called on Ben.

Stony-faced, plainer than ever, he gave his brief evidence. Grace Moss had failed to return after her weekly evening out on Wednesday, December 13. Lady Valeria had instructed him, should she reappear, to pay her whatever was owed and dismiss her. He had not set eyes on her again until he arrived at the Winter Garden yesterday as the body was identified. After arranging for the police to be called, he had stayed to guard the body until they arrived. He sat down.

Inspector Dunnett's impassive report added nothing new. Daisy's name remained unspoken, a delicate attention she did not appreciate. Her evidence was as good as any man's, if not better.

"Dr. Sedgwick."

The plump doctor revelled in obscure medical terms, but not for nothing had Daisy worked in a hospital office during the War. The deceased had been buried for several weeks, greater precision being impossible after such a passage of time. Because of the cold winter weather and the winding sheet, the body was in an excellent state of preservation.

As Sergeant Shaw had told Daisy, Grace had been hit on the back of the head by a blunt instrument, with enough force to crush her skull. An ordinary fall would be insufficient to produce the effect, and other injuries consonant with a fall from a height were absent. In fact, abrasions and contusions—scrapes and bruises, Daisy translated to herself—on the face, knees, and front of the body suggested that the victim had fallen forward, either immediately before or immediately after death.

Dr. Sedgwick paused for breath and the coroner interrupted to summarize in layman's terms for the jury.

"Is that correct, Doctor? Please continue."

"The deceased"—this time his pause was clearly for dramatic effect—"was three months pregnant."

With a wordless roar, Stan Moss jumped to his feet and shook a fist like a ham at the doctor. An excited clamour rose from the public and Press benches. The coroner rapped once on his table, gave up, and crossed the stage to speak to the jury.

As the hubbub died down, he returned to his seat and gave three smart knocks. An expectant silence fell.

"Gentlemen of the jury, have you considered your verdict?"

The foreman stood up. "That we 'as, sir, and we find murder, by person or persons unknown."

"Then I shall adjourn these proceedings for two weeks to allow the police to proceed with their enquiries."

Apparently Daisy was not the only one to feel a sense of anticlimax. Subdued chatter accompanied a general movement out of the hall. Inspector Dunnett and Sergeant Shaw climbed the steps to the stage to talk to the coroner. Ben and Daisy followed the flock down the aisle to the door.

Outside, people lingered, reluctant to return to their everyday affairs. Some of the Press photographers were snapping a few shots in a desultory way. As Daisy emerged into daylight, a tall, loose-limbed figure detached itself from the mass.

"Phillip! What on earth are you doing here?"

"What-ho, old thing. I read about this beastly business in the paper this morning and I thought I'd better toddle along and make sure you're bracing up. Hullo, what's going on now?"

Daisy turned. Behind her the two policemen had come up on either side of Owen.

"Mr. Morgan," said the Inspector, "I'm requesting you to come along with us to headquarters to help us with our enquiries."

"Murderer!" Stan Moss advanced, fists raised. As Sergeant Shaw interposed his bulk, photographers sprang to life.

"I'll see you in Hell for this, you dirty, sneaking Welshman," the blacksmith bellowed.

Dunnett's hand on his arm, Owen moved through the parting crowd like a sleepwalker, bewildered yet apathetic.

"Oh well," said Phillip, "if they've got their man already, I needn't have worried."

"They haven't arrested him," Daisy protested.

"Comes to the same thing, doesn't it? Watch those Press chappies run. They know what's what."

"Then they've got the wrong man," said Daisy fiercely. "Owen didn't do it. They've made him a scapegoat!"

"Here, I say, old bean, no need to bite a fellow's head off."

"No," Daisy admitted. "Sorry, Phillip. It's that ghastly man Dunnett I'm mad at, and myself. He wasn't interested in what I had to say so I tamely stood by and let him jump to the conclusion that suited him best."

"Why should it suit him—it's the busy we're talking about?"

"Inspector Dunnett," she said with loathing.

"Why does it suit him to pinch that particular laddie?"

"Because it lets the Parslows off scot-free and so saves him from Nemesis."

"Nemesis?" asked Phillip, puzzled. "Wasn't she that ghastly Greek female who turned people into stone?"

"That's Medusa. She'll do even better for Lady Valeria."

"She really is a battle-axe, eh? Look here, Daisy, I suppose you'd better tell me what this is all about."

"If you don't mind, Phil. It would help me sort things out for myself."

"Is there a Tea Shoppe in the village?"

"I don't think Occleswich runs to such gaiety. I'll ask. . . . Oh, where's Ben? I should have introduced him to you."

"Ben?"

"Sir Reginald's secretary, Ben Goodman. He had to give evidence so I came down with him."

"You call Sir Reginald's secretary Ben?"

"It's no good frowning at me. He's a thoroughly good egg and I like him and I'll call him Ben if I choose. There he is, talking to the coroner. Oh dear, he looks worn to a thread. He was gassed in the War."

"Was he, by Jove, poor devil! Expect I ought to offer to run him home in the bus."

"Will you? He has a bad leg, too. I'll squeeze into the dickey and we can go on into Whitbury for tea."

This plan was adopted, except that Ben insisted on taking the dickey seat. On the way back through the village after dropping him at the Hall, they stopped at the Cheshire Cheese and Phillip booked a room.

"Good job all those reporters are clearing out back to town," he said, returning to the Swift. "When I arrived, there wasn't a room to be had for love nor money."

"They've gone?" Daisy pulled a wry face. "So they really believe the case is closed."

"Yes, and without giving them much to sink their teeth into. This morning's headlines were along the lines of 'Beauty's Body Buried in Baronet's Border.' After that, 'Gardener Biffs Parlourmaid Sweetheart' just doesn't come up to scratch."

"If they print that, it'll be libel. He didn't."

"What makes you think not, old girl?" Phillip shouted over the racket of the car as he speeded up on leaving the village.

Daisy hung on to her hat. "I'll tell you when we get there," she yelled.

6

The small town of Whitbury boasted a genuine Cadena tea room. Over a pot of tea and hot-buttered toasted tea-cakes, Daisy gathered her thoughts and for the first time put her misgivings into words.

"For a start, Owen loved Grace and wanted to marry her. He was absolutely miserable because he thought she'd run away."

"How the deuce do you know that?" Phillip demanded.

"He told me. He was showing me the Winter Garden and we were talking about his family, and how lonely he was far from home."

Phillip shook his smoothly neat fair head in disbelief. "This assistant gardener, a total stranger, poured out his bally heart to you within minutes of meeting you?"

"Well, he did," Daisy said defensively. "I don't suppose Dunnett would have believed it, either, but I didn't even try to tell him because it didn't seem fair to expose Owen's private feelings. And worse, I didn't explain how that blasted bush got dug up in the first place. Did you hear the evidence?"

"Most of it. The head gardener ordered your Welsh chappie to dig it up."

"Yes, but only because Owen went to fetch him after inspecting the bush and finding it was dying. He could easily have passed it off to me as a late bloomer or something. And then he told Bligh his spade had hit an obstruction. I bet he could have got the bush out without ever mentioning it. Besides, what gardener would be fool enough to bury a body where it would kill plants and draw attention to itself?"

"That's a point," Phillip admitted.

"None of that came out at the inquest. I wonder if old Bligh was trying to explain when the coroner cut him off? I'll have to ask him."

"Dash it, Daisy, you're not going to get mixed up in this!"

"Someone has to stand up for Owen, and no one else will because they're afraid of Lady Valeria, and the more I think about it, the more certain I am Sebastian Parslow is in it up to his precious neck!" Daisy's teeth closed on a tea-cake with a resolute crunch.

"Sebastian? The beautiful son? Oh Lord, you're not going to start accusing *him* of murder?"

"Unlike the despicable Dunnett, *I* don't jump to convenient conclusions. I haven't any evidence, only heaps of hints linking Sebastian and Grace. Owen wasn't necessarily the father of her child."

"Which gives him a spiffing motive."

"Jealousy. Blast, you're right. But at least it opens the field up to other suspects. Lady Valeria and Bobbie are frightfully protective of Sebastian. Either of them. . . . Phillip, I've just remembered. Ted Roper didn't say Grace ran away to London, he said she'd gone off with a commercial traveler."

"Who's Ted Roper? Another suitor? Dash it, the girl must have been a regular Athena."

"I think you mean Aphrodite," said Daisy absently. "But Ted Roper's just the old chap who drives the station fly."

"I suppose he told you his family history, too," Phillip grumbled.

"Yes, and about the blacksmith's quarrel with Lady Valeria. And he said Grace left with a commercial traveler. Now why should he say that if she hadn't been seen with one just about the time she disappeared?"

"Can't imagine. Shall I order more tea? You've emptied the pot."

"Yes. No. Phillip, the obvious place for Grace to meet a commercial would be the Cheshire Cheese, wouldn't it? Lots of people must have seen her, and the locals are bound to be talking about it after the inquest. If you spend the evening in the bar, you might pick up all sorts of information."

"Here, I say!"

"And I must talk to Mr. Bligh before dinner. Come on, let's go."

Half an hour and a good many futile protests later, Phillip dropped Daisy at the wicket-gate at the top of the village street. She walked up the path across the park in the dusk. Her steps speeded up involuntarily as she came to the gravel walk and passed the door to the Winter Garden. The air was growing chilly, she told herself.

Ben had sent the two gardeners to Bligh's cottage, she recalled, and after taking their statements Sergeant Shaw had come round the end wall. Turning left through a gap in a laurel hedge, Daisy found herself among cabbages, cauliflowers, and cold frames. The air smelt of compost. On the far side of the vegetable garden a white-painted gate was visible in the growing gloom. Thither she hopefully picked her way between rows of Brussels sprouts.

"Miss!"

Daisy nearly jumped a mile. She swung round. Old Bligh stumped towards her from the direction of a potting shed she hadn't noticed.

"Mr. Bligh, I was coming to see you. I want to talk to you about Owen Morgan."

She was aware of a steady regard from beneath his appalling hat, then he said, "Right, miss. I be off home for m'tea. Do 'ee come along if 'ee will."

She followed him through the gate, set in a hawthorn hedge. A cottage crouched there, with a thin trickle of smoke rising from its chimney into the deepening blue of the sky.

There was just enough light left for Daisy to see that the tiny front garden was devoted to rose bushes, already putting out new red shoots. In summer the walls of the cottage would be a mass of climbing roses.

The gardener led her round the side. The back yard was occupied by a pump and an enclosure where half a dozen hens scratched and pecked idly at the ground. A ginger cat sprang down from a windowsill and twined around Bligh's ankles, mewing.

He opened the back door, ushered Daisy into the cottage, and lit an oil lamp. A single room dominated by a black cast-iron range combined the functions of kitchen, dining room, and sitting room. From rush-matted slate floor to whitewashed ceiling, everything was spotless.

"Set 'ee down, miss. I s'll just feed the hens afore I takes m'boots off, if 'ee don't mind."

"Of course not, Mr. Bligh. I don't want to be in your way. Shall I make a pot of tea?"

"That'd be right kindly, miss. There's water in yon kettle."

Daisy raised the cover on the hot side of the range and set the kettle to boil. A brown earthenware teapot was warming at the back of the range. She found a canister of tea in the larder. The sight of a large piece of pork pie reminded her that for country folk "tea" meant high tea, the main meal of the day. Taking a plate from the beautiful Welsh dresser, she set the table for one, laid out pork pie, pickled onions and beetroot, bread and butter and cheese. There was a crock of soup in the larder, too, so she ladled some into a pan and put it to heat beside the kettle.

Bligh came in, the cat at his heels. He stopped on the threshold to stare.

"I hope I've put out the right things," Daisy said. "I'm sure you must be hungry."

"I thank 'ee, missy, but won't 'ee join me?"

"I'm afraid I've just been making a pig of myself on

toasted tea-cakes, and I'm expected for dinner at the Hall later. I'd love a cup of tea."

She made the tea and served the soup while he took off his muddy boots and set them neatly on an old newspaper by the door. Before he sat down on a rush-bottomed chair at the table, the cat got a saucer of milk.

"How clean and tidy you keep the place," Daisy said, thinking of some bachelor flats she had seen.

"M'darter comes up fro' the village once a week to do for me, and me and Owen don't make no more mess than old Tibby there." He gestured at the lapping cat.

"Owen?"

"He lodges wi' me. Din't 'ee know? The other lads has homes in the village, but Owen stops here. A good boy, brung up proper. Chapel, but none the worse for that." His tone turned belligerent as he went on, "The babby worn't hisn, I'll lay my oath, and it worn't him as killed that poor young creetur. Apple of his eye, she wor, and any road Owen wouldn't set a trap to kill a mole if the lawn wor tore up like a ploughed field."

"I don't believe he killed Grace, either. That's why I wanted to talk to you. I don't know about the baby, but if it wasn't his, whose was it?"

She waited while, ruminating over his answer, he finished his soup. "I can't say for sartin-sure, miss, and it been't for me to go a-naming o' names."

"But you have a strong suspicion."

"Aye, that I do." The old man's bright, shrewd eyes regarded her with an assessing gaze. He nodded slowly as he decided to trust her. "Last summer it wor, missy, two, three, mebbe four times, I come upon Grace wi' the young master out and about in the gardens where a parlourmaid ha'n't no call to be. Owen seen 'em too, and he wor a-worriting, I don't deny. But it wor *him* he blamed, turning of a young girl's head wi' his handsome face and lying promises."

"Promises?"

"I can't swear to nothing, mind. Owen said Grace wor a-talking 'bout being a lady one day."

"Mr. Parslow promised to marry her?" Daisy asked, suddenly depressed.

"I dunno, miss, I dunno. Any road, Owen thought she'd come to her senses and wed him as loved her in the end. He wor saving up every penny."

"Did he know she was pregnant?"

Bligh's bent shoulders twitched in a shrug of impotent doubt. "There wor summat. The last days afore she disappeared, he wor quieter nor usual, and he bain't much of a talker best o' times. But I mind him saying as it's not fair to damn a girl forever for one mistake."

"I see. Of course, that could just mean he was finally certain she had . . . succumbed to Mr. Parslow's advances. Why on earth did he fall for her?"

"She wor kind to en, miss, when t'others laughed at the way he talked."

How lonely he must have been! Pondering what she had learned, Daisy worried her lip with her teeth. "The trouble is, there's nothing definite to tell Inspector Dunnett. He'll just put it all down as rumour and hearsay."

"Aye, miss," Bligh said sadly.

"Perhaps I can sow some doubts in his mind. At least I must make sure he realizes the body was only discovered because Owen drew attention to the dead azalea."

"That's what I wor trying to say to yon crowner, him making out digging wor my notion."

"I thought so. Anyway, I'll do what I can. Thanks for your help, Mr. Bligh, and for the tea." She stood up.

"Here, you'll need a lantern to light your way." He took down a hurricane lamp from a hook by the door, lit it, and adjusted the flame. "You'll tell me if there's owt I can do for the lad, missy?"

"I will, I promise."

Lamp in hand, Daisy walked swiftly towards the Hall.

Though the night air held a threat of frost before morning, it wasn't only the cold that made her shiver. She was afraid of Lady Valeria's ability to thwart any scrutiny of her family's involvement with Grace. Her ladyship wouldn't care if a mere gardener was wrongfully condemned as long as her darling Sebastian was safe. Perhaps he had nothing to do with the murder, but the dastardly Dunnett wasn't even going to try to find out.

The villagers didn't care about Owen, the "foreigner." Any of them who knew anything would keep his mouth closed rather than risk offending Lady Valeria.

They'd talk among themselves in the pub, though, about the commercial traveler if not about Sebastian. The traveler, supposing Ted Roper hadn't invented him, might prove of vital importance. Had Phillip taken seriously her request to listen in the bar tonight?

She was very tempted to go down herself to the Cheshire Cheese after dinner. The trouble was, even in this modern age a woman walking alone into a pub was looked at askance. Besides, since the inquest everyone must know of her connection with Occles Hall, so her presence would make them wary. No, it simply wasn't on.

She went up to her room and spent half an hour typing out the morning's shorthand notes before changing for dinner.

As she covered the typewriter and straightened her papers, Bobbie came in. "Owen Morgan's been arrested," she said gruffly.

"No, only taken in for questioning."

"Arrested and charged. The Inspector just phoned." She moved to the chest-of-drawers and fidgeted with Daisy's brush and comb. "They must have found evidence that he did it, mustn't they?"

"I don't believe it!" Daisy was on the point of asking straight out what had gone on between Sebastian and Grace when Bobbie interrupted with the obvious intention of changing the subject.

"Ben says a friend of yours is staying in Occleswich?"

"Yes, Phillip Petrie." A pang of guilt struck her. "Gosh, I'm afraid I've rather treated the Hall as a hotel this afternoon. Too rude, especially when your mother's dying to see the last of me."

"That's all right, Mummy doesn't know. The inquest was bound to delay your work so she won't expect you to leave in the morning, and Daddy's still frightfully keen on showing you the dairy. Is Mr. Petrie a particular friend?"

By the time Daisy had explained that Phillip was a childhood rather than a "particular" friend, they had to rush to change. Another chance to question Bobbie was lost.

Dinner was another uncomfortable meal, with Lady Valeria holding forth on the undesirability of hiring other than local servants, and Daisy holding her tongue with difficulty. She didn't want to have an outright row with her hostess so that she had to leave Occles Hall.

After dinner, she went to the telephone cubby and rang up Phillip. "Have you heard anything useful?" she asked eagerly.

"Dash it, old thing, I've just finished eating. Jolly good cheese your Sir Reginald makes, don't you know."

"Blast Sir Reginald's cheese!"

"Oh, right-ho, I did catch a word or two before dinner about your. . . ."

"Don't say it on the phone." Remembering how quickly the Press had arrived on the scene after her call to the Chester police, Daisy didn't trust the local exchange. She couldn't simply ring up Dunnett with her information. "Will you drive me into Chester tomorrow morning? I simply must . . . um . . . buy a new ink-ribbon for my typewriter."

"You and your writing!" Phillip sounded vaguely bewildered by what he evidently regarded as an abrupt digression. "Yes, I'll take you."

"Thanks, old dear. And you'll go on listening this evening?"

Reluctantly he agreed, and Daisy returned to the drawing room for coffee. Lady Valeria asked how her work was going.

"Quite well," Daisy said. Crossing her fingers under the table, she went on, "Unfortunately I find I need a new ink-ribbon for my typewriter. A friend who happens to be in the area has offered to drive me into Chester in the morning to buy one."

Suspicious of this fortuitous friend, Lady Valeria pursued enquiries with a zeal Inspector Dunnett would have done well to emulate. Her doubts were laid to rest when Daisy explained that, far from being a reporter, Phillip was a younger son of Baron Petrie of Malvern. "You may invite Mr. Petrie to dine with us tomorrow," she said graciously. "I know his mother."

Next morning, Phillip groaned when Daisy relayed this invitation. "I suppose I'll have to accept. The mater'll consider it treason." The Swift raced down the drive.

"Don't tell her. And there's no need to drive as if some frightful fiend does close behind you tread. I'd like to reach Chester in one piece. Well, what did you learn last night?"

"I wish you'd drop that bally business." He slowed for the gates, turned into the lane, and picked up speed.

"Then why are you taking me to Chester?"

"For a typewriter rib. . . . To see the police?" He groaned again. "Hang it all, that's a rotten trick to play on a fellow."

Soothing his lacerated sensibilities, Daisy managed to extract his bar gleanings. Grace had definitely talked at length with a commercial traveler shortly before her disappearance. He had treated her to either a half of shandy or a port-and-lemon, a subject of some controversy among patrons of the Cheshire Cheese. Not one of the regular, well-known suppliers of the village shop, he was thought to be a Londoner.

"And that's all," said Phillip. "I'll be hanged if I'll go

sleuthing to the point of asking nosy questions, even for you."

"That's enough," Daisy exclaimed. "Bless you, Phil. Even Dunnett will have to sit up and take notice."

"I can't think how you failed to twist him round your little finger in the first place," he grumbled.

"I might have if he wasn't scared stiff of Lady Valeria."

"Speaking of whom, a fellow in the bar-parlour last night was asking me about her. One of these long-haired poet chappies, but it turned out his brother is a man I know in the City. A downy bird, not like this fellow. He seemed a bit put out when I gave him the goods on Lady Valeria."

"How odd. You'll come in with me to see the Inspector, won't you? He may pay more attention to you than to me."

"Right-ho," Phillip agreed in a doubtful voice.

When they reached Chester, they found a photography shop and Daisy left a film to be developed and printed.

"It has the pictures Ben took in the Winter Garden," she explained. "I want to see how they come out before I try to interest Inspector Dunnett in them. I'll develop the rest in Lucy's darkroom when I get home."

They went on to the police station. The desk officer turned them over to Sergeant Shaw, who led them upstairs and along a corridor.

"Is it true Owen Morgan's been arrested?" Daisy demanded.

"That's right, miss. So you've got new information, 'ave you? Can't say as the Inspector's going to be 'appy. You wouldn't think to look at 'im 'e was a himpulsive man, but 'e tends to jump the gun a mite. Inspector Been and Gone and Dunnett we calls 'im."

Phillip snorted with laughter. Daisy was not amused. "Very appropriate. He's made a real bloomer this time," she said.

"You won't tell 'im I told you, miss?"

"Of course not." She smiled at him. "But I'm glad to know."

Sergeant Shaw became confidential. "What I 'ear is, the Super's raving mad and the Chief Constable's none too 'appy. I mean, it don't look any too good going round arresting people without enough evidence, and motive ain't evidence. Trouble is, neether of 'em fancies a set-to with 'er ladyship, and 'oo can blame 'em, says I? 'Ere we are."

He ushered Daisy and Phillip into a small office and made himself scarce. Behind a cluttered desk Inspector Dunnett rose to his feet, hanging up his telephone. He was in plain-clothes, a funereal black suit and navy blue tie. Daisy guessed he had worn his uniform to Occles Hall because its official nature stiffened his backbone to face the gentry.

"I gather you want to change your statement, Miss Dalrymple," he growled.

"Not so much change it as add to it, Inspector." Daisy tried to be tactful. "I suppose I was in a state of shock and may have inadvertently misled you by omission. Also, I've made one or two discoveries since then."

An expression of dismay crossed his long face, then he scowled and snapped, "One thing at a time." With a curt gesture he invited them to sit down. "What is it you failed to tell my sergeant?"

"First, long before we came to the dead bush, Owen told me the girl he hoped to marry had gone off. He was desperately unhappy."

"He was getting his story in before you asked about the bush."

Clenching her fists, Daisy kept her voice even. "But he could have told me it would bloom later in the spring. He was the one who said it was dying and insisted on calling in Mr. Bligh. And if he hadn't said his spade was hitting something, the body wouldn't have been disinterred."

"I'm afraid, miss, you don't understand the way a murderer's mind works," said Dunnett, with a cold sneer. "As often as not, they can't resist returning to the scene of the crime and poking around. And likely he'd be glad of witnesses to give him just the excuse you've provided."

"But he was horribly upset when he found her!"

"You can be sorry someone's gone even if you bashed her head in."

Daisy shuddered. Phillip leaned forward, angry. "Look here, my good man," he said, "Miss Dalrymple's come forward to help the police. The least you can do is treat her politely and take her statement."

"Yes, sir." The Inspector's tone was wooden. "I'll have a new statement typed up and Miss Dalrymple can sign it if you'll be good enough to return in an hour or so." He began to stand.

"I'm not finished!" Daisy wasn't going to let herself be dismissed yet again. "I'm pretty sure Grace Moss was having an affair with Sebastian Parslow, and the baby was his, not Owen Morgan's."

Dunnett paled, but he said sarcastically, " 'Pretty sure,' miss?"

"You can hardly expect me to provide proof. You'll have to investigate and find out for yourself."

"I'll thank you not to try to teach the police their business, miss. That sort of thing is hearsay, not admissible evidence. Still, Morgan may have believed it, which gives him another excellent motive: jealousy. Now, if that's all . . ."

"It's not." She almost spat the words out. "Lots of people saw Grace in conversation with a stranger, a commercial traveler, at the village inn on the day she disappeared. They thought she had run off with him. You'll find plenty of witnesses if you can be bothered to ask."

"Heard 'em talking about it myself," Phillip loyally confirmed. "You can't ignore that."

"Naturally we shall have this man traced, sir," said Dunnett, stiff with annoyance, "if he exists. No one else has mentioned him, but I'll get the Occleswich constable onto it." Reaching for his telephone, he paused. "Unless you have any more startling revelations, miss?"

"Not yet, Inspector." Daisy glowered at him as she stood up. "But you may be sure that I shall not allow anything I find out to be swept under the carpet!"

In fuming silence she marched along the passage and down the stairs, and swept out of the police station, Phillip trailing at her heels. On the pavement she stopped and turned to him.

"I need a phone," she announced. "I'm going to ring up Alec. Detective Chief Inspector Fletcher of Scotland Yard won't kowtow to Lady Valeria Parslow!"

1

Alec Fletcher's office in New Scotland Yard had a window overlooking the Thames. He rarely had time to admire the view, but today, after snatching a quick sandwich lunch in the canteen, he felt entitled to treat himself to a soothing thirty seconds of river and boats. In the past two days he had cleared up two major cases, a dock warehouse robbery gang he'd been working on for weeks, and a particularly nasty attempted murder.

Of course, in the meantime the paper had been piling up on his desk, and on Sergeant Tring's, at right-angles to his own. Tom Tring, mountainous in vivid blue and green checks, regarded the neat stacks with unmitigated loathing. With a sigh, Alec turned to his overflowing in-tray. He recognized the importance of paper-work but that didn't mean he had to like it.

The telephone on Tom's desk rang and the sergeant picked up the receiver. As he listened, his eyebrows rose towards the shining dome of his head.

"Put her through," he said. "Hullo? Yes, miss, Tom Tring here. What can I do for you?"

Again he listened. His little brown eyes began to twinkle and his luxuriant grey walrus mustache quivered.

Now what was amusing him? The distant, tinny female voice sounded vaguely familiar to Alec, but he couldn't make

out the words. Sighing again, he initialled the paper in front
of him and passed on to the next.

"Yes, miss," said Tom in a grave voice, "I do think that's
worth disturbing him for. Half a minute, I'll put you
through." Openly grinning, he pressed the button that transferred the call to Alec's apparatus, and put a meaty hand over
his own mouthpiece. "Miss Dalrymple, Chief. Got a job for
us."

Alec groaned. He might have known Daisy couldn't find
a murder on her doorstep without intervening. But this morning's headlines had reported the murderer arrested. What was
she up to?

As he lifted the receiver, he saw Tom switch his phone to
an internal line and start talking. Then Daisy's voice was in
his ear.

"Alec? Hullo, Alec, are you there?"

"Yes, Miss Dalrymple, Detective Chief Inspector Fletcher
speaking."

"Alec, don't Miss Dalrymple me. Oh, is Sergeant Tring
in your office with you? Not that he'd care. But never mind
all that, I haven't got an endless supply of sixpences. Alec,
you simply must do something. They've arrested the wrong
man."

"In the Occles Hall case? That's Cheshire police business.
Just hold your horses a moment and remember I can't interfere unless we're called in by the Chief Constable."

"I know, I know. You needn't think I've rung you up on
impulse. I was going to phone an hour ago but Phillip made
me wait and think about it until after we'd had lunch."

"Phillip?"

"Phillip Petrie. He read about the Occles Hall murder in
the papers and drove up here because he thought I might
need protection."

"Brave man," said Alec, who was of the opinion that Daisy
was more in need of protection from herself than from anyone else.

"Well, you know what a sweet old chump he is. He doesn't understand I can look after myself. But he does agree that Inspector Dunnett isn't investigating properly."

"Does he, indeed?" Of course, it took a strong man to stand out against Daisy's persuasive ways.

"Yes, he does. And Dunnett's sergeant told us neither his Superintendent *nor the Chief Constable* is satisfied with the arrest," she said triumphantly.

"I still can't butt in."

"And I've convinced Dunnett he has to trace a commercial traveler who's probably a Londoner so they'll be forced to ask for your help."

With considerable sympathy for Inspector Dunnett, Alec said, "It sounds as if they're doing everything they can."

"Oh no, they're not. They'll never ask the most important questions because they're all scared to death of Lady Valeria Parslow. That's why I want you to come. She won't frighten you."

"I see." In spite of recognizing the persuasive wiles aimed now at him, Alec was gratified by her confidence in his ability to withstand pressure exerted by the upper classes. And after all, she *had* sorted out the Wentwater Court affair, though the result had been decidedly unorthodox.

"Alec, there's an innocent man in prison! Blast, I'm running out of change."

"All right, Daisy, you win. I can't promise anything but I'll see what I can do."

"Angel! I'll see you soon, Chief," she said, and rang off.

He hung up the receiver, his face growing hot under Tom's quizzical gaze. "Don't say it," he warned.

"She's got her head screwed on right," the sergeant reassured him, adding slyly, "even if she can talk the hind leg off a donkey. Been seeing a bit of her since Wentwater, eh, Chief?"

Alec attempted nonchalance. "Once or twice, just to make

sure she's all right. That was a nasty business for a delicately bred female to be mixed up in."

"Delicate, ho!" Tom scoffed. "She's mixed herself up in a much nastier one this time. Pregnant parlourmaid got her skull stove in by her boyfriend, only our Miss Dalrymple don't believe it was the boyfriend, right? So whoever done it's still on the loose and she's in the thick of it. Seems to me, Chief, she needs someone up there to keep an eye on her."

"I can't just barge in," said Alec irritably, telling himself he couldn't possibly be jealous of that ass, Petrie.

"I reckon we can wangle it. I just rang down and a request's come in from Cheshire to trace a commercial, name of George Brown, would you believe it! You're the Super's blue-eyed boy right now. . . ."

"All right, all right, I told her I'd give it a try. I'll have to go upstairs to the A.C. though, because it means asking the Cheshire C.C.'s permission to invade his manor. Great Scott, what am I getting myself into?" He groaned but reached for the telephone. "At least Daisy—Miss Dalrymple claims the C.C.'s not happy with the arrest."

The Assistant Commissioner for Crime of the Metropolitan Police was one of the very few people who knew the whole story of Daisy's involvement at Wentwater Court. Alec was convinced he heard him wince over the wire when her name was pronounced. The thought of the Honourable Miss Dalrymple running wild in the middle of a murder case was enough to make the A.C. shudder—and send Detective Chief Inspector Fletcher to try to rein her in.

The Chief Constable of Cheshire, unaware—lucky man—of Daisy's proclivities, was only too glad for reasons of his own to have Scotland Yard take over a case that promised to turn into a disaster.

An hour and a half after Daisy's phone call, Alec hung up for the last time, sat back, and said in a voice full of misgiving, "Well, I'm off. Piper can drive me and I'll try to deal with some of this bumf en route." He gathered a sheaf of papers and shoved them into his attaché case, pretending not to notice Tom's expectant look. "And I'm leaving you, Sergeant, in charge of unmasking the mysterious George Brown."

"Right, Chief," said Tom, his broad face clouding. "Can't be more 'n ten thousand George Browns in London, give or take a couple. And not a clue what he sells."

Alec relented. "There must be some sort of listing of firms which use traveling representatives. Try employment agencies. I'll authorize three constables to help on the phones. Then when you've run the bloke to earth, hop on a train to join us. Don't take too long about it, Tom. Young Ernie deserves his chance but with a parlourmaid and a gardener involved we'll need to look below-stairs for answers, and there's no one to beat you in the servants' hall."

Tom stroked his mustache. "Right, Chief," he said again, slightly cheered. "My best respects to Miss Dalrymple."

With a load off her mind after speaking to Alec, Daisy went to find Phillip in the lounge of the Bear and Billet, the ancient inn in Chester where they had lunched. "He's coming," she announced.

"Just like that, because you asked him to?" Phillip said skeptically.

"Well, he said he'll see what he can do, and I know he'll manage it somehow."

"Hang it all, Daisy, I don't like it, inviting a busy in to pry into the private affairs of people like us."

"For heaven's sake, do stop calling Mr. Fletcher a busy," she snapped. "Murder is not a private affair and Lady Valeria is not 'people like us.' "

"You know what I mean. Oh, all right, I dare say Fletcher is a good enough fellow for a policeman, and Lady Valeria is in a class of her own. I can't say I'm frightfully looking forward to meeting her tonight."

"Just be your usual charming self. The Gorgon won't turn you to stone unless you start chaffing about the murder." An unnecessary warning; Phillip was far too well bred to dream of such a solecism. His social *savoir-faire* was impeccable. "It'll be a relief to have you there."

"I suppose we'd better be buzzing back."

"No hurry." Daisy found herself distinctly reluctant to return to Occles Hall. "I must buy an ink-ribbon first. Oh drat, I forgot to check what size the machine takes."

"That hardly matters since you don't really need one," Phillip pointed out, so they went in search of a stationer's.

Daisy was enchanted with the Rows, the shops whose roofs served as a galleried walk for another, set-back arcade of shops built on top. Exploring, she almost forgot the murder. Then they walked the circuit of the city walls, past the cathedral, the canal, the race-track, the castle, along the river and back. By then the sky was clouding over and she reluctantly decided she ought to put in an appearance for tea at Occles Hall.

As they drove up the hill through Occleswich, a few raindrops spotted the dust on the Swift's bonnet. Daisy saw a familiar stocky figure come out of the Cheshire Cheese.

"There's Bobbie Parslow," she said. "We'd better squeeze her in. It's going to pour any minute."

Phillip obligingly pulled up and Daisy introduced him. Scrambling back to the dickey seat, she induced Bobbie to take the front passenger seat. She thought Bobbie seemed oddly excited, at once guilty and defiant, but Phillip's affable social chatter quickly set her at ease. He dropped them in the entrance passage and put up the Swift's hood before reversing over the bridge and rattling off.

"He's jolly nice," said Bobbie as they went in.

"Yes, Phillip's a good egg. I've known him practically since I was born. His people's place shares a boundary with Fairacres and he was my brother's best chum."

"But you don't . . . I mean, he hasn't . . . ?" Bobbie flushed.

"Oh, he proposes every now and then. More because he feels it his duty to look after Gervaise's little sister than anything else, I think. But he hasn't a bean, any more than I have, just an allowance from his father. He does something in the City, and being a Micawber he. . . ."

"A what?"

"Micawber, the Dickens character who was always sure something would turn up. Didn't you do *David Copperfield* at school? Anyway, even if by a miracle Phillip did make a killing on the Stock Exchange, I wouldn't marry him."

"Oh. Don't you want to marry?"

Daisy thought of Michael, dead and gone; of Alec, a middle-class widower with a nine-year-old daughter she hadn't met yet: Alec, who was rushing from London to Cheshire at her behest. She sighed, smiled. "Under the right circumstances," she said, "I shouldn't have anything against it."

"Really? Because I. . . ."

"Oh there you are, Roberta." Lady Valeria lay in wait in the Long Hall. With a curt nod to Daisy, she turned back to her daughter. "I've been looking for you. Where on earth have you been?"

"I just walked down to the vicarage. I took Mrs. Lake the cake recipe you recommended to her." Bobbie shot a pleading glance at Daisy, who immediately started wondering what she'd been doing at the inn.

"Recipe? You've never taken the least interest in recipes, more's the pity. I want to talk to you about the Girl Guides' meeting next week." She drew Bobbie away and Daisy went upstairs to take off her hat and coat.

The typewriter ribbon was the wrong kind. She hoped the shop would give her her money back, or at least change it.

Picking up her comb to tidy her hair, Daisy gazed unseeing at the mirror. What had Bobbie been doing at the Cheshire Cheese that she didn't want her mother to know about? More than likely Lady Valeria would object to her going there for any reason, but if so, what had led her to defy the ban?

A taste for forbidden gin? Grinning, Daisy shook her head at herself. Not healthy, hearty Bobbie, and anyway the bars would not have been open at that hour.

Perhaps she had caught wind of the local constable's enquiries about the commercial traveler. She might hope for information which would exculpate her brother—except that she had no way of knowing anyone suspected him. Or she herself might suspect him and hope to suppress damning information.

Or she might have killed Grace to protect him.

Daisy shivered. Maybe Phillip was right and one ought to let well alone. But all was not well, she reminded herself sternly. A girl had been brutally murdered and an innocent man was in prison.

She squared her shoulders and reluctantly went down to tea. Everyone except Sir Reginald had gathered in the Yellow Parlour. No stranger dropping in could conceivably have guessed that a human body had been dug up in the garden two days ago.

Lady Valeria and Bobbie continued to talk about the Girl Guides—Daisy gathered Bobbie was a troop leader and Lady Valeria, naturally, headed some committee. Sebastian and Ben were in high spirits. They had been reading together about ruins on some of the smaller Greek islands whose archaeological significance had not yet been investigated.

"Even Ithaca has scarcely been touched," Sebastian told Daisy enthusiastically. "Schliemann only dug a trench or two. Think of it, Ulysses' own home!"

" 'It little profits that an idle king,' " Daisy quoted, trying not to think of trench-digging, " 'By this still hearth, among these barren crags. . . .' It's amazing how a poem learnt by heart years ago sticks in one's mind. I always liked that one."

"Tennyson's sequel to Homer," said Ben, grinning.

"Oh, Tennyson be blowed." Sebastian dismissed the late

Poet Laureate with a wave of the hand. "I don't suppose he ever actually saw the barren crags, or even set foot in Greece."

"If you like, Sebastian," said his mother indulgently, "we might consider going to Corfu next winter instead of the Riviera. I believe it's quite civilized."

"That would be a nice change, Mater," Sebastian said in a colourless voice, and exchanged a glance with Ben. Daisy presumed there was little or no chance of Lady Valeria agreeing to take the secretary with them.

However stunning, Sebastian could not be described as resolute or strong-willed. Was she crazy to think he might have murdered Grace? No; though she simply could not imagine him planning so dire a deed, in a fit of temper—on the spur of the moment—anything was possible.

After tea, he challenged her to a game of backgammon. She hadn't played for some time, and when she went astray he reminded her of the rules with such charming good humour that she was overcome with guilt at the prospect of setting Alec onto him.

Then he chivalrously let her win, which so annoyed her that she went up to change quite at loggerheads with him.

Phillip was not the only guest at dinner. Lady Valeria had also invited Lord and Lady Bristow, an elderly couple whose estate adjoined Occles Hall, and their middle-aged spinster daughter. Not by a word did any of the three indicate an awareness of the recent shocking events. With four outsiders present, everyone had on their social faces, and Daisy was amazed at the banality of the occasion.

Miss Bristow, for one, was never at a loss for a word. Addicted to good works, she was both garrulous and sanctimonious. Seated beside her at the table, Ben Goodman listened with admirable courtesy and patience, but he couldn't quite hide his relief when Bobbie claimed his attention. Miss Bristow addressed Sir Reginald, on her other side, and Daisy saw his eyes glaze as the flood washed over him.

Meanwhile, poor Phillip was undergoing interrogation by Lady Valeria, on his family, his schooling, and his prospects. She didn't seem to recall her row with his mother, but doubtless it had been nothing out of the ordinary for her. Nor, somewhat to Daisy's surprise, did she demand his reason for staying in Occleswich. Either she assumed he had an understanding with Daisy, or she was afraid the murder had something to do with it.

Good manners and an easy temper carried him through, but when he was able to turn back to Daisy, she had a distinct impression that he would have liked to wipe his forehead.

"Was there a Greek monster who melted her victims into a little puddle?" he asked in an undertone.

"Ask Ben, he's the expert. The nearest I know of is Phoebus, the sun god, who could be said to have melted the wax in Icarus' wings."

"I remember that story," said Phillip, pleased.

After dinner, following Lady Valeria and the Bristow ladies to the drawing room, Bobbie whispered to Daisy, "You really don't want to marry Mr. Petrie? You and he get on so well together. If I were you, I'd snap him up."

"Why don't you try?"

"Oh no, I didn't mean that. It's just that every time I see Miss Bristow, I can picture myself ending up exactly the same."

"She seems quite happy," said Daisy dubiously. She was sure she herself would never turn into a Miss Bristow, even if she never married, but if she'd been forced to live with her mother she might have. And if she'd stayed at Fairacres when those worthy, well-meaning fossils Edgar and Geraldine moved in, it would have been practically inevitable. Frightful thought!

The rest of the evening was decorously dull. Phillip discovered mutual Army acquaintances with Ben, but he buzzed off as early as he decently could and the Bristows did not long outstay him. Daisy was about to bid the others good-night and go up to bed when Moody plodded in to say Mr. Petrie wished to speak to her on the telephone.

She made her way to the Long Gallery. Could he have come across a clue? Or perhaps after meeting Lady Valeria he had decided to flee Occleswich at daybreak, she thought, shutting the phone cubby door behind her. Much as she had resented his arrival, she'd really rather like him to stay.

"Phillip? What's up?"

"A friend of yours has arrived, old bean. It'll be all over the county by morning but he asked me to put through the call so as not to wise up the natives betimes. Here he is."

Daisy smiled. However much Phillip resented Alec, he'd do as the detective asked.

"Miss Dalrymple?" The sound of his tired voice was infinitely reassuring.

"Good evening, Mr. Fletcher. Since you're here, I take it I did the right thing in squawking for help?"

"I certainly hope so. But I still know very little of your reasons. I'd like to talk to you before I see the big chief tomorrow. Can you come down to the inn early?"

"Eight o'clock? I'll join you for breakfast. I *am* glad you've come." Let him take that professionally or personally, whichever he preferred.

She hung up. Was it Vi who had told her no woman should consider marrying a man whose behaviour at the breakfast table she had never observed? Usually a house-party took care of that, but Alec was not likely to be invited to any house-party.

Not that she was considering marrying him. It was entirely Bobbie's fault the thought had even crossed her mind. She promptly banished it and instead considered what she was going to tell him tomorrow.

The awful truth was, she had nothing but intuition to explain her belief that Owen Morgan was not a murderer.

8

Under a pillar-box red umbrella, Daisy walked down to the Cheshire Cheese next morning. In the rain the village wasn't half so picturesque. In fact the forced sameness of the cottages gave it a rather sterile air, although more people were about, despite the rain, than there had been on Whitbury market day. An occasional roof of tile or thatch instead of slate, a row of leeks in a front garden, even an intrusive building of Georgian brick would have been welcome. At least the inn's half-timbering was genuine, of the same period as the Hall, to judge by the crooked beams, the wavering roofline, and the step down into the lobby.

Closing her umbrella as she stepped down, Daisy heard the church clock strike eight. Dead on time. A professional start to the interview the prospect of which was making her ridiculously nervous. She touched her coat pocket where reposed a sheaf of papers.

Alec and Phillip, crisp, dark hair and sleek blond, were already seated together at a table in the small dining room. Poor Phillip looked distinctly ill at ease. No doubt Daisy's friendship with Alec had put him in an awkward situation, making it difficult to treat the detective as a distant and far from desirable acquaintance.

Only one of the other three tables was occupied, by a thin, slightly shabby man of a type Daisy instantly recognized as all too common in Chelsea. Artistically dishevelled hair worn a bit too long, a green corduroy jacket and a flowing cravat, the faraway, rapt look of one expecting imminent inspiration: he must be the poet Phillip had mentioned.

Seeing Daisy, Alec rose and pulled out a chair for her. Phillip stumbled to his feet, not only uneasy but still not quite awake. Alec, broader of shoulder though not so tall, was alert, his clear, observant grey eyes smiling at her as he bade her "Good morning."

Her nervousness vanished and she returned the smile as she sat down. "Good morning, gentlemen."

"I was going to fetch you in the car," said Alec, "because of the rain, but Mr. Petrie explained that I'd probably miss you because of the shortcut to the village."

"You would have. It's all right, it isn't the beastly kind of cold, windy rain which blows in under an umbrella. The walk has given me a terrific appetite."

"They do a good breakfast here," Phillip assured her, "though I don't usually get to it till an hour later."

The peroxided girl who had showed her to the dining room came to take their orders. As she left, Daisy said to Alec, "Isn't Mr. Tring with you?" She bit back a giggle as she imagined Phillip's face had he been forced to breakfast with the vast sergeant.

"Tom'll be joining me later. Ernie Piper's eating in the kitchen and . . . er . . . gossiping." With a slight movement of his head, Alec indicated the poet. "But no business till after breakfast," he said firmly.

"By George, no," Phillip agreed. "In fact, unless you want me to stick around, Daisy, I'll see if I can borrow a pair of dungarees and have a go at the old bus. She was making a dashed sinister noise when I drove down from the Hall last night."

"She always does."

"A new noise," he said with dignity.

"You do your own mechanical work?" Alec asked, surprised. He confessed that his Austin Seven was serviced by the police motorpool mechanics, fortunately, as he had no mechanical aptitude. Not that he had had any trouble with it yet; it was only a few months old. Nonetheless he appeared happy to spend the rest of the meal discussing the quirks of the internal combustion engine and its various ancillary attachments. Daisy was bored stiff, but she observed Alec's low opinion of Phillip rising a notch or two.

The poet left as Daisy bagged the last slice of toast from the toast rack and finished off the marmalade. "I'll order some more," she said guiltily.

"Not for me," said Phillip. "It's stopped raining. I'll buzz along now, if you don't need me."

He addressed Daisy, but Alec answered. "Not at present, but don't leave Occleswich without letting me know, please. It's possible you may be able to confirm some of Miss Dalrymple's report."

"Not me!" Phillip hastily demurred. "I mean, I don't know anything about the bally murder, but I shan't skedaddle. Toodle-oo for now, then."

He left, and the girl came in to clear the table. Alec asked if they could use the room to discuss some business, and when she agreed he ordered more tea for Daisy and coffee for himself.

Daisy gave him her papers. "I typed it all out," she said, "so I wouldn't forget anything."

"Splendid. Do you mind if I smoke while I read?"

"Your pipe? Not at all, as long as you don't mind my spelling."

He grinned, reaching into his pocket for pipe and tobacco pouch. "Not at all."

"I didn't worry about spelling because I thought it was more important to make sure I wrote down absolutely everything which might be relevant, and I was up till one doing it anyway."

With a nod of approval, Alec flattened the papers on the table in front of him and started reading while he filled his pipe. The fragrance of fresh tobacco wafted to Daisy's nose. It was a pity people insisted on burning the stuff when it smelled so much better unburnt. The pouch was embroidered in blue with a crooked "A.F." Belinda's work, she guessed. Would Alec's daughter like her when they met?

Sipping tea, she watched him as he read, intent on her words, oblivious of her presence. Though the pipe went out after producing a few curls of blue smoke, he kept it clenched between his teeth while making occasional marks in the margins of the report with his fountain-pen. His face was set in stern lines and he frowned once or twice. Cool and competent, he was all policeman now.

He finished the last page. Straightening the papers, he said seriously, "You were right to call me in. You haven't got anything definite here, but quite enough to make me wonder why the deuce Inspector Dunnett is ignoring it."

"Don't blame him too much until you've met Lady Valeria."

His mouth tightened. "Whatever she's like, it's no excuse for a policeman neglecting his duty, let alone for wrongful arrest. You do realize though, don't you, that while there appears to be no real evidence against Morgan, nor is there any to clear him?"

"I know, but we'll find something."

"We? Daisy, you are absolutely not to interfere in this case."

"I shan't interfere, I'll only help. You must admit it's quite different from last time. I have no sympathy for whoever murdered an innocent young girl."

"Innocent?" he said dryly. "She was unmarried and pregnant, with at least two possible fathers for the child."

"Oh, Alec, don't be a prude. She didn't do anyone but herself any harm."

"On the contrary." His lips twitched. "She gave more than one person a lot of pleasure."

"And don't be coarse!" Daisy said severely.

"I beg your pardon." His voice was grave but those grey eyes laughed at her. Then he sobered and leafed through the papers. "I have one or two questions. First, who, besides Mr. Goodman, knew you were interested in the Winter Garden?"

Daisy thought back. "The subject came up at breakfast. Bobbie was there, and Sebastian."

"Neither of them, nor Goodman, made any attempt to dissuade you from visiting it?"

"No, but it would have looked awfully odd if they had, unless all three were in it together. Wait, Sebastian came in later. I'm sure we talked about the gardens in general in his presence—I refused an invitation to ride with him because I wanted to take advantage of the sunshine—but I can't swear to mentioning the Winter Garden specifically."

Alec made a note. "Now, Owen Morgan. It's a bit strange he should make a point of telling you about his girlfriend, that he wanted to marry her but she had deserted him."

"It's not strange at all. He sounds very Welsh, you know. I asked him where he came from, which led to his family, which led to his being lonely here, which led quite naturally to the missing sweetheart."

"I see. Well, I must interview him as soon as I've made my bow to the C.C. and my peace with the local coppers."

"Can you get him out of prison?"

"Probably. But he might be better off staying there." He flipped through her report. "You say here the girl's father threatened him."

"Because he thought Owen was the murderer."

"Even if he's released, he'll still be under suspicion. Anyway, that's not a decision I can make until I've seen him." Consulting his wristwatch, Alec pushed back his chair. "I must go, I have an appointment with the C.C. in Chester."

"Oh, I nearly forgot. Ben took some photos with my camera of the body in the trench." She wrinkled her nose in distaste at the memory. "It seemed like a good idea. I don't suppose they'll show anything useful but if you want to pick them up in Chester, here's the receipt. Don't lose my pictures on the same roll."

"I shouldn't dare." He pocketed the slip of paper. "Thanks. Unless something unexpected comes up, I'll see you this afternoon at Occles Hall. Daisy, you've done a good job but *don't* go asking questions while I'm gone. You never know what you might stir up."

"All right, I won't, if you promise not to cut me out of your investigation altogether."

Alec sighed and shook his head. "I'll keep you abreast of things," he said, "though I ought to be hanged for it."

Alec fetched his young constable, Piper, from the kitchen and they went out to the gravelled yard at the back of the inn. Petrie was flat on his back under his aging silver-grey Swift, invisible but for two long legs in oil-stained blue dungarees too short for them.

"Found the trouble?" Alec asked, striking a match and cupping his hands around the bowl of his pipe in an effort to relight it.

"I think so." Petrie wriggled out, his hands filthy, a smear of oil on one cheek, and wisps of his usually slick hair sticking up all over. Alec liked him the better for his dishevelment. "There's a nut fallen off," he said, sitting up. "I hope Moss will have one that fits."

"Moss at the forge? The bereaved father?"

"Yes, he lent me these dungarees. A good egg. He's got a load of bloody rubbish up there, but he swears he knows exactly where to find all the bits that might turn out to be useful."

"Good luck. You won't talk to him about anything to do with the case, will you? But if he should start on it, you might listen and remember."

Petrie began to scowl, then changed his mind and grinned. "All right, Chief Inspector. At least it's good to know I'm not on your list of suspects this time."

"You never seriously were, you know. Miss Dalrymple was quite convinced of your innocence, and Miss Dalrymple's convictions are damned persuasive."

"They are, aren't they?" Petrie agreed.

Alec drove to Chester. The Austin Chummy bowled happily along the country lanes at a steady thirty-five miles an hour while Ernie Piper reported on the Cheshire Cheese's kitchen gossip.

Most of what the young detective constable had heard merely confirmed already known facts about the commercial traveler: Daisy's account of what Petrie had learned in the bar, plus the Occleswich constable's findings as passed on by his superiors to the Met.

"That's not all, though, Chief," Piper announced importantly. "I found out why this here George Brown was in Occleswich even though he weren't trying to sell to the Village Store. He told the barmaid he'd been doing business in Whitbury, the market town. Summun there told him the village was worth a look and the Cheshire Cheese was a good place to stay, so he decided to try it, being headed this d'rection anyways."

"Well done! I'll ask the local people to make enquiries in Whitbury. The town can't be very big, compared with London at least, so you may have saved the sergeant a lot of work."

Piper's thin chest swelled with pride. "There's more, Chief. Seems he'd took a room for the night but he didn't stay, which is why they all thought the girl had hopped it with him. So what I reckon is, he done her in and then scarpered."

"It's a nice theory, except that he was a stranger in these parts. How would he have known the Winter Garden was there to bury her in?"

"Oh."

Alec glanced at Piper's crestfallen face and consoled him. "It's not inconceivable. I shan't dismiss the possibility that he may have visited Occles Hall at some time for some reason."

"Only then he'd've knowed about the village being pretty," said Piper gloomily.

"Probably. Just remember, in detective work recognizing the holes in your own theories is as important as coming up with them in the first place."

Piper perked up. "Right, Chief. 'Course, him saying that about coming to see Occleswich could've been a blind. S'posing he knowed the girl before and arranged to meet her, like. P'raps she worked in a shop in Whitbury for a while."

"It's worth checking. My impression is that she went straight from school into service at the Hall, but I don't know for certain."

Alec was both amused and pleased by the young man's imaginative reasoning. He knew how difficult it was for the average constable on the beat to earn the coveted transfer to the plainclothes branch. He himself, with a university degree, had entered the force expecting that transfer as a reward for the obligatory years on the beat. The War had interrupted the upward course, but a commission in the Royal Flying Corps and a DFC had not hurt his prospects.

Piper, under-educated product of a board school, had had a tougher row to hoe, but with a helping hand he might go far.

"Of course, it's possible the girl herself described the garden in arranging to meet him there for some reason," Alec conceded, adding, "But don't persuade yourself of George Brown's guilt to the point where you forget the other suspects."

"I won't, Chief. At least we know this gardener chappy's in the clear."

"We do?"

"Miss Dalrymple says so."

"Miss Dalrymple *believes* so." Alec laughed. "Don't mistake even Miss Dalrymple's beliefs for evidence."

Piper blushed. "No, Chief. One more thing I heard in the kitchen, Chief," he hurried on. "All the family at Occles Hall's suspects, aren't they? Seems Miss Roberta—that's what they call her; Miss Parslow she'd be—she's thick as thieves with that long-haired poet chap what's staying at the Cheshire Cheese."

"Is she indeed! That is odd. According to Dai . . . Miss Dalrymple, Miss Parslow is the hearty, sporting, outdoor type. She doesn't sound at all the sort to consort with long-haired poets."

"P'raps it's a disguise," said Piper eagerly, to Alec's relief failing to note his reliance on Daisy's description. "Or p'raps he knows summat about the murder and he's blackmailing her."

"I'll have to talk to him. You've done very well. Now, unless you have any more tidbits for me, let's have a bit of quiet while I think."

For the next few miles, he pondered not Piper's theories but Dunnett's astounding incompetence. Within a few hours of arriving in Cheshire, a very junior detective constable had opened up new lines of investigation which the Inspector should have followed up days ago. How on earth was Alec to handle the Chief Constable and Superintendent without entirely alienating them and losing their cooperation?

Before he had worked out an approach, they came to the River Dee and crossed the bridge into the city of Chester. Alec had visited and explored the ancient town while an undergraduate studying history at Manchester, so he felt less than his usual regret on arriving in an interesting place. His work had taken him all over the country but he was better acquainted with the interiors of police stations than with historical sights.

He gave Piper the receipt for Daisy's photos. "Pick these up," he said, "and wait for me at the desk at the station."

"Right, Chief."

On entering the Chester police headquarters, Alec was shown straight to the Chief Constable's office. Its furniture was upholstered in red leather, as was the C.C. himself—at least the observable bit of him from collar to receding hairline. An ex-colonial civil servant, recently appointed, he was inclined to be querulous about the differences in the administration of justice between Blighty and her overseas possessions.

"A lot of claptrap," he snorted, "all these formalities, warrants, solicitors, *habeas corpus,* wrongful arrest. I say, Chief Inspector, have you met the Parslow woman yet? Frightful female; I give you my word, simply frightful. Rather face a native uprising any day, what?"

Alec escaped as soon as he could and went to see the Superintendent of the Cheshire Constabulary Criminal Investigation Department. Mr. Higginbotham, a neat, spare Yorkshireman who must barely have met police height requirements, was delighted to welcome him. Nearing retirement, he found himself caught in the middle of a triangle composed of an inexperienced superior, a rash subordinate, and an influential termagant. Alec didn't envy him.

"I don't say I'd have called in the Met," he said defensively. "I could have sorted out the hugger-mugger, but I'm glad enough to have you on my patch since you offered. Here are the full reports." He pushed a slim folder across his desk. "Anything I can do to help, Mr. Fletcher, just ask."

"Thank you, sir. Of course it was your request for a tracer on the commercial traveler which brought us into the case." That should keep Daisy out of it. "I understand he may have been doing business in Whitbury before he went to Occleswich. I'd like permission to have some of your people check appropriate businesses in Whitbury to try if we can't get a line on him from this end."

Higginbotham groaned and clutched his head. "You've already discovered something Dunnett missed? If anything in this world is certain, it's that before I retire I'll put paid to any hope that man has of promotion. I've taken him off the case, by the way. He wouldn't even have known the fellow existed if it weren't for a young lady who laid evidence. A Miss Dalrymple. I'd like to have her on the force!"

"Oh no you wouldn't," Alec exclaimed incautiously.

"Aha, know her, do you? I did wonder just what it was brought the Met to our doorstep."

His eyes were twinkling, Alec noted with relief. "Miss Dalrymple seems to be developing a bad habit of falling over bodies," he responded ruefully, "and she . . . shall we say she has more respect for her notion of justice than for the forces of the law."

"No bad thing in this case," said the Superintendent, equally rueful, "but you might remind her that curiosity killed the cat. If the lad we have in custody is innocent, there's a killer out there."

"I have pointed that out, though perhaps not in sufficiently forceful terms."

"It'll bear repeating. Now, I'll have some men put onto the Whitbury search. What else can I do for you?"

"I'd like to speak to Owen Morgan, sir. He has a solicitor, I take it?"

"No. He was offered one at public expense but he refused. He won't say a word to anyone. I hope you'll have better luck. He'll come up before the beaks on Monday and unless there's some hard evidence by then, we'll have to let him go. Then the Press will scrag us either for letting a murderer loose or for arresting the wrong man. Either way. . . ." He shrugged.

"Out of the frying pan into the fire," said Alec with sympathy. The Met was by no means immune to such situations. He stood up. "I think that's all for the moment, sir."

"I'll call down and have Morgan taken to an interview room." Higginbotham rose and shook Alec's hand. "You'll keep me informed—and do try not to make my people look too bad."

"Of course, sir. Oh, one more thing. Do you know of any way George Brown could have been familiar with the Winter Garden?"

"Yes, the Parslows used to hold an Open Day to show it off, before the War. Always being postponed because of bad weather and they haven't started up again since. That's the way you're looking, is it?"

"I wouldn't go so far. It's not by any means the only line of enquiry I have to pursue."

Higginbotham grimaced. "Well, Occles Hall is a good deal farther off from London than from Chester. Good luck, Mr. Fletcher. If there's anything else you need, ask for me or Sergeant Shaw."

Alec found Ernie Piper in the lobby, chatting with the desk sergeant. He had Daisy's photographs, which Alec added to the thin file of police reports. A uniformed constable took them to a small, dingy room furnished with a bare desk and several hard wooden chairs lined up along the walls.

The desk chair, Alec was glad to see, was at least padded, if not the height of comfort. He sat down. Piper set one of the straight chairs to face the desk, and took his place on another in a corner where he'd be inconspicuous from the prisoner's point of view. He extracted his notebook and three well-sharpened pencils from the inside pocket of his modest brown serge suit jacket, placing two of the pencils in the outer breast pocket. Learning shorthand had been one factor in his promotion to the detective branch of the force and he was duly proud of it. Alec nodded approval of his arrangements.

Another uniformed constable brought in Owen Morgan. Alec studied the slight, dark youth who stood before him in a shabby coat, his shoulders drooping hopelessly, sallow face drawn, seeming to hold himself upright by a huge effort of will.

"Sit down, lad," he said gently. Morgan slumped onto the nearest chair. "Cigarette?" A weary shake of the head answered him. "Coffee? No, tea," he guessed. "Officer, three cups, please."

The constable saluted and went out.

"I'm Detective Chief Inspector Fletcher, from Scotland Yard. You know, I could have you out of here today."

Morgan looked up, a momentary flash of hope in his reddened eyes. Then he shook his head again. "What's the use, sir? I can't go back there and she'll never giff me a reference. It's home to Merthyr I'll haff to go and down the pit. It'll break me mam's heart, look you. I might as well stop here."

That didn't sound like the answer of a murderer, Alec thought, as the tea arrived, slopped in the saucers. He sipped from his cup. It was stewed, tepid, and over-sugared, and white flecks suggested the milk had seen better days. He abandoned it, but Morgan drank his thirstily.

Alec waited till he had finished before he said, "Tell me about Grace."

Silent tears began to course down Morgan's face. He scrabbled in his pocket, came up empty-handed. Alec moved around the desk and gave the boy his handkerchief, hoping his mother, a quick-packing expert, had remembered to put in a spare. He perched on the corner of the desk.

"You saw her on the day she disappeared?"

"No, sir. Busy all day she wass. After tea at the Hall, her evenings off, she'd go down to the fillage to make her pa's tea."

"And then to the Cheshire Cheese. You didn't go with her?"

"Saving to be married I wass."

"You didn't mind her chatting with other men at the pub?"

"I loved her," Morgan said with a defiant air. "It's not I will tell tales on her."

"You can't hurt her now," Alec said brutally. "Everyone

knows she was expecting a child. The only question is, whose?"

"Not mine, but gladly I'd haff giffen the babe my name."

"You knew before the inquest that she was pregnant?"

"She told me."

"And she told you the name of the father?"

"No need. Wassn't she in love with the young master, and him promising to marry her?"

Alec glanced from the corner of his eye at Piper, to make sure he hadn't broken the leads of all three pencils at the wrong moment. "The young master?" he probed.

"Mr. Sebastian."

"Sebastian Parslow."

"Aye, him."

"How do you know?"

"Didn't she tell me everything? How her ladyship wass always after pushing her at him and. . . ."

"Wait a minute. You're saying Lady Valeria encouraged her parlourmaid to chase her son?"

"Grace told me," said Morgan stubbornly. "Her ladyship ordered her to take up Mr. Sebastian's early morning tea, because the housemaid was a silly girl who embarrassed him with her giggling. And his whisky nightcap, too, when he rang for one, which Mr. Moody ought to haff done, or Mr. Thomkins, who's so careless and lazy he cannot be relied on to answer the bell."

"Good Lord!" Alec said, flummoxed. The only explanation that came to mind was that Grace had made up the story to excuse herself to her suitor.

The boy was in full flood now, reticence forgotten. "And Grace thought it meant her ladyship liked her. She wouldn't believe me when I said her ladyship'd neffer let her precious son marry a servant, whateffer he promised. You can't blame her, sir, with her pa after her too."

"You mean she told you her father also encouraged her to . . . ah . . . sow her wild oats?"

"All *he* cared about wass making trouble for her ladyship," said Morgan bitterly.

That at least was more explicable than Lady Valeria's behaviour, if hardly paternal. According to Daisy, Stanley Moss had a virulent grudge against Lady Valeria. He'd expect his daughter's affair with her son not only to cause trouble but possibly to lead to a monetary settlement.

On second thoughts, maybe Lady Valeria felt the same way about Grace's fall bringing trouble on her father. Had the girl's reputation—and eventually her life—been sacrificed to the unforgiving malevolence of two cold-blooded egotists?

"But you said Grace was in love with Mr. Parslow."

Morgan shrugged his thin shoulders in a gesture of helpless incomprehension of the mind of woman. Thereafter he responded in miserable monosyllables and Alec learned nothing new. The unhappy gardener was conducted back to his cell.

Had Lady Valeria and Stanley Moss between them pushed Grace into Parslow's bed? Alec was inclined to believe Owen Morgan, but most of what he'd said was pure hearsay, repeating what Grace had told him, and Grace was as far beyond human enquiry as she was beyond human judgement.

The Parslows, however, were not. Daisy was right, as usual. He was going to have to tackle Lady Valeria.

9

Piper drove the Austin back to Occleswich while Alec pondered the meaning of Morgan's revelation. For a father to try to wipe out the shame of a promiscuous daughter by doing away with her was uncommon but not unknown, yet if Moss drove Grace to seduce Parslow he had no cause for outrage. Bang went his already weak motive. As Daisy had mentioned, he had lost her pay and his free housekeeper by Grace's death.

As for her ladyship, Alec needed to know far more about her family before he could begin to untangle motivations.

He turned to the local police file on the murder. By the end, he shared Daisy's opinion of Inspector Dunnett. The report of the inquest gave the impression that the coroner, too, had done his best to cut off any witness who might point to evidence distressing to Lady Valeria.

He glanced at Daisy's photographs. Wrapped in a mud-sodden sheet, the body could have been an Egyptian mummy. Only the face was visible, well-preserved, protected by the sheet and the winter's cold according to the doctor, recognizable to those who knew her well. To a stranger the slackness of death and time robbed it of all individuality. Grace was not there.

Back at the Cheshire Cheese in time to order a late lunch, Alec sent Piper to the village constable's one-room police station with a note. He himself telephoned Occles Hall and asked for Daisy.

"The lad confirms most of what you've told me," he said, remembering her warning about the local exchange.

"I knew it." Her voice was triumphant, not unnaturally. "Did you get him out?"

"Not yet."

"But. . . ."

"Just listen a minute, will you? I liked him and I think he's telling the truth, but he's not out of the wood yet. We still have only his word for it. Besides, he's no unhappier there than anywhere else, and he's sure he's lost his job."

"Oh dear, I expect he's right. I'll have to write to a few people and see what I can arrange."

"Do." With luck that would keep her out of trouble for a while. "I'm coming up after I've had a bite to eat. Is everyone at home?"

"No, you're in luck, *she's* popped off to one of her committees. I don't believe there's a committee in the county she doesn't run. She's not expected back till teatime and the more you can do by then the better. Oh, and my friend is out, too. She didn't come in to lunch."

"But the person I want most to see is there?"

"Yes." The crackling sound coming over the wire might be a sigh. "I quite like him, you know, in spite of everything."

"Daisy, *someone* did it," Alec expostulated.

"I know. I shan't interfere."

"Good. I'll see you later, then, to bring you up to date. Cheerio."

He hung up as Piper returned to report that P.C. Rudge was expected to return soon from his bicycle rounds. Mrs. Rudge promised to give him the note when he came in.

They sat down to oxtail soup, an excellent cauliflower cheese, and a couple of pints of mild. No one else was in the dining room, so Alec was able to give Piper the instructions Tom Tring would not have needed. The young detective kept his notebook open beside his plate.

"When we get to Occles Hall, I want you to talk to the servants," Alec said.

"You won't need me to take notes, Chief?" Piper asked, disappointed.

"It's more important to get to the staff before Lady Valeria realizes what we're up to and forbids them to speak to us."

"That'd be obstructing the police in the course of their duties."

"Something tells me that will cut no ice with her ladyship. As it is, they may not be willing to talk about young Parslow or the rest of the family anyway, but see what you can do. What I want to know is what they were doing that evening, family and servants both, and whether anyone saw Grace up at the Hall after she left here. With times, of course. Do we know what time she left?"

"Round about ten o'clock, Chief," Piper answered while scribbling reminders to himself. "The barmaid noticed because if Grace came at all, she always used to stay till closing time—half past. She didn't have to be back at the Hall till eleven."

"Hmm. Why did she leave early that night? She needn't do so to meet anyone resident at the Hall. Had she arranged to meet someone in or near the Winter Garden? I wonder what the weather was like."

"Summun'll know."

"There's always the *Meteorological Record.* Even if it was too cold or wet for an outdoor rendezvous, perhaps someone walked her home, Morgan or maybe George Brown. We'll ask this evening whether he or anyone else left the bar at the same time she did."

"I should've asked at breakfast, Chief."

"Never mind, you can't think of everything. Let's see: other servants may have had the day or evening off and gone down to the village. If so, ask whether they saw Morgan or any of the family, or Grace walking up the hill, alone or in company."

"It's a long time to remember," Piper said doubtfully.

"Your barmaid remembered the time, didn't she? With luck it would stick in their minds because Grace vanished, especially if she was seen with someone other than the stranger she was later reported to have left with. They'll surely at least remember whether she came in. So far we have no evidence as to whether she died soon after leaving the pub or later that night. Incidentally, ask whether she made a practice of returning to the Hall on time, by eleven that is, and what time the doors are locked. Perhaps we can narrow down the time still further."

"Right, Chief."

"Also, try to find out whether there were rivalries and jealousies between the girl and her fellow-servants." Alec frowned. That was the sort of thing Tom was so good at ferreting out. He wished he hadn't left him behind. "Do your best, Ernie," he said.

"Of course, Chief." The detective constable sounded injured. "What about the outside men?"

"Good point. If you have time, see the head gardener. You may have to hunt about the grounds for him."

"It's raining again."

"Then try potting sheds and greenhouses, though I imagine gardeners are out in all weathers, like policemen. Ask the same sort of questions, especially whether any of his underlings had an eye to Grace, and more particularly whether he saw or heard Morgan going out that night."

"Right, Chief."

"Oh, and you'd better find out whether Grace went to work at Occles Hall straight from school. It's always difficult at first to work out what we need to ask about. After today's enquiries we'll have a better idea of what line to follow, unless Miss Dalrymple is all at sea and Morgan turns out to be the obvious culprit."

"She wouldn't never go that far wrong, Chief!"

"Well, we wouldn't be here if I wasn't inclined to trust her judgment," Alec agreed, amused. "This evening we'll see what we can pick up in the bars, from the village people. I'd rather not go door to door if we can help it." He turned his head as heavy footsteps entered the room behind him. "Ah, Constable Rudge, I presume?"

"Yes, sir, Chief Inspector, sir." The man saluting was the epitome of the country bobby as seen in innumerable melodramas, farces, and music-hall skits. Middle-aged, ponderous, with a round, red, bovine face, he'd have got a laugh simply walking on stage at the Palladium, before the audience heard his slow voice and thick local accent.

Such men were the backbone of the law, Alec was well aware. Rudge would know everyone in his district, at least by sight. A stolen chicken, a pub brawl, a Peeping Tom—ninety-nine times out of a hundred he'd resolve the matter without recourse to the courts. But to put him on a murder enquiry was ludicrous.

"Thank you for coming so promptly, Constable. I didn't want to trespass on your patch without informing you." Alec introduced Piper.

"Owt I can do to help Scotland Yard, sir." Rudge remained rigidly at attention.

"I take it Chester let you know we've been called in on the Moss murder. I'm hoping you might have observed the movements of some of the people we're interested in on the night in question."

"Nay, sir. I looked it up in me book for yon sergeant from Chester. On the night in question, sir, I were out to Oakwood Farm. Mr. Simpkins's head cowman, he. . . ."

"So you saw nothing in the village?" Alec hastily interrupted.

"Not a blessed thing, sir," the constable admitted with a heavy sigh, "but owt else I can do to help. . . ."

"What was the weather like?"

"Dry, sir, and mild for the time o' year. When you rides a bicycle, you notices."

"Yes, thanks. Have you got a typewriter? D.C. Piper may need to borrow it. That's all for now, but I may well call on you later."

"Aye, sir. The wife gen'rally knows whereabouts I be, sir."

Alec dismissed him, entertained by Mrs. Rudge's obviously essential share in his work, whereas he himself felt guilty every time he discussed a case with Daisy. Of course, he wasn't married to Daisy—nor ever likely to be, however friendly she was. The daughter of a viscount, even if she did choose to earn her own living, and a middle-class copper, ten years older, a widower with a child. . . . Forget it, he told himself, swigging down the last drop of ale.

Piper followed suit and they went out to the Austin. A light but steady drizzle forced Alec to open the upper half of the windscreen to see the way as he drove up the hill. Nonetheless, as they passed the forge, the seats of two pairs of damp and oily dungarees presented themselves, the wearers' heads invisible beneath the bonnet of a silver-grey Swift two-seater.

Petrie consulting Stan Moss. Daisy described the bereaved father as a frightful brute; either a mutual interest in things mechanical made up to Petrie for any defects in Moss's character, or else more than a missing nut ailed the Swift.

At some point Alec would have to speak to Moss, though at present it was more urgent to see Parslow before his mother's return. It might be useful to have Petrie on good terms with the blacksmith.

The high, spiked gates to Occles Hall were closed. Alec honked his horn and an aged gatekeeper appeared at the door of the half-timbered lodge.

"No reporters," he announced and turned away.

"Police," said Alec loudly. "Scotland Yard."

The old man gaped. "Oh lor', what'll her la'ship say?" he moaned, but he scuffled through the rain to open the gates.

As they approached the house, Alec could see why Daisy had wanted to write about it, and especially to photograph it. The Tudor half-timbering was as splendidly fanciful as the much better known Little Moreton Hall. His particular interest had been the Georgian period, but that didn't stop him appreciating this.

"Cor," said Piper, "talk about jazzy!"

Laughing, Alec pulled up alongside the rain-wrinkled moat. They walked across the bridge into the tunnel under the gatehouse and Piper rang the front-door bell.

After a considerable wait, the door was opened by a bilious-looking butler who regarded them with dispirited disdain.

"Scotland Yard." Alec knew how to deal with obstructive butlers. He moved inexorably across the threshold as he presented his identification card. "Detective Chief Inspector Fletcher. I'm investigating the murder of your parlourmaid, Grace Moss. Your name?"

The butler stared in dismay at the notebook and pencil which had appeared in Piper's hands. "Moody, sir. I can't take it upon myself to. . . ."

"Detective Constable Piper will be talking to the staff. I shall interview the family, beginning with Mr. Sebastian Parslow."

"If you'll be so good as to wait here, sir, I'll see if Mr. Parslow is at home."

Ignoring this, Alec and Piper followed Moody across the small, paneled room and into another. The butler glanced back at the sound of their footsteps. His thin lips pursed but he made no demur.

He led them to a long room with windows all down one side and a multiplicity of doors leading off it. Stopping before one of these, he opened it and announced in doom-laden tones, "A policeman to see you, Mr. Sebastian."

Thereupon he beat a hasty retreat, with Piper at his heels. Alec stepped into a pleasant sitting room. Above waist-high wainscoting the walls were hung with a golden yellow brocade which made the room seem sunny. A small table in front of the fireplace bore a game of backgammon in progress, with Daisy seated on one side, smiling at him, and on the other. . . .

Why the hell hadn't Daisy warned him that Sebastian Parslow was a Greek statue come to life? No wonder Grace Moss had bestowed her favours. The wonder was that she had needed her father's and his mother's encouragement. No wonder Daisy "quite liked him in spite of everything." What woman could resist him?

There they sat at backgammon like Ferdinand and Miranda over their game of chess—and Alec had less than no right to be jealous. He was going to have to be extraordinarily careful to treat the young man fairly.

The colour in Parslow's face drained, leaving in truth the cold white perfection of marble, save for blue eyes and golden hair. He pushed back his chair and stood up, leaning with one hand on the table.

"Yes?"

"Detective Chief Inspector Fletcher, Scotland Yard. I have one or two questions to ask you, sir, regarding the death of Grace Moss."

"I'd better go," said Daisy, rising with visible reluctance.

"No," Parslow said unexpectedly, his voice uneven, "do stay, Daisy. I don't suppose this will take long, and then we can finish our game."

How the deuce did she do it? Alec could have asked her to leave, but when she looked at him with her head cocked like a robin hoping for a worm, he hadn't the heart. She wasn't wearing powder or lipstick, he noticed. The tiny mole which looked like an eighteenth-century "Kissing" patch was unmasked. He liked her that way.

If Parslow thought her presence would forestall awkward questions, he was in for a shock.

"Do sit down, Mr. Parslow," he suggested.

Daisy discreetly retired to a chair in a corner, while Parslow, after glancing around with a helpless air, waved Alec to her relinquished seat and resumed his own. Alec moved the backgammon board aside, taking care not to upset the men, and placed his notebook on the table though he doubted he'd need to make notes at this stage. It was a nuisance they'd be sitting at the table—he wouldn't be able to see Parslow's hands—but the gas-brackets above the mantelpiece lit his face well enough.

Interrogation was a game at least as complex as backgammon, the significant difference being that it was only necessary for one player to know the rules. Himself. And if he was any judge, Parslow's backbone was less marmoreal than his features.

"Grace Moss worked here at Occles Hall for several years, did she, sir?" he began mildly.

"Yes, I suppose so. I don't know exactly how long."

"So you knew her well?"

A hint of colour tinged Parslow's pallid cheeks. "Hardly. I don't suppose I ever exchanged more than a word with her while she was a housemaid. Dash it, one doesn't, you know."

"I'm aware of that, sir. And when she was promoted to parlourmaid?"

"One saw more of her, of course, serving at table and so on. My mother was pleased with her. She was a very competent parlourmaid, a rare creature. But as for conversation. . . ."

"It's not conversation I'm concerned with, sir, but a rather more intimate relationship. I've been given to understand the deceased was your mistress."

The marble crumbled like chalk. Burying his face in his hands, Parslow said hopelessly, "I suppose you were bound to find out."

"Tell me about it," Alec coaxed. "A pretty, lively maid, a vigorous young man, it's not unnatural."

Parslow shuddered. Then he pulled himself together and

sat up straight, though the rigidity of his shoulders told Alec his hands were clenched in his lap.

"As you say, it's not un . . . uncommon. She used to bring my morning tea, and sometimes a nightcap if I was feeling restless. The mater didn't like me to keep whisky in my room, so. . . ."

"Just a minute, sir. Were those among the usual duties of a parlourmaid?"

"Good Lord, how would I know?" Parslow sounded genuinely mystified, but then he frowned. "No, come to think of it, it's usually a housemaid brings the tea and I'd expect old Moody to toddle up with the whisky and soda. What are you suggesting?"

"It's not for me to suggest anything, Mr. Parslow."

"Well, Moody's not so brisk on his pins as he was, and it's impossible to get footmen since the War. It wouldn't surprise me if Grace carried it up for him as a favour. She was a good-natured girl, at least until. . . . She was an obliging girl, it was the sort of thing she'd do."

Alec let the "until" lie for the moment. "So you don't think she was making a dead set at you?"

"It's possible," Parslow said thoughtfully. "That would explain . . . Well, I didn't have to make much effort to . . . to. . . ." He flushed.

"To seduce her." Alec pronounced the word without embarrassment, but for some reason knowing Daisy was listening to his next question brought the heat to his own cheeks. "Was she a virgin?"

"No!" Parslow shook his head violently. "She told me she'd had a sweetheart, a village boy, who was killed on the Marne right after he was shipped across. She must have been just out of school herself, but in those circumstances. . . ." He shrugged, regaining his fragile composure.

"You did have a certain amount of conversation with her, then. Did she ever talk about another sweetheart?"

"No."

"About your mother?"

"Hardly. She'd know better than to try. A chap doesn't listen to that sort of stuff."

Alec bit back a smile at the obvious inference that anything Grace might have said about Lady Valeria was unlikely to be complimentary. "About her father?" he asked.

Unexpectedly, that rattled the young man. "Stan Moss? Only that he was a rotten blighter—'a ruddy bastard,' I think she said, actually—which I already knew. I dare say you've heard about his quarrel with the mater."

"Yes. What else did she tell you?" Alec pressed him.

"About Moss? Nothing."

He was lying, but again Alec left the question for the moment. "And you're certain she never mentioned Owen Morgan to you."

"I didn't know she was walking out with him until after the inquest."

"She wouldn't want to spoil a good thing with the young master, no doubt. After all, you'd promised to marry her."

"How the deuce do you know that?"

"We have our sources." The noncommittal phrase covered rumour, hearsay, innuendo, gossip. Alec hadn't known for sure until Parslow confirmed it.

"It wasn't till much later I . . . I said that. Not before, to persuade her."

"Not until she told you she was pregnant."

Parslow groaned. "Yes, she told me. She said I'd ruined her and I had to marry her or her father would kick up an almighty stink and make her sue me. So I agreed."

"With the intention of carrying out your promise?"

"No, of course not, not if I could help it," he said wildly. "I *couldn't* marry her, but I didn't know what else to do!"

He had been in just the sort of situation to make a weak man crack and hit out, Alec thought. He was on the edge now. Would he confess to murder?

Alec fixed Parslow with his coldest stare. "You didn't

know what to do, but there was one obvious and decisive way to rid yourself of the threat."

"Rid . . . ? Murder her?" The young man was distraught, his voice emerging in a croak. "God, no, I didn't! I swear I didn't. It didn't even cross my mind."

"What did you do, then? Sit back and wait to see what happened next?" Alec asked witheringly.

"I told my sister."

The answer was so unexpected, Alec was momentarily struck dumb.

Yet Daisy's report had hinted that Roberta Parslow was protective of her younger brother. Daisy had seen through the handsome façade to the weakness within. How could he have doubted her? How could he have supposed for a moment that she admired this milksop?

No, Sebastian Parslow brought out *her* protective instincts too. Alec was all too well acquainted with Daisy's protective instincts. He could only hope that in this case her sense of outrage was stronger.

He sighed. "You told your sister. Everything?"

"Y-yes. I think so. I was . . . in a bit of a state, but she said I wasn't to worry. You do believe me, don't you, that I didn't kill Grace?"

"My beliefs are irrelevant, sir," Alec said, not quite truthfully. "It's the evidence that matters. What were you doing on the evening of December 13th?"

"I was packing," Parslow said eagerly. "Or rather, I was telling my man, Thomkins, what to pack. You see, the mater and I popped off to Antibes the next day, so I remember it well."

"You left the packing until the evening before your departure?"

"We'd been going to leave on the following Monday, but the mater changed her mind at the last minute. She didn't tell me until dinner time."

"How long did the packing take? What time did you finish?"

"I-I couldn't say for sure."

"Never mind." For the first time, Alec wrote briefly in his notebook. "Thomkins will know, or one of the other servants will remember when he reappeared in their midst. Who else did you see after dinner?"

"Bobbie came in, just for a moment, to give me a tie-pin she'd bought me for Christmas. That was quite early. Then later on, after the packing was done, I went along to the mater's room . . . to say good-night."

"What time was that, do you remember?"

"Half past eleven? Thereabouts. I'd already climbed into my pyjamas. He was being evasive about something, Alec was sure.

"Lady Valeria was in her room?"

"Oh yes."

"Dressed for bed?"

Parslow shrugged. "I don't recall."

"Your parents have separate rooms?"

"Since I was a child."

"You didn't go to wish your father good-night?"

"He'd have been asleep long before that. The pater gets up at crack of dawn to see his jolly old cows milked."

"Ah. Did you see anyone else?"

"Not that I recall." Again he was evasive, not meeting Alec's eyes.

"Not even a servant? You didn't ring for a nightcap?"

"No, I was tired and ready to sleep without one. I didn't see *anyone,* let alone *her."*

"So the next morning you went off to the Riviera, safe from Grace's demands. You simply put the episode behind you."

"That's right, and when we came back I heard she had cleared out to London, to the bright lights."

"Let me get this straight. You informed your sister of the mess you were in. She advised you not to worry, so you left the country, trusting her to cope with the situation during your absence."

"I would have. She's a dashed good sort, Bobbie, and not one to stand any nonsense. But while we were talking about it, my mother came in and. . . . Well, I told you I was in a bit of a state. The mater blamed Bobbie for upsetting me. I couldn't let her think it was Bobbie's fault, so I told her everything, too."

"And no doubt she too told you not to worry."

"She said she'd deal with Grace." Parslow's pale face grew livid. "My God, you don't think *she* . . . ?"

"I don't know," said Alec grimly, "but you may be sure I shall find out."

10

Daisy was dismayed, if not surprised, to hear Bobbie knew all about her brother's affair with Grace. However, at present she was more concerned with Sebastian. From her corner seat she couldn't see his face, but he sounded alarmingly distraught.

She was relieved to hear Alec say, "Thank you for your cooperation, Mr. Parslow. That will be all for now, though we shall have to take a formal statement and I may have more questions for you later."

Swiftly she crossed the room. "You look as if you could do with a bracer, Sebastian. Shall I ring for Moody?" She put a hand on his shoulder as he started to stand up.

Subsiding, he shook his head and managed a travesty of a smile. "No, thanks. I'm all right. It's just all been rather a shock. To tell the truth I'd forgotten you were there. I'm afraid I must have shocked you, too."

"Not at all," she said kindly. "I'm no wishy-washy Victorian damozel, thank heaven."

Alec's eyes laughed at her. "I shall need a word with you, Miss Dalrymple," he said, "about the discovery of the body."

"Of course. You stay here, Sebastian, and don't put the game away. I'll beat you honestly yet. Shall we go to the library, Chief Inspector?"

"Ben's in the library—Ben Goodman, my father's secretary—writing some letters for my mother."

"That will do very well," Alec said. "Since the rest of your family is out, I might as well speak to him right away."

"To Ben?" Sebastian lost what little colour he had regained. "You don't need to tell him all I've told you, do you?"

Alec raised his fearsome eyebrows. "I don't imagine so. My business is collecting information, not distributing it. Miss Dalrymple?" He opened the door and held it for her, closing it firmly behind them as they went out into the Long Hall. They walked slowly towards the library.

"I knew it," said Daisy, "though I didn't expect him to cave in so quickly and admit it."

"You quite shocked him by not being shocked. You don't care for 'The Blessed Damozel,' I take it."

"Of all the ghastly sentimental tripe we had to learn at school, that took the biscuit." She hoped Michael wasn't drooping around Heaven weeping for her to join him. No, he wasn't that sort. He'd have found some way to make himself useful and he'd be wishing her a long and happy life.

"I had quite a shock myself," Alec said. "I wish you'd warned me about Parslow's looks!"

"You did rather gape when you came in." Daisy giggled. "But I don't suppose he noticed. He's not at all vain."

"He had other things on his mind when he heard a policeman announced. You didn't warn me he was such a jellyfish, either."

"Oh, not quite that bad, though he's wetter than I thought. But I did tell you he lets Lady Valeria boss him about."

"So, I gather, does half the county."

"And that Bobbie tries to protect him. Ben, too."

"Can he possibly believe Goodman doesn't know Grace was his mistress?"

Daisy frowned. "I don't see how he can. Ben was so particular about being the one to break the news to him of Grace's death. I expect he meant he didn't want Ben to know all that beastly stuff about her trying to force him to marry her and running to Bobbie for help and his mother being involved. They're friends, but after all Ben is his father's employee."

"True. Could Miss Parslow or Lady Valeria have killed Grace?"

"Physically, yes. As far as character is concerned—" Daisy grimaced. "Well, not normally, but for Sebastian's sake . . . I don't know, Alec. They might. Here's the library," she said, with relief.

"Is there anything you haven't told me about Goodman?"

"Did I tell you he limps from a war wound? He was gassed, too. Oh, and before the War he was a Greek scholar, a don at Oxford. Perhaps I ought to warn you," she added teasingly, "he's decidedly plain, at least until he smiles, but by no means a walkover like Sebastian."

Alec smiled. "Thanks for the warning. Just a minute, before we go in. Do you want to keep it a secret that we've met before?"

"No, that would be frightfully bad form. Oh dear, we didn't tell Sebastian, did we? I'll have to explain to him later."

"Leave it to me," Alec said firmly, and reached for the door handle.

"Wait. Once they know, it's going to be harder than ever to stay on here. I've been putting off inspecting Sir Reginald's dairy but I can't use that as an excuse for ever."

"I'd much rather you were out of it."

Outraged, Daisy glared at him. "How can you say that when I called you in in the first place and gave you practically all the information you possess?"

"Alternatively stated, you embroiled me in this mess; nonetheless I feel obliged to consider your safety."

"Do you really think I'm not safe?" she asked uncertainly.

Alec capitulated with a sigh. "No, now that I'm here and know everything you do, you're probably perfectly safe—as long as you keep your promise not to interfere. I'll advise them no one in the house, including you, is to leave the area. I don't suppose even Lady Valeria would expect an unaccompanied young woman to stay at the inn."

Daisy bristled. "I could perfectly well stay at. . . . Dash it, you beast, I don't *want* to stay at the inn. Between you and Phillip, I'd be completely out of it. I'm staying here until I'm thrown out." She opened the library door and marched in.

The library was a modest one, low-ceilinged like the rest of the house and with only one wall entirely covered by bookshelves. Apparently none of Sir Reginald's ancestors had been intellectually inclined.

Ben sat at a leather-topped writing-table, surrounded by neat heaps of papers. He looked up as they entered.

"Miss Dalrymple," he said, rising. He wouldn't call her Daisy before a stranger. "Can I help you?"

"Not me. This is Detective Chief Inspector Fletcher of Scotland Yard. He wants to ask us both some questions about finding Grace. I don't believe Owen killed her," she added resolutely, "so I phoned him. I met him when he was in charge of another case."

Nodding, Ben capped his fountain-pen. "I find it hard to believe Owen did it," he admitted. "Do pull up chairs and sit down."

Alec placed a Windsor chair for Daisy and brought up a second. He stood for a moment with his hand on its back.

"You want my place, Chief Inspector?" Ben asked perceptively, with a faint smile.

"No," Alec said, grinning. "It's just that it feels unnatural to be on this side of the desk. There's no need to switch." He sat down.

He took Daisy and Ben through the events of Tuesday morning, in much more detail than Inspector Dunnett or Sergeant Shaw had wanted. All the same, Daisy didn't think he learned anything new that mattered. Reaching the point where Dunnett had dismissed Ben from the Winter Garden,

Alec said, "I suppose I'll have to go and inspect the place some time," and he glanced with distaste at the windows. Rain streamed down th diamond panes. "Thank you for taking the photographs, by the way."

"Did you learn anything from them?" Ben asked.

"Not really," Alec said frankly.

"I doubt seeing the place will teach you anything more. Lady Valeria had the trench filled in and the bed replanted the moment Inspector Dimwit left the premises. I beg your pardon, Chief Inspector, her slip of the tongue, not mine. I don't mean to imply any lack of respect for the police—in general."

"I'm sure you don't," Alec said dryly.

Daisy debated telling them Sergeant Shaw's nickname for his superior but decided it might get the friendly sergeant into trouble. Besides, Alec's last few questions had been directed at Ben and for the moment Ben had all his attention. Any moment he'd move on to more interesting questions. If Daisy drew his notice he'd probably ask her to leave. If she managed to remain silent and invisible he might let her stay rather than disturb his rapport with Ben.

She was sure they liked each other, but Alec wouldn't let liking compromise his investigation.

"I may have to have the flowerbed dug up again," Alec went on, "or even the entire garden, but it can wait. Any buried clues aren't going anywhere. Now, to return to the night we must assume Grace Moss was killed, the 13th December last, can you tell me what you were doing that evening, Mr. Goodman? A matter of routine."

"As it happens, I remember that evening very well. Lady Valeria had unexpectedly moved up her and Mr. Parslow's departure for Antibes, and after dinner she had reams of instructions for work she wanted done in her absence."

"You're Sir Reginald's secretary?"

"I was hired as Sir Reginald's secretary. I take care of the paperwork for the dairy. He asks very little else of me. Lady

Valeria, on the other hand, sits on a dozen committees or more, all of which require extensive correspondence, minutes, agendas, et cetera. I also handle the household accounts; that is, paying tradesmen and servants and so on."

"I see. Just clarifying. So you spent the entire evening with Lady Valeria?"

Daisy was disappointed. That is, she was glad Ben had an alibi, not that he needed one, but sorry Lady Valeria was equally cleared. She made a good villainess.

Then Ben said, "Not all evening, no. At about ten, maybe a bit earlier, she left me to complete some odds and ends for her to sign in the morning. At eleven I decided to stop for the night and go to bed, though it meant getting up early to finish before she came down."

"You were alone—in here?—from ten till eleven?"

"I was."

Alec made a note. "Did you see anyone else that evening?"

"Everyone was at dinner, all the family, from eight to eight forty-five, say. Then no one but Lady Valeria until about a quarter to midnight."

"You were still up?"

"I took a long, hot bath." His mouth twisted in a wry smile. "My gammy leg was playing me up rather, aching like the blazes."

"The War? Where did you catch it?"

"On the Somme. Was there anywhere else?"

"I certainly spent a lot of time flying over it. I was a spotter."

"Well, it wasn't all fun on the ground—in it, rather—but you couldn't have paid me enough to get me up in one of those canvas and piano-wire crates."

"It had its interesting moments," Alec acknowledged. "But back to business, I'm afraid. Whom did you see at quarter to twelve?"

"Young Parslow came to my room." Ben spoke coolly, but

with a hint of wariness, Daisy thought. "He had begged Lady Valeria, not by any means for the first time, to take me to the South of France with them. I find English winters trying, you see, and he's a kind boy. He came to tell me his mother still wouldn't hear of it."

He didn't like to reveal himself as an object of charity—attempted charity—Daisy decided. And Sebastian had been sensitive enough to know it and to keep the business to himself even though it meant lying to the police. She'd have to make sure Alec understood.

"Was Parslow with you long?"

"A few minutes. I wish I could say we'd spent the night . . . playing cards together. I don't know what time you're interested in, Chief Inspector?"

"We're not sure ourselves as yet, though we hope to narrow it down. In eight weeks memories fade and evidence vanishes." Alec ran his hand through the crisp, dark hair that had first attracted Daisy to him. "How would you describe Parslow's state of mind when he came to your room?"

The wariness was more pronounced: "Lady Valeria's intransigeance had upset him a bit."

"He was agitated?"

"I wouldn't go so far. Mildly disturbed. Perhaps 'ruffled' is the word I want. I suggested he have a whisky to settle his nerves before he tried to sleep."

"Do you know if he took your advice?"

"No idea. My position in the household is not such that I make a habit of ringing for servants to come to my bedroom. He wouldn't have done so until he returned to his own room. By then I had calmed him down."

"Apart from his distress at his inability to persuade his mother to invite you to go along, he was happy to be leaving in the morning?"

Ben hesitated. "Certainly. In general, his life is rather 'cabin'd, cribb'd, confin'd.' He seldom goes up to town. The annual visit to the Riviera is, to a certain degree, an escape."

"Do you know of any other reason he was particularly glad to get away from Occles Hall?"

"Chief Inspector," said Ben steadily, "please don't play games with me. I'm sure you are aware, as I am, and as I was then, of Sebastian's involvement with Grace Moss."

"No games," Alec blandly assured him. "Mr. Parslow asked me not to divulge his disclosures to you."

Ben seemed puzzled. "Then I don't know what he has told you, but I knew he felt his position had become untenable and he was decidedly relieved to get away."

"You knew before the inquest that Grace was pregnant?"

"N-no." For a moment he looked older, tired and ill, then he rallied. "Only that he was anxious to break off with her. I suggested he should find a pretext to ask Lady Valeria to give her notice, but he dreaded his mother learning about the affair. Besides," he added ironically, "whatever her faults, Grace was an excellent parlourmaid whom even Lady Valeria would not lightly dismiss."

"Her ladyship was ignorant of the affair?"

"He thought so. I thought not, but of course I couldn't be sure."

"Mr. Parslow seems to confide in you a great deal, Mr. Goodman."

"You have obviously learned a great deal about the family, Chief Inspector," Ben said pointedly. "In his circumstances, are you surprised?"

"Perhaps not," Alec admitted.

He went on to ask a few questions about Sir Reginald. Ben obviously regarded his nominal employer with fond amusement, mingled with respect for his expertise in his chosen sphere and a touch of exasperation at his inability to stand up to his wife.

Daisy doubted whether Sir Reginald, a benevolent but inattentive father, had more than an inkling of what was going on in his household.

"I'd better see him next," Alec said, "since the ladies of the house are out. How do I get to the dairy?"

"You can drive," Ben told him, "but you have to go right around the park so it's much quicker to walk if you don't mind the rain. It's less than half a mile on foot—just far enough for the noise and smells not to trouble her ladyship. Ask Moody for an umbrella if you haven't brought one." He explained how to find the footpath Sir Reginald used several times each day.

"Thank you for your help, Mr. Goodman." Alec stood up. "We'll leave you to your paper-work. I just wish I could send you to London to deal with mine."

Daisy smiled at Ben, then she and Alec left the library together.

"He's worth ten of Parslow," Alec observed as they returned to the Long Hall. "It's a pity Lady Valeria refused to take him south. He looks a bit dicky to me."

"He seemed quite well when I first met him," Daisy said. "I think seeing the body in the trench must have revived memories of the War. I know people who still have nightmares about the trenches."

"Yes, I was really better off up there in my paper and string kite. Oh, here are your photos, minus the body in the trench."

"Thanks. How much do I owe you for them?"

"It's on Scotland Yard."

"Spiffing!" Daisy returned to business. "I'm glad Ben couldn't have done it."

Alec raised his fierce eyebrows at her. "He couldn't?"

"I shouldn't think he's strong enough, for a start."

"With the right weapon, it doesn't take vast strength to crush a skull. As for the digging, desperation lends strength, and whoever did it must have been desperate to conceal the body."

"But he had no motive."

"We may yet discover one."

"And he needn't have shown me the Winter Garden, nor told Owen to show me when he was called away."

"That's not a convincing. . . . Great Scott!"

"You there!" From the Yellow Parlour a whirlwind in a purple rain-cape erupted and stormed towards them. "You! Inspector Treacher, or whatever you call yourself."

"Detective Chief Inspector Fletcher, ma'am, C.I.D." Despite his start on seeing Lady Valeria, Alec spoke calmly. Daisy decided he'd be better off without her to worry about so she stepped aside, pretending to study one of the portraits on the wall. Nothing in the world could have made her leave.

"What the dickens do you mean by it, Fester," she trumpeted, eyes glittering in a face suffused with fury, "sneaking into my house without permission in my absence? That's a crime, C.I.D. or no C.I.D."

"Your servant admitted me, Lady Valeria. I have spoken to your son, who is not, I think, a minor."

"Without a solicitor present!"

"There's no question of charges," said Alec mildly, "at present."

"Charges—I should think not!"

"But if you wish to contact your solicitor. . . ."

"Certainly not. That pusillanimous poltroon would only advise me to cooperate with the police, which I have no intention whatever of doing. Your presence in my house is absolutely unjustifiable. Kindly leave at once."

"I'd prefer not to have to invite you to accompany me to a police station for an interview, ma'am. Certain matters which have been brought to our attention. . . ."

"Rumours! Gossip! Since when do your precious police listen to tittle-tattle?"

"Oh, since forever, ma'am. How else should we ever find out what's going on? But in this case, Mr. Parslow has confirmed that he was . . . intimately connected with Grace Moss. You cannot expect us to overlook that."

Lady Valeria attempted a frank bonhomie. "Young gentlemen have been seducing serving maids since forever, In-spector. It hardly calls for a police investigation."

"When the serving maid becomes the victim of murder, ma'am, it most certainly does. Further, when the young gen-tleman admits that she extracted a promise of marriage, which he had no intention of carrying out; when he admits to. . . ."

Bonhomie vanished. "How dare you!"

"When he admits to having told his sister and his mother of his plight and claims they offered to deal with. . . ."

"You have bullied my poor boy into making up these ri-diculous stories! You seem to believe you can treat me and my family as you treat the riffraff, forcing false confessions for the sake of solving your case. I'll have you thrown out of the force for threatening respectable people. If you don't drop this nonsense at once, I shall telephone your superiors at Scotland Yard."

Alec's response was blandly unconcerned. "Go ahead, ma'am."

Daisy couldn't contain her ire, though she did her best to hide it, knowing it would not impress Lady Valeria. Joining them, she said sweetly, "I shouldn't waste the effort if I were you. I'm perfectly prepared to swear on oath that Chief In-spector Fletcher's behaviour was perfectly proper. If you complain, they'll only assume you have something to hide."

"I have nothing to hide." All the same, her bombast was noticeably diminished. "I found my son distraught. I merely wish to protect him from Machiavellian manipulation and protest against. . . ." Her protest died away as she turned a sudden scowl on Daisy. "But what is your role in this, Miss Dalrymple? You are a guest at Occles Hall. What do you know of this wretched business?"

"At Sebastian's request, I was present when the Chief In-spector interviewed him." Daisy was perfectly prepared to reveal her part in summoning Scotland Yard, but as she opened her mouth to continue, Alec silenced her with a barely perceptible shake of the head.

"Miss Dalrymple has observed my work in the past," he said smoothly. "She knows I threaten no one. I ask questions. Since. . . ."

"You're in league with this detective?" Lady Valeria demanded, outraged anew. She drew herself up to her full, impressive height and said haughtily, "I'm afraid, Miss Dalrymple, I must ask you to leave."

"I'm afraid, Lady Valeria," said Alec, "I must ask everyone to stay until my investigation is completed."

She gaped at him, apparently too taken aback by his presumption to think of suggesting that Daisy remove herself to the inn.

"Since you have nothing to hide," he continued, "you can have no objection to answering my questions."

But that was trying her too high. "Bosh!" she exploded. "If you're expecting me to pay the least heed to your impertinent inquisition, you may wait until Doomsday." And in a swirl of purple cape she stalked out.

11

"Whew!" Alec wiped his brow with an exaggerated gesture.

"Oh, rot," said Daisy, "she didn't rattle you in the least. You didn't turn a hair."

"Well, no, though I was quite glad to have you as witness to the propriety of my behaviour. Can you imagine young Adonis in the witness box swearing to police brutality?"

"You see, I *am* useful," she hastened to point out. "Thanks for not letting her give me the old heave-ho. I really thought I'd had it, though in the circs I can't honestly blame her."

"Not for that, no, but what a virago! I can see why half the county cries craven at the prospect of crossing her. And while she may not have rattled me, nor did she give me any answers. I particularly want to know why she suddenly put forward their departure for the Riviera."

"You'll get what you want. You're irresistible." What could have been a horribly embarrassing statement was spoken so absently that Alec didn't feel called upon to blush. It quickly became apparent Daisy was still pondering the social implications of staying on in a house where her hostess wished her gone. "I feel like a frightful snake in the grass, or cuckoo in the nest, or something. On the other hand, I'd feel worse if Lady Valeria had ever really welcomed me or gone out of her way to help."

"She hasn't?" He had a sudden sense of being poised on the edge of understanding this curious family.

"Not at all. Bobbie invited me, with her father's concurrence, and her mother was furious because she hadn't been consulted. Also, she disapproves of working women—'well-bred' women, that is," Daisy added apologetically. "I gather she's afraid Bobbie might follow my example."

"A truly shocking example."

Daisy wrinkled her adorably freckled nose at him. Irresistible, indeed! "Well, my mother feels the same way," she admitted. "The other thing is, I think Lady Valeria may also wish me away because she doesn't like Sebastian to meet eligible girls. She's fearfully possessive, and if he married he'd escape from under her thumb, at least to some degree. Not that I flatter myself he's at all attracted to me!"

"No?" Alec made his voice carefully casual. "And you to him?"

"No, though I was just a bit at first. But he hasn't got the character to go with his looks, has he? Still, he did make me welcome and I listened to his confession to you under false pretenses. I think I'd better make my peace with him myself, if you don't mind."

"And even if I do, no doubt. All right, go and talk to him, but no questions, mind. And make sure he knows I know you're with him. I don't want to be digging your body out of the Winter Garden."

The freckles stood out on her suddenly pale face. She shook her head violently. "No, he wouldn't! I don't think he possesses a temper, and even if he does, the only thing in the Yellow Parlour he could hit me with is the backgammon board."

Alec smiled but said seriously, "Be careful, Daisy. I'm pretty sure you're in no danger now that I'm here, but I'd never forgive myself if you were hurt. I'm going down to the dairy to see Sir Reginald."

Since she didn't beg him to wait for her, he guessed she considered the baronet a highly unlikely suspect. He might have useful information, though; or she might be wrong.

The moment Daisy saw Sebastian, she was sure she wasn't wrong about him. No one could have looked less like a brutal murderer. He was still sitting in the chair by the backgammon board, his forehead pillowed on his folded arms on the edge of the table, his bowed shoulders shaking.

She was about to back hurriedly out but he heard her and raised his head, though he kept his face turned away from her. "Daisy?" he said in a thick voice.

"Yes, I. . . ."

"I knew you'd come back to finish the game. I'm afraid I've knocked the pieces all over the place."

"It doesn't matter. I have something to say to you but it can wait."

"No, it's all right. Come in." He straightened, made a half-hearted effort to rise.

"Don't get up." She crossed to the chair opposite him and sat down. Fidgeting with the backgammon pieces, she carefully kept her eyes from his face, but a brief glimpse had showed her red-rimmed eyes and eyelashes spiked with tears. "I want to apologize. I ought to have made it clear to you that I know Chief Inspector Fletcher. In fact, I asked him to come because I don't believe Owen Morgan killed Grace."

"That's all right. It doesn't make any difference. Nothing makes any difference," Sebastian said hopelessly, "except that somehow my mother manages to make everything seem ten times worse."

"I know what you mean," she said with sympathy. "My mother's difficult, too, though in a different way." Mentally she begged pardon of the Dowager Lady Dalrymple, who was a saint compared to Lady Valeria.

"Is she?" He brightened, as if it had never dawned on him that other people had awkward parents. "Does she treat you like a child and stop you doing everything worthwhile or interesting or . . . or just that you want to do?"

"She tries. I don't let her." Daisy had not forgotten her promise not to interfere, but her promise was to Alec and concerned the case. What was on her mind now had nothing to do with the case. "Lady Valeria can't really stop you, if you stand up to her and stick to your guns. You're of age and Bobbie told me you have money of your own."

"Not a great deal."

"I'm sure she said you have enough to live on."

"Yes, but. . . ." He bit his lip fiercely, fighting for composure. "Thank you for your encouragement, but you don't—you *can't* understand. There are other problems. . . ."

Lady Valeria came in. Daisy could have killed her.

She looked as if she could have killed Daisy. If looks could kill, Alec would have had to dig up another body in the Winter Garden.

"So, Miss Dalrymple, you have taken your accomplice's place in victimizing my son."

"Oh no, Mater, Daisy. . . ."

"My poor boy, you have been hoodwinked in the most despicable fashion. Miss Dalrymple is in league with the police. Don't worry, your mother will make sure no harm comes of it. Miss Dalrymple, I must ask you to pack your bags at once. If Inspector Fetter refuses to allow you to leave, no doubt you will be able to persuade the Cheshire Cheese to give you a room."

"No!" said Sebastian loudly, stepping between Daisy and his mother. "Daisy isn't trying to hoodwink me. She has told me she's acquainted with Chief Inspector Fletcher."

"Nonetheless, she cannot remain at Occles Hall."

It was against Daisy's principles to let a man defend her, but she decided the experience was good for Sebastian. She congratulated herself on the unexpectedly rapid effect of her words of encouragement.

"You'd never let Bobbie stay alone at an inn," he expostulated.

"I see no reason why Miss Dalrymple should not, since she chooses to set herself up as an independent woman. I dare say she frequently puts up at hostelries, and at least one

of her gentleman friends is already in residence at the Cheshire Cheese."

"Oh yes, Petrie. Then she can't possibly go there."

"Of course she can, Sebastian. She *claims* Phillip Petrie is
like a brother to her. Don't be difficult, there's a good boy."

Treated as a child, Sebastian lapsed into childish sulkiness.
"But I want her to stay here. I like her. She's a friend. You
never let me have any friends."

Lady Valeria threw Daisy an ingratiating smile, which
nearly succeeded where her murderous look had failed—in
killing Daisy from shock. "Now stop being silly, dear," she
said. "Of course you may have friends. I suppose it can't
hurt if Miss Dalrymple stays another day or two. I expect
you have work to do on your article, Miss Dalrymple," she
added pointedly. "Shall you and I have a nice, quiet game
of backgammon, Sebastian?"

He looked as if he'd have liked to refuse but under his
mother's gaze, at once steely and indulgent, he wilted and
agreed. Daisy went upstairs, wondering whether Lady
Valeria would let her little boy win the game.

She did in fact have work to do on her article, so she sat
down at her typewriter, rolled in a blank sheet of paper—and
sat staring at it. What on earth had Sebastian been talking
about? If he had enough to live on, what other problems had
he besides his inability to withstand his mother's ragging?
Why was he so nervous and so desperately miserable?

All she could think of was that he had killed Grace and
lived in imminent expectation of arrest.

After half an hour, the sheet of paper was no longer blank.
One and a half sentences stared back at her. Nor was she
any wiser with regard to Sebastian or the murder, having
passed the time watching a pair of newly arrived mallards
swimming happily on the moat in the rain. In spite of the
continuing drizzle, she decided to go to meet Alec.

Leaving her room, she saw Gregg just going into Bobbie's
room with a pile of clean laundry.

"Oh, Gregg, has Miss Roberta come home?" she called.
The maid turned, looking flustered. "No, miss."

"Do you happen to know where she went?"

"I'm sure I couldn't say, miss." Her gaze dropped evasively.

"You mean you don't know?" Daisy demanded.

"That I don't, miss, honest."

"You know something about her absence though, don't you?"

"Oh miss, she made me swear not to tell, for fear her ladyship'd find out."

"You must be aware the police are in the house, asking questions," Daisy said sternly.

"Yes, miss, I already saw that Detective Piper, but it wasn't today he asked about. He wanted to know did I see Miss Roberta or her ladyship the evening Gracie disappeared. Or anyone else, come to that."

"And did you?"

"No, miss. I packed her ladyship's trunk, but she always takes just the same stuff every year so she didn't have to be on the spot. Then I went to pack my own bag. They don't neither of them hardly ever need me at bedtime so I stayed in my room, resting up for the journey. Travelling with her ladyship's no picnic, miss."

"The very thought boggles the mind," Daisy conceded with a shudder, and she went on her way. She couldn't see how extracting Bobbie's secret from Gregg would help Alec, since all he had to do was ask Bobbie when she returned, if he was interested. A secret to be kept from Lady Valeria was not necessarily of any significance to anyone else.

Under her red umbrella, she set off down the path Ben had described. It took her through a copse, winding between leafless oaks and ashes, and hazel bushes bright with dangling yellow catkins. She emerged from the trees to the sound of cattle lowing. A slow procession of black-and-white cows, followed by a matching dog and a man, was approaching a collection of low brick buildings surrounded by a wooden rail-and-post fence. As they entered the enclosure by a wide gate to Daisy's left, Alec came through a kissing gate straight in front of her.

She wished she had arrived just a few minutes sooner. Of course, Alec was a townsman and might not know the swinging gate in the V-shaped enclosure was called a kissing gate, and even if he did. . . .

He raised in greeting the hand that wasn't holding up a huge black umbrella. "Hullo! Nothing the matter, I hope?"

"No, I just felt like a breath of fresh air." She turned back as he joined her.

Their umbrellas kept bumping, so she closed hers and moved under his. Walking became much easier when she tucked her hand through his arm. He smiled down at her.

"Did Sir Reginald say anything useful?" she asked, trying to pretend they always walked arm in arm.

"Not a word. Grace's disappearance and the departure next day of his wife and son altogether failed to impress December 13th on his memory. His records did confirm that it was a mild day, and revealed that a champion milker by the name of Gloriosa had a near-record percentage of butterfat in her milk."

Daisy giggled. "I can't say I'm awfully surprised."

"He's a nice old buffer with a one-track mind, who goes to bed at ten because his cows get up early. How did Sebastian take your confession?"

"Actually, he didn't care. He really has the wind up and he seemed to think my part in your arrival was pretty irrelevant." She decided Sebastian's troubles with his mother and her own advice were irrelevant to Alec.

"Do you think he's in a flap on his own account? Or because he knows or fears his mother or sister killed Grace for his sake?"

"Goodness only knows! I should think that might be enough to give him the willies."

"Incidentally, is Miss Parslow back yet?" Alec asked as they left the copse and approached the house.

"She wasn't when I left."

"I'll have to leave her until tomorrow, then. I must see what Piper has to report, and this evening we're hoping to pump the villagers."

"The pump being a beer-pump, no doubt," Daisy said tartly.

Alec grinned. "Yes, of course. Alcohol lubricates tongues. I'll come back up here as early as is decent in the morning."

"If your head allows."

"Mine's a hard head. As I was saying, I'll be here early because there's the funeral later on."

"I don't think I'd better go. It would look a bit pushy as I didn't know her. Not that I'm exactly keen on funerals at the best of times."

"Unfortunately, attending the funeral of murder victims is one of the inescapable duties of a detective. Someone just might break down and confess."

"You're out of luck if you're hoping to catch anyone from the Hall. Lady Valeria has said no one's to go, neither family nor servants. It's a bit thick really, considering Grace worked here for several years and the other maids were her friends."

"It does seem rather harsh. Well, I'll have to go anyway. We can't be sure yet it was someone from the Hall, and I want to catch Moss for a word afterwards. He sounds like a thoroughly awkward customer—a rude mechanical, you might say—but. . . ."

"A rude mechanical?" She looked at him enquiringly, her head tilted in a way that for some reason made him want to kiss the tip of her nose.

"A Midsummer Night's Dream," he said briefly. "But I hope his daughter's funeral will make him anxious to cooperate in catching the murderer."

Daisy took her hand from his arm as they reached the

shelter of a small back porch. "I should think Moss'll be overjoyed to find you suspect Lady Valeria!" she observed.

"I'm not." He groaned. "Why do I always end up dealing with the nobs?"

"According to Piper, because you have a degree and talk posh."

Laughing, Alec shook and closed the umbrella. "There are occasional compensations," he conceded with a smile. *"Some* of the nobs are really quite nice to know."

They went into the house and made their way to the Long Hall. Before going to look for Piper, Alec once more warned Daisy against meddling, thus ruining the effect of his compliment.

Piqued, she went off to the Yellow Parlour. She was glad to find Phillip there. Having called to thank Lady Valeria for last night's dinner, he had been pressed to stay for afternoon tea. His presence did much to lessen the inevitable sense of constraint.

Neither Bobbie nor Ben came in, but Sebastian appeared to have recovered his equanimity, at least outwardly, and Lady Valeria had donned a veneer of cordiality. As she sat there dispensing tea and cake, no one would have guessed how recently she had freely dispensed hints of an improper relationship between Daisy and Phillip.

Her ladyship's assumed complacency was not destined to last. Phillip started talking about his motor-car, always one of his favourite subjects of conversation. Stan Moss had not only tuned up the Swift so that the engine ran as smooth as silk, he had taught Phillip how to do it himself. Stan Moss was a mechanical genius. Stan Moss could make a fortune if he just had a proper service-station with modern equipment.

Lady Valeria's face regained its familiar thunderous aspect. Sebastian looked more and more amused, and Daisy had to avoid his eye or she'd have burst into fits of giggles.

"Dash it," said Phillip, "just think how convenient it

would be for you to have a petrol pump on your doorstep instead of having to drive into Whitbury to fill up."

"Never," pronounced Lady Valeria in tones of doom, "never shall there be a petrol pump in Occleswich as long as I . . . that is, as long as Sir Reginald owns the village!"

"Right-ho," Phillip obligingly agreed. "Smelly things, what? The whole village belongs to the estate, does it?"

"Sir Reginald was unwise enough—before we married—to dispose of the leasehold of the smithy and the inn in order to finance modern equipment for his dairy. Even with a clause forbidding material alterations without permission, it has caused nothing but trouble."

Phillip nodded. "You lose control," he said. "The gov'nor sold quite a bit of the freehold of Malvern Green to pay the death duties when my grandfather died."

A discussion of the iniquities of death duties and the income tax so far restored him to Lady Valeria's favour that she invited him to Sunday lunch. "If you are still in the neighbourhood, Mr. Petrie," she added with a peevish glance at Daisy.

Phillip also looked at Daisy, but anxiously, as he answered, "Thanks awfully, I'll be here and I'm happy to accept, but I'm going to have to toddle off back to town on Monday. Business, and I didn't bring my man with me. Simply can't do without him much longer, don't you know."

He was reluctant to leave her here with Alec and with the murder unsolved, Daisy guessed. However, she didn't see how she could decently prolong her own stay at the Hall beyond the weekend, whatever Sebastian and Bobbie wanted. Alec's insistence on her remaining didn't really hold water, and the dairy excuse was not simply wearing thin but already in rags—she'd had plenty of time to inspect the place. And though considerations of propriety wouldn't stop her staying at the inn, she couldn't really afford even the Cheshire Cheese's modest tariff.

At least she'd be able to bag a lift with Phillip and get a

refund on her return ticket, she thought, brightening. Of course she'd pay him back the difference between first and second class, but she'd still come out a few shillings ahead. A new pair of silk stockings?

Phillip rose to take his leave.

Sebastian stopped him. "I say, won't you hang about a bit longer and give me a game of billiards?" He was like a little boy begging for a treat.

"Right-ho, old man."

A flash of dread crossed Lady Valeria's heavy features, so quickly suppressed Daisy wasn't sure she hadn't imagined it. Her ladyship's mouth opened, but if she meant to voice a protest she was forestalled as Phillip went on, "What d'you say we make it snooker and ask Daisy to play with us? She's not bad, for a girl."

"Not bad!" Daisy squawked. "I've jolly well trounced you more than once."

Sebastian laughed. "I'd have asked you before, Daisy, as a change from backgammon, if I'd known you play. Come on."

Could that possibly be relief on his mother's face now? Disconcerted, Daisy went off with the men, feeling thoroughly perplexed.

Lady Valeria's curious reactions faded from her mind as she struggled to persuade both Sebastian and Phillip not to cheat in her favour. The result of her efforts was that they continued to do so with more and more outrageous openness, until they were all so helpless with laughter they could barely hit the balls.

Daisy had never seen Sebastian so relaxed and happy; she was pretty sure he rarely had the opportunity to enjoy himself with his peers. It was criminal the way his mother kept him mewed up at her side. No wonder he had turned to an unsatisfactory affair with a sympathetic parlourmaid, with such disastrous results.

She couldn't believe he was a murderer. He simply hadn't the spunk. Someone else had done the deed.

Lady Valeria? Bobbie? The mysterious commercial traveler? Surely not Bobbie. Girls one had been to school with didn't turn out to be murderers, especially forthright, sporting types like Bobbie. Murder just wasn't cricket.

Yet murder had been done, and its daunting effects settled once more on Daisy and Sebastian when Phillip departed. They went up to change for dinner in dispirited silence.

The grey silk frock matched Daisy's mood. Anticipating another long and uncomfortable evening, she went down to the drawing room. As she approached the door, she heard Moody's cheerless accents within and hesitated a moment.

"No, my lady, Miss Roberta hasn't come in yet. Miss Gregg asked me to give your ladyship this note she left for you."

"Note? Roberta left a note? And Gregg has only just decided to give it to me?" Lady Valeria sounded astonished, indignant, and apprehensive all at once.

"I understand, my lady, that such were Miss Roberta's instructions."

"What does it say, Valeria?" Sir Reginald asked, mildly curious.

Daisy couldn't have stopped eavesdropping to save her life. Fortunately Lady Valeria didn't send Moody out before she read Bobbie's note and in her shock she relayed the contents to her husband without considering the butler's presence.

"Good heavens above! Reggie, she's staying away tonight!"

"Where?"

"She doesn't say, and she can't say for sure when she'll be able to come home!"

Bobbie fleeing the police? But she had nearly fainted when Daisy told her Grace had been murdered—or was it because Grace's body had been discovered?

However treacherous she felt, Daisy had to tell Alec.

12

When Alec and Ernie Piper left the Hall, the rain had stopped and a streak of red from the setting sun showed below the clouds in the west. Petrie's elderly Swift was parked beside the Austin, which looked nice and new but very staid next to the nifty two-seater. As Alec started up his practical family car, Piper pulled out his notebook.

"I covered the lot, Chief," he said with satisfaction. "All them questions you had."

"They actually talked to you, in spite of Lady Valeria?"

"That butler said they was told not to talk to the police, so I up and says we're not just police, we're *Scotland Yard* and we don't pay no heed to country bigwigs. So he looks gloomier than ever and tells the rest to cooperate."

Alec grinned. "A bit of an exaggeration, but well done. Just run through what you've written down. We'll sort it out later." It was no good asking Piper to pick out the relevant bits, as he would with Tring. The lad hadn't enough experience to know what might be significant.

"Moody, that's the butler, after dinner he served coffee to Sir Reginald and Miss Parslow in the drawing room and her ladyship and Mr. Goodman in the library. Then he went to his pantry and put his aching feet up till he went round locking up at half eleven."

"He locked up at half past eleven?"

"Yes, Chief, same as always. There's a side door with no

bolt, just a Yale lock and the family all has keys, so I didn't reckon much to that."

"Except that if Grace came back into the house at all, it must have been before eleven thirty—unless for some reason she came in with one of the family. Suppose young Parslow met her in the village and took her for a drive in hopes of sorting things out, then returned home and told his mother or sister he'd failed. How many motors do they own, and were any out that night?"

"I dunno, Chief," said Piper, anguished. "I didn't even think to see the showfer."

"No one ever asks all the questions first time round," Alec told him bracingly. "That's what tomorrow's for. Let's get back to Moody."

"Right, Chief. He says Mr. Parslow's vally, Thomkins, popped into his pantry for a drop of port after packing for Mr. Parslow. A bit after ten, it was. He remembers acos they was talking about the packing only taking an hour or thereabouts, Mr. Parslow being so easygoing. Seems Thomkins's last master was a fusspot as never could make up his mind. Thomkins agrees it was just after ten."

"So Parslow has no alibi from ten until eleven thirty," Alec mused, "and I have only his word for eleven thirty since Scotland Yard fails to impress his mother. Not that I'd believe any alibi she gave him. If he'd been with his sister he'd have said so, for her sake as well as his own. Did any of the servants see him during that time, Ernie?"

"No, Chief. They keeps pretty much to their own quarters after dinner, even the personal servants, unless they're rung for."

"No maid taking round hot-water bottles?"

"Her ladyship don't hold with hot-water bottles."

"Curses upon her ladyship! Go on. No, wait a bit," Alec said, drawing up in front of the smithy. "There's no light visible, but just pop round the back and see if Moss's lorry is there."

Piper popped, and returned to announce no lorry, no lights.

They reached the Cheshire Cheese and went up to Alec's room long before Piper came to the end of his list of those who had seen nothing and nobody.

No one had seen any of the family after ten o'clock. No one had seen Owen Morgan. The powder old Bligh took for his rheumatics made him sleep so soundly he wouldn't hear a herd of wild elephants, let alone Morgan leaving the cottage. The other three under-gardeners had girlfriends in the village; their only interest in Grace was to tease Morgan about her.

No one had been down in the village after six, when the housemaid whose day off it was had come in.

No one had seen Grace come in, but she could have gone up to her room unseen. She always returned on time because she liked her job and didn't want to lose it. Though she had worked in a shop in Whitbury for a few months after leaving school, five or six years ago, she had been glad to get a position at the Hall. It was nearer her father but at least she didn't have to go home to him every evening. As it was, he took most of her pay and expected her to cook, clean, and launder for him on her days off. She seldom had a chance to go into Whitbury to shop or to the pictures as the others did.

"A right bastard he sounds," Piper opined, "but he was sitting pretty. He wouldn't want to do away with her."

In spite of her unpleasant home life, Grace was always cheerful and helpful. She was popular with her fellow servants, though mildly envied by the young and indulgently frowned upon by her elders for her "way with the fellows." The only indoor menservants were the butler and two valets, but she flirted with the postman, the butcher's boy, the grocer's and baker's deliverymen. No one believed her relationship with the young master had gone beyond a flirtation. The news of her pregnancy had come as a shock and general opinion in the servants' hall blamed the foreigner, the Welsh gardener, not Mr. Sebastian.

In fact, everyone but Bligh was so sure Morgan was the

murderer, they couldn't understand what Scotland Yard was doing at Occles Hall.

"Is Miss Dalrymple wrong this time, Chief?" Piper asked, his faith shaken.

"Not she. Parslow was having an affair with Grace all right. Tell me, were Grace's things missing from her room? Never mind," he said as Piper's face fell, "we'll find out tomorrow."

All the same, Tom would never have missed such an obvious question. If Grace had left her belongings behind, why did everyone assume she had run away? If they were gone, someone in the household had removed them, someone who knew she was dead and who wanted people to think she'd run away.

"That's all very well," Alec said slowly, "but what made them believe she had run away when she liked her job and they didn't know she was in trouble? They said she was always cheerful?"

"Always till the last couple of weeks, Chief. One of the housemaids—lessee—Edna her name is, Grace's best friend like, she says she seemed a bit mopish. This Edna asked what was wrong and Grace said her pa was being even awkwarder'n usual. She didn't like being asked, though, so she tried to behave like normal; only when she disappeared, Edna told the rest she'd been in the dumps."

"Poor kid." For the first time Alec was beginning to see Grace as a real person, in some ways an admirable person despite her fall from grace (and that was a bloody awful pun he'd being trying not to make). With an altogether obnoxious father, she had somehow managed to grow up sunny-tempered and kind-hearted, and competent to boot. Whatever her mistakes, she hadn't deserved to die.

He wanted badly to nail her killer. Daisy expected no less. The trouble was, unless he got hold of some real evidence soon, the A.C. was going to call him home. The Met couldn't spare a chief inspector for a two-month-old murder that the locals hadn't even started to investigate properly.

At least he'd see Owen Morgan released. There wasn't a shred of real evidence against him, and the Parslows had quite as much motive.

"I'd like to get this cleared up before the magistrate's hearing on Monday," he said to Piper. "Unless we find something definite against Morgan, he ought to be let out without going to court, for the sake of the reputation of the local police, and police in general. If we can arrest someone else that'll be all to the good, but if we can't manage it, I want to be sure we've left no stone unturned."

"Not digging up the garden!" said Piper, aghast.

"It may come to that. The murder weapon may be buried there. We won't get prints by now, but just knowing what was used might help. But I hope we shan't need to, and if we do you can supervise a crew of local officers." He grinned as Piper breathed again. "I wonder whether the locals have dug up George Brown's traces in Whitbury? It's just possible he had met Grace before if she worked there, but it was rather a long time ago. I'd better go and ring up Sergeant Shaw and. . . ."

"There's one more thing, Chief."

"Yes?"

"The housekeeper, Mrs. Twitchell, I saw her last and mostly what she said was just the same as the others. Then she asked was it only that night we was interested in, 'cos a week before she saw Mr. Goodman talking to Grace."

"Goodman deals with the servants' pay and so on," Alec said impatiently. "He must talk to all of them quite often."

"But this was different, Chief," Piper persisted. "She says he was talking ever so serious, and then Grace laughed at him and ran away, so I thought maybe he fancied a bit of slap and tickle and she turned him down and he got mad and. . . ."

"Bloody hell, another suspect! Just what I need. All right,

Ernie, it could be important. We'll have to follow it up to-morrow. Right now, you go and open your ears in the public bar. I'm going to telephone Sergeant Shaw."

On his way down the narrow stairs, Alec met the plump landlady puffing up. "I were just coming to fetch you, sir," she said. "You're wanted on the telephone.

He thanked her and squeezed past. The telephone hung on the wall in a tiny booth at the back of the lobby. Putting the dangling receiver to his ear, he announced himself into the mouthpiece.

"It's Tom, Chief. We got him. Well, nearly."

"George Brown? What do you mean, nearly?"

"A Sergeant Shaw rung me up from Chester, said he'd tried to get hold of you but you wasn't there. His laddies tracked Brown to one of his customers in some little town up there. . . ."

"Whitbury. As a matter of interest, what does he travel in?"

"Ready-to-wear ladies' corsets, Chief." Tom snickered.

"Great Scott! That explains why he wasn't trying to sell to the village shop and why he didn't announce his line to the people here. Poor chap, I bet he catches a lot of ragging. Shaw found out what company he works for?"

"The Clover Corset Company, known to bosom friends as CCC." The sergeant's cackle crackled down the wire. "Their head office is in Ealing. I phoned 'em up and talked to the top bloke in the sales department. Brown's territory's the Northwest. Seems he's pretty free to ramble around, hunting down new customers. He's not married and he only gets back to London every couple of weeks, but he rings up on Satur-day evening to report in. So they'll find out tomorrow night where he is and let us know."

"You told them not to warn him we want to see him?"

" 'Course, Chief, wotcha take me for?"

Alec smiled at his injured tone. "I beg your pardon, Tom."

"And I asked 'em to telephone the Chester police if I'm not here."

The broad hint broadened Alec's smile. "Well, if Brown's up north, you're finished in town, and I need you. Hop on a train in the morning."

"I c'd come tonight, Chief. There must be a night train."

"You *are* married, Tom."

"Worse luck. Proper cramps me style, does the old trouble and strife."

"I hadn't noticed it." If Grace had had a way with the fellows, Tom had a way with the ladies, or a least with a certain class of females. Nonetheless, despite his use of derogatory rhyming slang, Alec knew he was deeply devoted to the equally mountainous Mrs. Tring, from whom he was too often reft by the demands of his profession. "Tomorrow will do. Let me know the time and I'll send Piper to meet you at Crewe."

"Ta, Chief. Miss Dalrymple all right?"

"Miss Dalrymple thrives on trouble and strife," Alec said acidly. Her annoyance at his repeated warning against meddling had not escaped him.

He rang off.

The sound of voices from the bars was increasing as men came in for a pint after work. Glancing into the public bar, Alec saw Piper sit down with a couple of farmhands. The youthful detective in his brown serge suit looked out of place among collarless, stubble-chinned labourers, and Alec doubted he'd be able to make himself at home as Tom would.

He shrugged. He himself would be still less welcome there. He went into the bar-parlour next door, which was where Grace and George Brown had had their *tête-à-tête*.

The small, cosy room, all polished wood and brass, fell silent as he entered. Not only was he a stranger, he'd have bet a month's pay every soul in the place knew he was a police officer. It was inevitable in so small a village, he supposed, but it meant he had little hope of getting anything out of them short of formal questioning. He wasn't likely to do any better than Ernie.

"Good evening," he said to the room in general, crossing to the bar.

A pair of moderately prosperous farmers in country tweeds and leggings nodded to him and returned to a discussion of the prospective price of spring lamb. A man seated alone at the bar ignored him after a glance. A middle-aged couple sitting by the fire answered his greeting. He recognized them as the Taylors, proprietors of the Village Store where he had replenished his tobacco pouch.

"What will you have?" he asked them genially.

After consulting her husband with a doubtful look, Mrs. Taylor said, "I wouldn't say no to a sherry, Chief Inspector. Just a small one, mind, and thank you kindly."

"The name's Fletcher. What's yours?"

"Half of bitter, thanks, Mr. Fletcher."

The improbably blond barmaid came through from the public, which shared the long bar-counter. He gave his order and carried the two tankards and a glass over to the Taylors' table.

They proved friendly, perfectly willing to talk about the murder, but quite unable to help. Their custom was to call in at the Cheshire Cheese for a drop before dinner (no proletarian tea for the Taylors). They very seldom came back later, preferring to listen to the wireless when there was not stock-taking or accounts to be dealt with. On the evening of December 13, as usual on a Wednesday, they had been in the shop restocking shelves, but the blinds had been down and they had seen nothing in the street.

"It's no picnic running the only shop in the village," said Mr. Taylor impressively. "People expect to find everything under the sun, and then there's the Post Office, too. Well, we'd best be off, Doreen. Take my word for it, Mr. Fletcher, you're wasting your time. It was the Welshman did it."

Alec had much the same result from the less amicable farmers and the solitary fellow at the bar, a clerk who worked in Whitbury and lived with his parents in Occleswich. Three or four others came and went without adding to his store of information.

"Likely you'll do better after you've ate, sir," the barmaid told him when she summoned him to dinner. "There's them as comes in early and them as comes in late."

"And never the twain shall meet," Alec said resignedly. "Perhaps you can help me with a couple more points, Rita. I know you wouldn't have seen anything outside, but did you notice whether anyone left at the same time as Grace, or thereabouts?"

"I couldn't say, sir, I'm sure. There was people coming and going same as usual, and I only noticed Grace 'cos she gen'rally stayed till closing."

"Did her father come in at all?"

"Don't think so, sir, though I wouldn't swear to it."

That agreed with the local police report. Moss told Dunnett he came home late; Grace had left his tea in the oven and he did not see her.

"What about the commercial traveler? He was a stranger and supposed to be staying here, so you might have been aware of his movements. When did he leave the bar?"

"Oh, yes, he did stay till closing, I 'member that. He were knocking back the whisky like water. After Grace went off, he talked to some others, but he kept taking out his watch. It seemed a bit odd to me, seeing he'd booked a room. Must've been after the bars closed he picked up his bags and scarpered. I were cleaning up and I din't see him again."

"Do you by any chance recall who else he talked to?"

Rita's eyes went blank as she thought. "No, sir, I'm that sorry."

"Never mind, you've been a great help."

"Well, sir, if it weren't Owen Morgan done it, I'm sure I hopes you catches whoever it were, or we're none of us safe in our beds."

As Alec crossed the lobby to the dining room, Petrie came down the stairs in his dinner-jacket. Probably Petrie, as was rumoured of his class, would dress for dinner in a clearing in the jungle, whereas Alec hadn't even brought his dinner-jacket with him to the wilds of Cheshire. He suddenly felt underdressed, but after all he was dining with Piper, who undoubtedly didn't even own such esoteric garb.

"Hullo, Fletcher," Petrie greeted him. "Heading for the old feeding trough? Mind if I join you?"

"I'd be delighted, except that my young officer may have a report to deliver while we eat."

"Right-oh. Don't want to butt in, old man." But Petrie looked disappointed. He was a sociable chap, and pleasant enough when he forgot to stand on the dignity of his father's rank.

With a touch of malice, Alec decided to see whether the Honourable Phillip would decline to dine with a mere constable. "Here comes Piper now," he said, turning at the sound of footsteps behind him. "If his luck was as bad as mine and he has nothing to tell me, you're welcome to sit with us."

Petrie's dismay was obvious, but he rallied and said stoutly, "Jolly good. I say, young fellow, anything to report?"

Piper's mouth dropped open. "N-no, sir," he stammered, then turned gloomily to Alec. "I mean, no, sir, I didn't get nothing useful. The ones as come in early, they're the ones as is hen-pecked, as you might say. They stops by for their pint afore their tea acos once they've gone home, they're not let out again, so they wasn't here when Grace was."

Alec laughed. "I drew a blank, too," he consoled. "With luck we'll do better after dinner. I'd really rather not have to do a house-to-house."

They went into the dining room. At first Piper was a bit overawed by their dinner-jacketed companion, but when Petrie started talking about football and cricket, he joined in eagerly. In fact, he knew far more about sport than did Alec, who was left to enjoy his meal in peace.

Afterwards, Petrie accompanied Alec to the bar-parlour. "A sound chap, that constable of yours," he said, as they made their way to the bar. The room was now too full for their arrival to create a hush. "What are you drinking, old man?"

"Allow me," Alec said. "Tonight's on expenses. All I have to do is point out to my Super that a few rounds come cheaper than overtime for a horde of uniformed locals knocking on doors."

"B-and-s, then. Thanks, old chap. Don't worry, I shan't get in the way of your enquiries."

But Alec's enquiries, though watered by several rounds, still failed to bear fruit. Everyone denied having noticed the movements of either Grace or George Brown, let alone having spoken with the traveler. Nor had they seen anyone in the street other than the cronies with whom they had left the pub. None of them even claimed to have seen the despised Welshman.

By half-past nine, Alec was resigned to a wasted evening. Having made a pint of stout last till then, he ordered a whisky from the landlord—as unobservant as any of his customers—who had joined Rita behind the bar. Glass in hand he turned to survey the room, hoping to spot someone he hadn't yet spoken to.

Then Daisy walked in, with Ben Goodman limping after her.

From her face Alec knew at once that she had news, and that from her point of view it was bad news. And what the deuce did she mean by going out alone with one of the suspects? Had she no common sense whatsoever?

Throughout a sombre dinner at the Hall, Daisy had been wondering how to convey her news to Alec without broadcasting it via the telephone operator. She suspected he'd be less than pleased if she delayed until the morning. Of course, having proclaimed her right to stay unaccompanied at the inn, she could hardly cavil at entering the place alone. It was the walk down to the village in the dark she didn't look forward to. After all, a girl had been killed out there quite recently. Bobbie's unexplained absence didn't prove Bobbie had done the foul deed. Some maniac might be lying in wait for another victim.

Alec himself had warned her to be careful.

She was still trying to decide whether to telephone or risk the walk when Ben announced his need for exercise.

"I've been cooped up all day," he said. "Do you want to pop down to the Cheese with me for half an hour, Sebastian?"

"How thoughtless of you," said Lady Valeria coldly. "You can't imagine the dear boy chooses to expose himself to the vulgar curiosity of the yokels. Sebastian, why don't you put a record on the gramophone. We haven't listened to any music in a long time."

"All right, Mater," Sebastian said without enthusiasm.

Daisy jumped up. "I'll go with you, Ben. I'll just fetch my coat. I shan't be a moment. You'll excuse me, Lady Valeria."

"Naturally I cannot control your movements, Miss Dalrymple." Her ladyship's censorious voice followed Daisy to the door. "Such odd behaviour, these modern girls."

Bloody cheek, thought Daisy, when her own daughter had just cleared out on the arrival of Scotland Yard.

As she and Ben left the house, he smilingly apologized. "I ought to have invited you, as well as Sebastian, to go with me. I'd forgotten you modern girls refuse to be limited as were the young ladies of my youth. You must think me a frightful old fogy."

"Not at all. I'm afraid you'll think me a frightful traitor. You see, the reason I want to go to the inn is to tell Mr. Fletcher about Bobbie going missing."

"Missing? Lady Valeria just said we wouldn't wait for her as she might be late. By Jove, you don't suppose she's been mur. . . . No, that wouldn't make you a traitor."

"She wrote a note to her mother. She left of her own accord and couldn't say when she'd return."

"So you think she's lying low, hiding from the police? You can't believe she's a murderer!"

"I don't want to. It's possible she knows something she doesn't want to tell, isn't it?"

"Something about Sebastian," Ben said dully.

"Or Lady Valeria." Daisy realized she was hurrying her pace as they passed the Winter Garden, and Ben was having trouble keeping up with her. She slowed down. "This whole affair is so beastly."

"I imagine murder is always beastly. You're perfectly justified in telling the police anything which might help them find the killer, and Bobbie's absence could hardly be kept from them for long anyway. You need not feel treacherous."

"Thank you, Ben," she said, reassured. "At least I know Mr. Fletcher won't jump to conclusions as the dreadful Dimwit did."

"You know the Chief Inspector pretty well, don't you?"

"Yes, rather."

"He's not quite what one expects of the police, not that I've ever come across the upper echelons of Scotland Yard before. But he struck me as well educated, not your narrow-minded guardian of the law."

"He's a gentleman," said Daisy in hot defense of Alec. "He may not have gone to Eton and Oxford, but he has a degree in history from Manchester University. I dare say he knows as much about eighteenth-century England as you do about ancient Greece."

She heard the smile in his voice. "I expect he does, and all about detecting crime, into the bargain. He's young to be a Chief Inspector, isn't he?"

"I can't say I'm acquainted with many police officers, but he's much younger than the Dimwit, who's only an Inspector."

"You'd better stop using that name for Inspector Dunnett," Ben advised, laughing as he opened the wicket-gate in the park wall. "You might call him Dimwit to his face by accident."

"I hope I never meet him again," said Daisy, passing through into the lane, "but if I ever do address him as Dimwit, it won't be by accident!"

She glanced at the smithy as they passed. A light flickered in the downstairs window next to the forge itself. Presumably Stan Moss was at home, not at the pub, and she was glad of it. She ought to feel sorry for the bereaved father, but after seeing him threaten Owen she found him more alarming than pitiable.

Before they reached the Cheshire Cheese, the street door of the public bar at the front opened as someone went in. They heard a cheerful hubbub of voices. Ben ushered her past and through the lobby to the bar-parlour at the back.

Alec stood with his back to the bar. He saw her at once and smiled. Then his smile turned to a frown. He came to meet them.

With a curt nod to Ben, he said to Daisy, "What's the matter?"

"I have to talk to you." She glanced around the crowded room.

"Not in here. We'll go to the dining room. It should be empty. I'd like a word with you later, Mr. Goodman."

"I'm at your service, Chief Inspector." Ben looked exhausted. Daisy wondered whether his desire to walk down to the village was due more to a wish to escape the Hall for a while than to a need for exercise.

Phillip joined them. "What-ho, Daisy, Goodman."

"Hullo. I'm just going to the dining room to talk to Mr. Fletcher."

"I'll come with you," said Phillip promptly.

"Don't be an ass, Phil. I *don't* need a chaperon, nor a protector. We'll only be a couple of minutes."

As she and Alec left, she heard Phillip asking Ben, "What's yours, old chap?"

Alec closed the dining-room door behind them. "What is

it?" he asked, taking down two of the chairs which had been up-ended on the tables to facilitate sweeping the floor.

"Bobbie." Daisy sat down and told him about overhearing Lady Valeria reading her daughter's note. "I feel utterly despicable eavesdropping and tale-bearing," she finished, "but I thought you ought to know."

"You're quite right, it's definitely fishy. I'll put out a general call to keep an eye out for her, but not to stop her unless she tries to leave the country. Describe her, please." He took out his notebook.

"I can do better than that. I pinched this photo." She produced a shot of Bobbie in the centre of a group of Girl Guides, abstracted from Bobbie's room when she went to get her coat. "This was the most recent I could find. She's taller than me, blue eyes. Alec, if you're not going to tell them to stop her, that means you don't necessarily think she's the murderer, doesn't it?"

"Not necessarily. After all, since she was already gone, I hadn't actually requested that she inform me before leaving the area. I take it you don't believe she's our villain?"

"No, I *can't* believe it."

Alec glared at her and said in a biting voice, "In which case, with the murderer still at large and nearby, what the dickens did you think you were doing going out alone at night with Goodman?"

"Ben?" Daisy stared in astonishment. "I'm safe with Ben, of all people!"

"We can't be sure of that. Piper dug up a possible motive."

"Not Ben!" Her eyes filled with tears. "This is a *beastly* business!"

He took her hand in a warm clasp. "Go back to London, Daisy, won't you?"

"No," she said stubbornly. "I'll see it through."

Sighing, he passed her his spare handkerchief. "Then for pity's sake at least take elementary precautions, you little idiot!"

B

Alec watched with fond exasperation as Daisy blotted her eyes and turned on him an indignant gaze.

"I'm not quite an idiot. Everyone at the Hall knew I was going with Ben, so he wouldn't be so stupid as to try anything. Anyway, I'm sure I'm at least as strong as he is. In fact, I don't believe he could have carried Grace to the garden, let alone dug a hole and buried her."

"From the path outside he might have dragged her, and a well-prepared garden bed is comparatively easy to dig, not like undisturbed soil. Besides, he might have had help."

"He's the secretary, not a member of the family, remember. What's his motive supposed to be?"

"He was seen talking seriously to Grace, a week or so before her death. She laughed at him and ran away. A man whose advances are ridiculed by a girl known to be . . . no better than she should be has to join the list of suspects."

Daisy bit her lip. "Ben's not like that."

Alec felt a flash of jealousy. "You hardly know him," he pointed out tersely.

"I know he's kind and sympathetic."

There it was again, that hint of a sorrow in her past, which she had never confided to him but had apparently revealed to Ben Goodman—Goodman, who was of her class despite his menial position. Alec's jealousy intensified and he struggled to subdue it.

"There may well be nothing in it," he conceded, "but I have to talk to him."

"Yes, of course. But you must admit, under those circumstances Grace wouldn't have agreed to meet him, and he's not well enough to lurk about waiting for her on a winter's night, however mild."

"He walked down tonight, didn't he? You really shouldn't have risked coming down alone in the dark with him. If you had telephoned, I'd have driven up there."

"Oh Alec, I didn't even think of that! I was so determined not to let the switchboard girl know Bobbie was missing. Yes, Ben did walk down tonight, but he is fearfully tired, I'm afraid. Would you mind driving us back? I'd ask Phillip, only his car is a frightful squeeze with three."

"I'll take you, provided Goodman doesn't confess within the next few minutes." He started to stand up.

Daisy clutched his arm. "You haven't told me what else Ernie found out from the servants!"

"Very little. They all seem to stick pretty close to their own quarters after dinner."

"Servants expect to be treated like human beings these days. Mother's always complaining that hers have the nerve to demand more than a half day off once a month. Didn't you learn *anything* from them?"

Succumbing, as usual, to the appeal in her blue eyes, Alec told her what little Piper had found out. "He didn't get around to seeing the chauffeur," he finished, "so we don't know whether a car was out that night. Do you happen to know how many motors the Parslows own?"

"A Daimler and a Morris. Bobbie and Sebastian both drive the Morris, but I don't think either of them goes anywhere very often."

Alec sat up. "Bobbie—Miss Parslow *has* gone somewhere. Did she take the car?"

"I've not the foggiest."

"Dash it, I'll have to ring up and ask the chauffeur before

I send out a description. I'm afraid your switchboard girl is soon going to know all there is to know."

"Inevitable." Daisy sighed. "At least I tried."

She returned to the bar-parlour while Alec went to the telephone. Moody was at length persuaded to fetch the chauffeur, Brady, to the telephone. Alec didn't ask about December 13, but he found out that Miss Parslow was indeed driving the Morris, a blue, bull-nosed "Oxford," of which there were hundreds on the roads. He wrote down the number-plate, rang up Scotland Yard, and ordered a description of car and driver to be circulated to all police forces. He was well aware, though, that if Miss Parslow stuck to country lanes or had gone to earth at a friend's country home she'd be very hard to find.

Could she be the murderer? He'd had no opportunity to judge for himself. According to Daisy she was strong enough, and protective enough of her brother to provide a motive. Nor was Daisy anywhere near so convinced of her innocence as she was of Goodman's.

If Miss Parslow hadn't turned up by Sunday night, he decided, he'd have her detained if found, not merely watched. But he hadn't nearly enough evidence to justify ordering a full-scale hunt.

He went to find Ben Goodman.

Petrie and Goodman were deep in conversation over a couple of tankards. To Alec's surprise, Daisy wasn't with them. He scanned the room and saw her chatting with an elderly man in an old-fashioned knickerbocker suit who had the outdoor look of a smallholder. She saw him and waved him over.

"Mr. Fletcher, this is Ted Roper, proprietor of the station fly."

"And me grandson drives a motor-lorry," said Ted Roper with pride. His deepset eyes twinkled maliciously at Alec, who had already talked to him without eliciting more than an "ar" or a "nay."

"Mr. Roper was here when Grace was talking to the commercial traveller," said Daisy.

"Just like her ma," Roper said unexpectedly. "Runned off wi' an artist fella came to paint the village, Elsie Moss did. 'Cepting Grace didn't, seemingly."

"Her mother ran away with an artist?" Alec sat down. Trust Daisy to get the close-mouthed old fellow chatting. "When was that, Mr. Roper?"

" 'Bout when Gracie turned fourteen and left school, it'd be, old enough to look after her pa, any road. No one din't blame Elsie too much, mind. Stan Moss were always a cantankersome bugger, beggin' your pardon, miss. A flaming row they had, and Elsie up and walked out."

"So that's why everyone was so sure Grace had gone off with Brown." Alec had never been quite satisfied with the collective certainty. "Did you see Grace leave the pub?"

"Aye, that I did. Din't reckon nothing to it, then."

"Did anyone else leave at the same time, or shortly after?"

"Not as I saw, sir. All alone, she were. Arterwards, us reckoned she went to pack up her bits and bobs and come back later to meet the fella."

"Did you talk to the man, or see who did?"

"Not I."

"Oh, come on, Mr. Roper," said Daisy coaxingly. "You told me which men he talked to, and I bet I can remember some of the names. Mr. Fletcher doesn't think any of your friends killed Grace, only that they may have heard something which will help him if the commercial did it. Don't you want him to catch the murderer? It could be your granddaughter next!"

"Now, now, missy," Roper growled, "my girls be good girls."

"I'm sure they are, but who's to say the murderer knows or cares? Until Mr. Fletcher works out who it was, he can't tell why he did it."

"Perhaps Grace made someone angry by refusing him," Alec suggested. Daisy frowned at the reference to Goodman's possible motive.

"Fair enough," said Ted Roper reluctantly. "Them as talked to him was Walt Ferris, Ned Carney, Peter Jiggs, Albert Bartholomew." He pointed out each man as he named them. "And Harry Middlecombe."

Old Uncle Tom Cobleigh and all, Alec thought. "What a memory you have, Mr. Roper," he said, slightly sceptical.

"Oh aye." The old man preened, then admitted, "They han't none on 'em never stopped jawing 'bout it since."

They hadn't jawed to Alec, though he'd already questioned four of the five. Hoping Roper's loquacity had broken the dam of silence, he excused himself and went to try the fifth, Peter Jiggs, who was Sir Reginald's chief dairyman.

Alec had met Jiggs briefly when he went to the dairy to see Sir Reginald. Asked not whether he'd spoken to Brown but what had been said, Jiggs scratched his head and thought the weather might have been mentioned. "Mild it were for December. Good for the pasture. Cows milk better on green stuff nor ever they do on fodder. Yon fella said it made his job easier, too, dashing all over in one o' they motor-cars."

"Oh aye." Ned Carney had drifted over to join them, no doubt having seen Ted Roper point him out to the detective. He met Alec's gaze with bland unconcern. "Fella told us a yarn 'bout getting stuck in snow up Cumberland way. Took three horses to pull his motor out o' the drift." He snickered.

"They get much more snow up in the hills than we do down here." That was Albert Bartholomew, a young clerk with a job in Whitbury, a ploughman's son who had bettered himself. He had the grace to give Alec a sheepish look.

"Did he seem familiar with this area?" Alec asked.

The three men glanced at each other doubtfully.

"A Londoner, he were," said Carney.

"Cheshire was part of his territory," said Bartholomew, "and he liked to explore the countryside when he had time. He said village inns often did him better than fancy hotels. But I'm pretty sure he'd never been to Occleswich before."

The other two shook their heads. "He were asking 'bout village fairs and such," said Jiggs.

"He said he enjoyed quaint rural jollifications," Bartholomew said distastefully.

"A Londoner, he were," Carney repeated with scorn.

"What did you tell him?"

"Church bazaar."

"Whitsun fête."

"Bank holiday Open Day up at the Hall."

"Harvest festival."

"Someone said something about the old Winter Garden Open Day they used to have before the War," said Bartholomew. "That's what you want to know, isn't it, Chief Inspector? Whether he knew about the Winter Garden?"

It was indeed. None of the three, nor the other two named by Roper, could recall what had been said about the Winter Garden, but there was a fair chance George Brown had known its rough whereabouts and that it was walled.

Perhaps he had in fact arranged to take Grace to London. She had gone up to the Hall to sneak in and fetch her belongings. Suppose he parked his motor by the wicket-gate and walked up the path to meet her. . . .

No, more likely he'd wait for her. She's late—delayed by a last effort to persuade Sebastian to marry her? Impatient, Brown walks up the path, meets her near the Winter Garden. They quarrel.

What did they quarrel about? Maybe she had changed her mind and was on her way to tell him. From what Alec had learned of her, it was the sort of thing she'd do rather than leave the fellow up in the air. But he knew nothing of Brown's temperament, couldn't guess whether the commercial might be triggered to violence by his blighted hopes.

According to Rita he had been drinking heavily, which could also account for the murder weapon. Unsteady on his feet, he'd want a walking-stick to help him up the path. After his adventure in the snowdrift, he'd probably keep a hefty walking-stick in the car against future need—and a spade.

Brown collects his bags, drives up to the wicket-gate, gets fed up waiting in his car, walks up the path and meets Grace. Perhaps she even takes him into the Winter Garden to ensure privacy. She tells him she isn't going with him. As she turns away to hurry back to the Hall before the doors are locked—having decided to stay, she wouldn't want to risk being locked out—he hits her.

The timing was tight, but by no means impossible. Brown left the inn shortly after ten thirty; Moody locked up at the Hall at eleven thirty. Time enough, and once she was dead he had all the time in the world to bury her.

Thin motive, Alec thought. He'd have a better idea what was what once he'd seen Brown. Right now, Goodman was waiting for him.

While he worked out Brown's possible movements, the men had been arguing about precisely who said what. He asked them a few more questions, which they answered with apparent candour if unhelpfully. Everyone who had been at the Cheshire Cheese that December night had been debating it ever since the body was discovered. No one had seen anything worthy of note or they'd have told each other, if not the police.

Alec was about to buy his informants one last round when Carney said, "Yon fella never told us what he were a-selling of. I 'spect you'll know that, Chief Inspector?"

Alec pondered for a brief moment. Brown's job was hardly a secret and anyway the chances were excellent he'd never return to Occleswich. "He sells ready-to-wear corsets," he informed them.

This was met with such delighted mirth—broad grins, raucous laughter, and slapping of thighs—he wished he'd told them sooner. He might not have had to rely on Daisy to break the ice. As it was, she'd hold her assistance over his head whenever he tried to disengage her from the investigation.

He looked around for her. Just as he spotted her, sitting

with Goodman and Petrie now, the landlord called out, "Time, gentlemen, please."

Too late for Goodman tonight. He did look exhausted. With luck the offer of a lift up the hill would put him in a helpful frame of mind tomorrow.

When Alec returned from driving up the hill, he was astonished to find Petrie and Piper together in the bar-parlour. They were talking sports again, over a legal-to-residents nightcap. Petrie was a simple soul at heart, his snobbish notions a thin veneer over a friendly, modest chap inclined to like everyone he met, even Stan Moss.

Piper had seen the blacksmith earlier in the public bar, the only point of interest he had to report. Moss came in looking surly. As Piper approached, some helpful soul pointed him out as a detective investigating Grace's death, whereupon Moss had scowled, spat on the sawdust-covered floor, and stalked out.

"I says to the bloke I was with, 'That's a bit odd, seeing we're trying to find the chummie what done his daughter in.' And he says as Moss don't like the police on account of her ladyship setting 'em on him. 'Sides, he's made up his mind Morgan done it, and he's afraid we're going to let him out. Seems he's got it in for the Taffies, Chief, ever since his wife ran off with a Welshman."

"So the artist was a Welshman, was he? Well, like it or not, I have to see Moss sooner or later, and after the funeral tomorrow is as good a time as any. We'll go up to the Hall first, though."

Daisy would be out of the way while he interrogated her new friend. She had said she was at last going to visit the dairy.

First thing next morning, Alec reported by telephone to his Super at the Yard. As he expected, he was given until Monday to clear the case up or turn it back to the local police. "You've set 'em straight," grunted Superintendent Crane. "That's what you're there for. I can't spare you to do their work for 'em.''

The day was overcast but dry and mild. As Alec drove out of the inn yard, he glanced down the hill. Lady Valeria's unmistakably imposing tweed-clad rear view was receding along the track by the church, towards the vicarage and school.

"Excellent," he said to Piper. "I'll see young Parslow first, while she's out. In fact, we might as well get statements from both him and Goodman, so you'll take notes. You can carry on with the servants while I'm at the funeral. If you have time, start typing up the statements on Constable Rudge's machine. We'll meet at the Cheshire Cheese at one for lunch."

"Right, Chief."

Moody admitted them with his usual sour face but without comment. Parslow and Goodman were strolling on the terrace, the younger man accommodating his long stride to the other's limping pace. Intent on their conversation, they both started when they turned at the end and saw Alec waiting for them, watching them.

Goodman resigned, Parslow frightened, they approached.

"I'd like a word with you first, Mr. Parslow, if you please. Then with you, Mr. Goodman."

Parslow looked around wildly. The secretary touched his shoulder and said, "Why don't you use the library, Sebastian? Shall I go with you?"

"I'd prefer not, sir," Alec said in his most stolid, policemanly manner. "Mr. Parslow is at liberty to refuse to speak to me without his solicitor present."

"No! I don't need a lawyer." The young man managed a wavering smile. "I'll come quietly, Officer."

In the library, in his preferred place behind the desk, Alec explained that Piper would be taking notes to be transcribed into a formal statement. Piper seated himself at the long library table, behind the suspect, where his unobtrusive presence would be forgotten by all but the most self-possessed, which Parslow was not.

Alec took him through the sorry story he had told the day before. The only material change was that this time he reported, with attempted nonchalance, his visit to Goodman's bedroom at eleven forty-five.

"Why didn't you mention that yesterday?"

Parslow flushed. "It seemed irrelevant. Ben didn't need an alibi. He obviously had nothing to do with Grace's death."

"I decide what is irrelevant, Mr. Parslow, and what's obvious."

"Ben couldn't have done it! He's not strong." He didn't claim Goodman had no motive, Alec noted with interest. "All right, if you want to know the truth, I didn't care to tell you about the mater refusing to take him with us, when another English winter could kill him." Having said this, he looked horrified, as though he had never quite put the thought into words before. The colour in his cheeks ebbed, leaving him sickly pale.

"That's more like it." Alec was noncommittal. The answer was reasonable, given that Parslow felt no need for an alibi for himself. Though not entirely satisfied, he had no idea in what direction to probe. "I gather it was not the first time you had approached Lady Valeria on the subject. This was a last-ditch effort, I take it, because she had unexpectedly put forward your departure for France. Why did she suddenly change the date?"

Parslow shrugged his admirable shoulders. "The mater isn't in the habit of explaining herself. I assumed she wanted to get me away from Grace. She can be difficult at times," he said awkwardly, "but she's only doing what she thinks best for me."

"Including 'dealing' with Grace."

The possibility that Lady Valeria was the murderer had been broached before. This time her son simply shook his head wearily. "I don't know. It's not the sort of thing one can believe of one's mother, is it?"

Alec thought of his own kind, fussy mother, who had kept house for him and Belinda since Joan died in the '19 influenza pandemic. The only way she'd ever kill anyone was by over-cosseting. Lady Valeria was another kettle of fish, but he could see Parslow's point.

"How did you imagine she meant to deal with Grace?"

"Oh, by paying her off, I suppose. That's what Bobbie said I should do. I didn't think it would work."

"Because Grace was determined to marry you?"

"Because Stan Moss was determined to cause as much trouble as he possibly could."

"Ah yes, Stan Moss." Alec was becoming more and more eager to talk to the blacksmith. He glanced at his watch, which reminded him of another question. "What were you doing between ten, when your manservant left your room, and half past eleven, when you went to your mother's room?"

For a question that must have been foreseen, it rattled Parslow excessively. "N-nothing in particular," he stammered.

"You didn't try to see Lady Valeria about taking Goodman with you?"

"Oh yes." Now why was he relieved? "I'd forgotten. I went down to the drawing room, but I didn't go in because the mater and Bobbie were in the middle of a row."

"What about?"

"I just heard raised voices. I didn't stay to listen."

"What time was that?"

"Right after Thomkins left. Ten did you say?"

"If you didn't listen, that can't have taken long. What next?"

"I-I went back upstairs and . . . oh, fidgeted around. I wanted to give the mater time to cool down before I tackled her, so I listened for the creaky board outside her room. I . . . I know, I hunted for a missing cuff-link, one of a favourite pair I wanted to take with me. Thomkins is deuced careless."

He announced this with an air more of inspiration than remembrance. What the devil had he really been up to? Alec didn't think he'd been murdering and burying his mistress. He relied on his mother and sister to save his bacon—and he quite simply hadn't the guts.

But he was hiding something. Perhaps Goodman would provide a clue.

"Thank you, Mr. Parslow, that will be all for now. A statement will be typed up and I'll be asking you to read and sign it. At that time, you'll be able to make any changes or additions you wish."

"Right-oh, Chief Inspector." He stood up, looking almost lightheaded with relief. "Anything I can do to help. She was a good girl, really. I'll send Ben in, shall I? You'll find he hadn't anything to do with it."

Yet Goodman, for all his ill-health, was a much stronger character. He limped into the library with a calm, friendly smile on his homely face, though Alec noted that his eyes were watchful. Still, few indeed were those capable of facing a Scotland Yard murder investigation without visible qualms.

Remembering his "don't play games with me," Alec advised him straightforwardly that he had been seen with Grace and asked for an explanation.

"I was warning her, Chief Inspector. Warning her that Lady Valeria would go to any lengths to stop her son marrying a parlourmaid."

"You knew Grace was demanding marriage?"

"Sebastian had told me."

"And that he had promised to marry her?"

Goodman flinched. So that was what Parslow had not wanted him to find out—but why should he care? "No, I didn't know that," he said unhappily. "He's . . . high-strung, irresolute, but what can you expect of the way he's been brought up?"

"It's not for me to judge him. You didn't know of his promise, but you feared he might give in to Grace's importunities and that her ladyship would then take a hand?"

"Exactly."

"I suggest in fact you had taken a fancy to the girl yourself, you approached her, and she ridiculed your advances."

He laughed, with obviously genuine amusement. Alec suddenly saw why Daisy might find him an attractive man.

"Oh, Chief Inspector, unwilling women have never been a problem to me, I assure you. I'd have to be in dire need to pursue the mistress of my employer's son."

"It does seem unlikely," Alec conceded, smiling. Dammit, he *liked* the chap. "You understand, we have to follow every possible lead."

"I don't envy you your present job, any more than your stint in the R.F.C."

"It suits me well enough. All right, let's go back. Parslow kept from you his promise to Grace. Now he's keeping something from me. Any idea what he's hiding?"

"Hiding, Chief Inspector?" Goodman spoke lightly, but the wariness had returned to his eyes. "Poor Sebastian is so used to hiding minor matters from his mother, I dare say simply being questioned is enough to make him look shifty."

"Perhaps it's from Lady Valeria more than from me that he's trying to conceal what he was doing between ten and eleven thirty on December 13th," Alec said, irritated.

"Very likely."

"You don't know?"

"No." Was there the slightest hesitation before the firm denial? No doubt Goodman, too, was bent on protecting Parslow from his mother. Confound the woman!

"You told Grace that Lady Valeria would go to any lengths to prevent a marriage. Did you mean it?"

"Do I consider her ladyship capable of murder? In all honesty, I couldn't rule it out. I hope I'm not speaking from personal dislike. Lady Valeria has . . . virtues isn't the word . . . qualities one must admire. She is not capricious;

she does nothing without what seems to her good and sufficient reason, and Sebastian's welfare is her prime motive—whether or not one agrees with her notion of what's best for him. If she believed Grace posed a threat to him only to be removed by her death. . . . But I hardly think the situation had reached such an impasse."

"Do you know when and why she suddenly changed the date of their departure for the Riviera?"

"She ordered me that afternoon to telephone Cook's to change the bookings, and to tell no one. Lady Valeria is not accustomed to explain her decisions to the hired help, nor, in all fairness, to her family. Miss Parslow and I assumed her aim was to remove Sebastian from a painful predicament. He was in a bad way."

"Ah yes, Miss Parslow. In your opinion, would she be capable of murder?"

"Bobbie? Good Lord, no. It wouldn't be playing the game. Simply not cricket." His irony was affectionate.

"Yet she disappeared when I arrived. I ought to have asked last night whether you know where she went."

"Neither where nor why, but I think you'll find she was unaware of your arrival and the reopening of the enquiry. Miss Parslow is a sensible young woman."

"Who has disappeared without informing her family of her whereabouts or her plans."

"Without informing her mother."

"Everything comes back to Lady Valeria. I shall have to try again this afternoon to get a few answers from her, but now I must dash off to the funeral." Alec pushed back his chair and stood up. "I understand the Hall will not be represented."

"No," said Goodman with regret, then added dryly, "Her ladyship went down to the vicarage this morning to make sure Mr. Lake's plans for the service are appropriate. Not that he'll pay her much heed."

"No? A bold man! Thank you for your cooperation, Mr.

Goodman." Not that he was quite finished with the secretary. However much Daisy trusted the man, Alec was quite certain that, like Parslow, Ben Goodman had something to hide.

14

Reluctant to witness Ben's response to a conjecture that Grace had scorned his advances, Daisy hadn't even tried to persuade Alec to let her be present. Instead, she had arranged with the delighted Sir Reginald to tour his dairy. Now, though, she was eager to find out how Ben's interview had gone. She hurried back up to the Hall.

He wasn't in the library. She went to the Yellow Parlour. Pushing open the door, she stepped in, then stopped, her hand to her mouth to hold back a gasp of shock.

Ben sat in a chair by the fire with Sebastian huddled on a footstool at his feet. Sebastian's face was hidden in his folded arms, resting on Ben's lap. Ben had one arm about Sebastian's shuddering shoulders, and his other hand caressed the golden hair.

The loving tenderness on Ben's face made Daisy's breath catch in her throat. As she stood frozen in the doorway, Ben looked up. His expression changed to resigned regret. "Miss Dalrymple's here, Sebastian," he said gently.

Sebastian raised a tear-devastated face and reached for Ben's hand.

Daisy hurriedly shut the door behind her. "You're . . ." she began, then stopped, unable to think of a polite way to phrase her question.

"We're in love," said Sebastian defiantly.

"That explains a lot." So many little oddnesses came together in her mind. She crossed the room to drop, weak-kneed, onto the sofa opposite them. "It must be absolutely frightful trying to keep it hidden."

"I've grown accustomed to concealment," Ben said wryly. "It's been hell for Sebastian. You aren't beating a horrified retreat?"

"I live in Chelsea; we have all sorts of . . . unusual people living around us," Daisy explained. All the same, she was rather proud of her *sang-froid*. She had met two or three male couples at parties, but somehow suddenly discovering someone one regarded as a friend to be that way inclined was rather more difficult. "Lady Valeria knows, doesn't she?"

"She certainly suspects." The grim set of Ben's mouth made him plainer than ever. "She inveigled Sebastian into the affair with Grace to try to prove her suspicions were unfounded."

"You can't be sure of that, Ben. In any case it wasn't all her doing," Sebastian said with remorse. "I wanted to prove to myself that I wasn't . . . different. It didn't work. I was more than ready to admit that to myself when Grace told me she was pregnant and all the fuss started."

"Escaping to Antibes must have been a vast relief," said Daisy.

"It would have been, if only Ben could have come too. I was desperately worried about him. When Bobbie wrote to say Grace had cleared out with a stranger I wanted to come home but . . ."

"Bobbie wrote to tell you?"

"Yes. She's not much of a letter-writer but she knew how much it meant to me."

"When did she write?"

"Oh, about a week after we left. It takes a couple of days for village gossip to filter up to our ears, and she waited a day or two longer to be sure Grace didn't reappear."

Daisy noticed Ben was amused. She lifted an enquiring eyebrow at him.

"Fletcher has an apt pupil," he said.

She blushed furiously. "I'm sorry."

"It's all right, I don't mind telling you," said Sebastian. "It's an enormous relief to have it all out in the open." He leaned back against Ben's knees.

"I'm glad, but . . . Ben, you know I have to tell Mr. Fletcher?"

His eyes were full of weariness and pain. "I know," he said quietly. "But he's a clever man, your detective. He'll find out anyway, and I'd rather you told him than I."

"I'm sure he won't. . . . No, I can't be sure," Daisy admitted, downcast. "I think Alec's broadminded enough not to make things more difficult for you just because of that. If it weren't for Grace's murder. . . ."

Ben nodded. "As it is, you have no choice but to tell him."

"I'll try to persuade him not to tell anyone else," she promised.

Sebastian was in better form than Ben now. His cheeks had regained their colour and the signs of tears were fading. "Why do you want to know about Bobbie's letter, Daisy?" he asked curiously.

"Because it seems highly unlikely that if she had killed Grace she'd write you a letter which might well bring you home into the middle of a murder investigation. She couldn't know so soon that it was safe. Therefore she didn't kill Grace, not that I believed for a minute she did."

"Anyway, the mater refused to come home. Jove!" Sebastian clutched his dishevelled golden locks and groaned. "I suppose that makes it look even more as if she. . . ."

Heavy footsteps outside the door silenced him. In an instant he sprang to his feet and sat down again on the sofa beside Daisy. When Lady Valeria clumped in, the three were discussing Greek architecture—and Daisy had just had a brilliant idea.

For the moment she had to keep her idea to herself. Lady Valeria stayed with them until they all moved to the dining room for lunch. Besides, though as an afterthought, Daisy decided she'd better hold her tongue until Alec was convinced of Ben and Sebastian's innocence of Grace's murder.

She wondered whether he'd be frightfully shocked by her discovery about them. No, a policeman was not so easily shocked; but she hoped he wouldn't be disgusted. Slightly to her own surprise, she found she liked Ben as much as ever, and Sebastian was nice enough when he pulled himself together. They obviously cared deeply for each other.

Surely Alec would not arrest them? Even if he wanted to, he'd have to have proof of "misconduct," not just an admission of feelings, wouldn't he? But she refused to believe he was a bigot.

It wasn't something she could discuss over the phone. If he didn't return to the Hall soon, she'd walk down to the inn.

Alec returned to the inn sooner than he had intended. The only remarkable thing about Grace's funeral was that her father had attended wearing greasy dungarees and a surly scowl. Stan Moss did not accompany his daughter's coffin to the graveside, as Alec realized very nearly too late. When he reached the street the blacksmith was revving up a small, dilapidated motor-lorry.

Over the noise of the engine, Alec bawled, "I'd like a word with you, Mr. Moss." He reached through the glassless window to present his credentials. "Scotland Yard."

Moss glowered but he took his foot off the accelerator. The roar diminished to a loud rumble. "Ruddy Lunnon busies think you know better'n the local coppers? That Taffy done it."

"Did you see him?"

"Di'n't get home till late that night, did I?"

"Then what makes you think Morgan killed your daughter?"

"Bloody obvious, innit! She got a bun in the oven and whether 'twere his or not he'd cause."

"You knew she was having an affair with young Parslow."

"Mebbe I did and mebbe I di'n't."

"I understand you encouraged her to seduce him."

Moss's sullen face crimsoned. "It's a bloody lie!" he bellowed. "Look here, mate, I can't stop here chatting all the ruddy day. I got business." He revved again and released the brake.

"I'll need to see you again," Alec shouted, hastily removing his hand from the door and jumping back.

The lorry roared off down the hill, leaving Alec certain the blacksmith was lying. He had pushed his daughter into the affair. However, far from making him a murderer, that gave him every motive to keep her alive for his unpleasant purposes.

Annoyed, Alec walked back to the church for a word with the vicar. He felt a spark of hope when Mr. Lake told him Wednesday was choir practice night. However, the practice ended at nine, a good hour before Grace was last seen alive. Another dead end.

On the point of leaving, Alec turned back. "Owen Morgan isn't in the choir? The Welsh are known for their singing."

"And for their Methodism, Chief Inspector. I believe Morgan often walked into Whitbury to Chapel on a Sunday. A good lad, by all reports, and I'm glad you have reopened the case."

A charitable man as well as a bold one, Alec thought.

Stan Moss, on the other hand, seemed absolutely convinced the police had already arrested his daughter's murderer. He might change his mind if he realized his enemy, Lady Valeria, was now a suspect. Alec wanted to talk to him again.

Not nearly as badly, however, as he wanted to talk to Lady Valeria Parslow, and Miss Roberta, and George Brown.

Back at the Cheshire Cheese, he reread the scanty reports of the local police. He noticed Ben Goodman had said at the inquest that Lady Valeria told him to sack Grace if she re-

turned. When had she so instructed him? Either her ladyship
reckoned the girl's running off removed any claim against
Sebastian, or she knew Grace would not be seen again.
Which? Alec wondered.

He telephoned Sergeant Shaw to clarify one or two points.
Ernie Piper came in with his typed report and clarified a
couple more points. Grace's belongings were still in her bedroom at the Hall, he announced, but since they consisted
only of her parlourmaid's uniforms no one had wondered at
it.

Something curious about that caught Alec's attention, but
before he could chase down the thought, Piper continued.
"And the chauffeur swears no one took a motor out the night
of December 13th."

"He's quite certain?"

"Yes, Chief. His room's right over the garridge, an old
hayloft it is, the garridge being part of the stables. He was
there all evening, having to drive to London next day."

"Any witnesses? Any sign he was interested in Grace?"

"No witnesses, Chief, but he's engaged to a girl in Whitbury, which he don't want her ladyship to know about. I got
her name and address, case we need to check."

"Well done, Ernie. Let's go and eat before you leave for
Crewe. I'll go over your report later."

They had the dining room to themselves. Petrie had gone
off to call on a distant, elderly cousin at his mother's behest.

"It's odd, Chief, that long-haired bloke not being here. I
mean, with Miss Parslow gone missing and all."

"Great Scott, I'd forgotten. You said they knew each
other."

"I only remembered acos of typing up my notes, Chief,"
Piper said modestly. "D'you think he went with her?"

"It's a possibility I shouldn't have overlooked. Everyone's
hunting for a woman on her own, not a couple. Mrs. Chiver,"
he said to the landlady as she brought in their soup, "has
our resident poet left?"

"Mr. Wilkinson, sir? He's booked another three nights and left one of his bags. Said he might be gone a night or two. You don't think he's skipped, sir, without paying?" she asked anxiously.

"I don't suppose so," he soothed her, "but I'd better take a look at that bag, make sure it's not empty."

"After lunch, I hope, sir. The cutlets are browning nicely."

"I wouldn't want them to spoil. The bag won't run away." And if Mr. Wilkinson had run away, he'd not get much farther in half an hour. The landlady left and Alec said to Piper, "If the bag's empty, or full of rubbish, I'll add him to the wanted notice, but all he has to do to make himself unrecognizable is cut his hair. Chances are, though, he's just dodged the bill and his departure has nothing to do with Miss Parslow."

The small portmanteau turned out to be full of books, surprisingly neatly packed shirts, and a cheap but respectable lounge suit. Alec had a feeling that Wilkinson was a red herring, his acquaintance with Miss Parslow probably distant and certainly nothing to do with Grace. Lady Valeria was sufficient reason for any air of conspiracy surrounding their meetings.

He set off to walk up to the Hall, Piper having already left in the Austin to meet Tom Tring's train at Crewe. The light overcast had taken on a yellowish tinge which, together with a distinct chill in the air, threatened snow. Alec hoped it would hold off until his precious motor-car was safely back in Occleswich.

Despite the chill, well-muffled children played in the front gardens of several cottages. Most ran to the fence to stare as he passed, and one bold little girl waved. He waved back, which sent her and her companions giggling and shrieking into the house. The shop and post office were closed on Saturday afternoon, so few adults were out and about. One or two of those he met nodded and smiled, others ignored him.

The smithy looked deserted, and no one answered the door

when he knocked. Out of curiosity he walked right around it, picking his way between the piles of rusting junk. The yard behind the cottage was also paved, with a considerable area clear of rubbish. Moss must keep his lorry here, and perhaps do such mechanical work as he obtained. In fact, a farm tractor standing near the back door of the forge was obviously being worked on, and a decrepit harrow had a shiny, newly forged bar holding it together.

No sign of the blacksmith, however. Alec walked on.

By the time he reached the Hall, an icy wind had sprung up and begun to disperse the clouds. He was glad to be admitted to the comparative warmth of the house.

"Miss Dalrymple requests a word with you, sir," said Moody grudgingly, "before you see anyone else. Miss is in the Red Saloon, if you'll please to come this way."

Before Moody opened the door, Alec heard the rattle of typewriter keys under vigorous attack, punctuated by the ping of the carriage return warning. Daisy sat at a Regency writing-table, a silhouette against the window, bashing away at her machine. She paused and peered across the gloomy room.

"Alec? Give me half a jiffy to finish the paragraph."

The butler had vanished on silent feet. Alec dug in his pocket for a box of matches and lit a couple of gas-lights. The painting above the mantelpiece sprang to life, a gruesome scene with guns blazing and the bodies of British soldiers and half-clad natives bleeding all over the place. Alec turned his back on it.

"Isn't it ghastly?" Rolling the paper out of the typewriter, Daisy gave him a rather strained smile.

"Frightful, but frightfully heroic, I expect."

"Probably." She came around the desk. "If we sit here and turn our chairs just a little, we needn't look at it."

"Do you mind if I smoke?" He took out pipe and tobacco pouch as she shook her head. "What's wrong, Daisy? It's not Victorian gore that's upsetting you."

"Oh no. It's just that I have something to tell you and it's rather difficult. Would you turn off your searchlight gaze for a bit?" she begged.

"Sorry. Copper's bad habit." He busied himself with filling his pipe and trying to persuade it to light. "It's Goodman, isn't it?" he asked between puffs.

"How did you guess!"

"Because you've taken him under your wing, as you did Lady Wentwater, and because I know he's hiding something."

"It's nothing to do with the murder, Alec, honestly. He's . . . You know about men who don't like women?"

"Great Scott, so that's it! Goodman and Parslow? Of course! No wonder the poor lad's been in such a rotten funk."

"They love each other. You don't have to arrest them, do you?"

"People are arrested for actions, not inclinations, and I've no evidence of misbehaviour. You do realize this gives them both excellent motives to get rid of Grace? Goodman must have been jealous, and Parslow wouldn't dare risk being forced to marry. Parslow *was* the father? Trying to prove he is what he is not?"

"Yes," said Daisy mournfully, "and I know it looks bad for both of them, but I really think the only thing they were hiding was . . . that."

"Neither has an alibi for ten to eleven," Alec pointed out, running through their statements in his mind. "Unless . . . yes, that would explain quite a lot . . . unless they were together. But I can't accept either's testimony about the other, and if they were together they may have been committing murder together. I must see them both—together."

"Let me stay, Alec, if they don't object. I'll take shorthand notes for you."

He pondered a moment. "All right. Highly irregular, but they have already confided in you, and this isn't something

I'd want Piper to hear unnecessarily. Anyway, he's meeting Tom at Crewe."

"Sergeant Tring's coming?" She beamed. "I'm glad. I like him."

As he rang the bell by the fireplace, he wondered at her ability to find pleasure in little things even in the midst of upheaval. Joan had been the same, cheered by a daffodil in the middle of a Zeppelin raid.

Moody shuffled in and was sent to fetch the two men. Daisy went to the desk to get her notebook and pencils.

"Why aren't you in hysterics?" Alec enquired, following her and moving her typewriter aside. "I'd have thought most women of your class wouldn't know such unnatural tendencies existed. I'm sure the middle classes don't; my mother, for instance." He sat down behind the desk.

"Well, public schools, and having a brother—one can't help hearing things. And I live in Bohemia, remember."

"Still, I'm amazed at your calmness when you've just discovered a friend to be that way inclined."

"It was a bit of a shock, actually. But after all, they're still the same people they were before. I don't believe they can help it, so you can't really say it's unnatural, can you? It's like blaming someone for a squint, or for going prematurely bald." She eyed him thoughtfully. "All the same, I'm glad you're not going bald yet."

"Yet!" he said in mock outrage, and they were laughing when Parslow and Goodman came in.

Both men looked disconcerted. Goodman limped forward, saying sardonically, "I take it you're not about to haul us off to prison, Chief Ins. . . ." His words were swallowed up in a raw, painful cough which doubled him up.

Parslow hurried to him and took his arm. "It's the cold wind," he explained anxiously. "Draughts everywhere. Come and sit by the fire, Ben."

"Yes, do," said Alec, regretfully abandoning his pipe, which had just caught and emitted a curl of smoke undoubtedly injurious to gas-corroded lungs. The reminder of Goodman's war service shattered the shards of contempt he had carefully hidden from Daisy. Also he was surprised and impressed by the young Adonis' care for his crippled companion. The relationship was not at all as one-sided as he had imagined.

Daisy had hurried to help Parslow settle Goodman in a chair by the fire. With dismay, Alec noted the determined light in her eye. She whispered something in Parslow's ear. He looked in turn startled, enlightened, entranced, and then her determination was reflected in his eyes. Alec nearly groaned aloud. What on earth was she up to now?

He ought to send her away before whatever it was went any further. Instead, subjected to a blue, appealing gaze, he found himself saying, "You don't mind if Miss Dalrymple stays to take notes?"

"Not at all," said Parslow firmly. He took a leather-covered flask from his pocket, unscrewed the top, and held it to Goodman's pale lips. A few sips brought a tinge of colour to the wan cheeks, but Goodman leaned his head back on the high back of the chair and made no attempt to speak. Pulling up a straight chair, Parslow sat down beside him, one hand laid comfortingly on his arm.

Alec took a seat opposite them as Daisy retreated to the desk. "Right," he said, "we'll take what Miss Dalrymple has told me as read and go on from there. Do you wish to amend your statement in any particulars, Mr. Parslow?"

"Yes. Ben and I were together most of the time between ten and eleven o'clock on December 13th. I went to the library and. . . . It was the first time we'd really talked about . . . things. About what we mean to each other," he amended, raising his chin.

"Why didn't you tell me each of you could give the other an alibi?"

"My fault, Chief Inspector." Goodman's fragile voice was rueful. "I thought it more important to conceal our . . . desire for each other's company than to provide alibis, since neither of us killed Grace. My encounter with Inspector Dunnett didn't prepare me to expect intelligence, let alone perspicacity, in a police officer."

Alec nodded impassively in response to the compliment.

"I muffed it," said Parslow. "I couldn't remember whether we'd agreed not to mention my going to Ben's room later to tell him what the mater said. That must have made you suspicious."

He seemed unworried, even confident, no longer a frightened, easily upset boy. It looked to Alec as if his terrors had all been connected with the fear of exposure of his relationship with Goodman, nothing to do with Grace's death. The exposure had come, and was not half so terrible as he had expected. His present lack of fear reinforced Alec's admittedly unfounded belief in the mutual alibi.

The self-confidence was another matter. That had come since Daisy's whisper. What the devil had she said?

"As far as I can see," he said with a sigh, "you're both out of it. However, I must ask you not to leave Occles Hall without informing me."

"We shan't go." Parslow grimaced. "One runaway in the family is more than enough. By Jove, I wish I knew where Bobbie went, and why. It can't be anything to do with Grace, Chief Inspector. I'm sure it can't!"

"Does your sister know about you and Mr. Goodman, sir?"

"No, not a thing. Bobbie's a thoroughly good sport, but she's too straightforward to see anything that's not shoved right under her nose. Like my father, only he's still more so; he manages not to see things even when they *are* shoved under his nose. But Bobbie didn't guess about Grace until I told her."

"And Lady Valeria?"

"I think she has suspected," Parslow said slowly, "even before I was sure myself. It would explain why she has hemmed me in since I left school, wouldn't it? Protecting me from myself. And Grace . . . I've been thinking about what you said, about her bringing my nightcap and the early morning tea. Do you think my mother put her up to it, to try to change me?"

"To try to prove to herself exactly what I imagine you were trying to prove to yourself," Alec suggested gently. "Grace told Morgan her ladyship encouraged her to seduce you—as did her father."

"Moss? Just to create trouble for us?" That was too much for Parslow's new-found equanimity. "Oh Lord!" he groaned, hiding his face in his hands. It was Goodman's turn to offer comfort. After a moment, the younger man recovered enough to say, "Poor Grace didn't stand a chance, did she? I liked her, you know, even though I didn't *want* her."

Alec nodded. "I dare say your mother's doubts explain why she refused to take Mr. Goodman with you to the South of France. She wasn't just being difficult. I'm only surprised she didn't dismiss him."

Goodman said dryly, "To do so would have amounted to acknowledging to herself her son's nature."

"Yes, of course. Did anyone else know or suspect?"

"Thomkins, my valet, knew about Grace, not about Ben."

Ernie Piper hadn't picked up on that, Alec thought. What else had he missed? Tom Tring would have to have a go at the servants.

The answers to the rest of his questions tended to confirm their innocence of Grace's murder. Lastly, he asked Goodman when Lady Valeria had told him to dismiss Grace if she returned.

Goodman thought. "It was the next morning," he said slowly, "when Grace was not there to serve breakfast before her ladyship left for France."

Before she could possibly have heard the rumour of Grace running off with a commercial—another suggestive point against her ladyship. Otherwise there was nothing new, noth-

ing to incriminate Lady Valeria or her daughter, equally nothing to exonerate. Those two, with George Brown, remained
Alec's chief suspects.

"Thank you," he said at last. "I'm not about to haul you
off to prison, and I see no reason at present to reveal your
secret to anyone—even my sergeant—other than Lady
Valeria. I assume you're resigned to confirming her suspicions?"

"It's inevitable now, and I'll be glad to have you break the
news," Parslow said candidly.

"However, I must warn you that if you are required to
give evidence at a trial, I may not be able to keep it out of
my report."

"Thank *you*, Mr. Fletcher," said Goodman, wearily lever-
ing himself out of his chair with Parslow's assistance. "You
have been most understanding. I know you'll do your best
for us."

After a moment's hesitation, he held out his hand, and
Alec shook it without, he hoped, noticeable hesitation on his
part. It wasn't a contagious malady the man suffered from,
after all.

Supporting Goodman, Parslow had no free hand to shake,
but he too thanked Alec. And, as they turned towards the
door, he winked at Daisy, who grinned back.

What the exchange portended Alec was determined to discover, but just now he urgently wanted to see to Lady Valeria.
At last he had a lever which might dislodge her from her
refusal to speak to him. He rang the bell.

"Lady Valeria?" asked Daisy.

"Yes; or at least I hope so."

"*She* won't let me stay in the room. What a shame! I'd
like to see her face when you let the cat out of the bag." She
pondered a moment. "No, that's not fair. It'll be beastly for
her."

"I'm surprised Parslow didn't go to pieces when I said I'd
have to tell her. Won't she hit the roof?"

"Probably, but he's used to it. That's the trouble with blowing people sky-high for every little thing. When something big comes along, you have no ammunition in reserve."

"True, but at the least she'll surely sack Goodman."

"Oh, that doesn't matter any. . . ." She stopped as Moody trudged in.

"Please tell Lady Valeria I'd like a word," said Alec.

The butler's face somehow managed to combine triumph and despondency. "Her ladyship has gone to a committee meeting, sir. In Chester. The Bishop's Crusade against Crime, I understand."

Daisy collapsed in peals of laughter.

15

"The Bishop's Crusade against Crime!" repeated Daisy, when the affronted butler had stalked from the Red Saloon, closing the door with rather more force than was butlerianly proper. A last giggle escaped her. "Too, too shocking if you have to arrest the chairwoman for murder!"

Alec groaned. "She's in the chair?"

"I don't believe she'd sit on a committee where she wasn't invited to take the chair. I don't believe there's a committee in existence would dare refuse to invite her. Oh, Alec, I'm so glad Ben and Sebastian are in the clear."

"They aren't absolutely cleared," he warned, "though I'm inclined to believe them. I could tell when they were lying before, so I hope I'm right in thinking they're not now."

"I've remembered something else. When we found poor Grace, I had the impression Ben was relieved, which he wouldn't have been if he'd done it, or he wasn't quite sure Sebastian hadn't. I suppose he'd been afraid Grace might come back and make more trouble."

"It's another point in their favour. Goodman certainly doesn't seem strong enough, and Parslow appears to have relied entirely upon his mother and sister to extricate him from his problems."

"Yes, but things are going to change," she prophesied blithely.

"Daisy, what are you plotting now? You needn't think I didn't see you whispering to Parslow. Come on, out with it."

She shook her head, regretful. "I was going to tell you. Then you said you were going to tell Lady Valeria about Ben and Sebastian. It's nothing to do with Grace, I promise, but you just might decide to use it to persuade Lady Valeria to talk, and the longer she's kept in ignorance the better."

"Deuce take the woman! I'd positively enjoy arresting her, Crusade against Crime or no. And if I can't get anything out of her because of your secret. . . ." Looking exasperated, Alec ran his fingers through his hair. "Blast it, why didn't I stick to my own precept? Didn't I swear never again to have anything to do with you on a professional basis?"

Daisy was hurt. "If I hadn't phoned you, you wouldn't even be here," she pointed out.

"Which would be a great improvement! Oh, I'm sorry, Daisy, but if I'm going to have to explain away another botched investigation to the A.C. . . ."

"All right, I'll tell you what I suggested to Sebastian if you still haven't had any success with Lady Valeria by—say after church tomorrow?" It was time to remind him of her usefulness. She waved her notebook at him. "Shall I type up the notes I just took?"

He gave her a rueful grin. "You'd better, since you claim your version of shorthand is unreadable by anyone else. No, wait a minute." He pulled a sheaf of papers from his pocket. "I brought this morning's statements for them to sign. Do you think you could retype them, adding the necessary new bits in such a way that they don't contradict the previous evasions Piper's aware of? I don't want to advertise your friends' idiosyncrasies unnecessarily."

"Bless you, Alec!" She suppressed an urge to throw her arms around his neck and kiss his cheek. "You've been frightfully nice about that. Of course I can do it. I'm a writer."

"Just remember this is supposed to be fact, not fiction,"

he grumbled, then sighed. "Well, failing Lady Valeria and Miss Parslow, I'll walk down to the dairy to see if Sir Reginald's remembered anything useful, though the man seems to live in another world."

"He'd be happier in a world inhabited solely by cows, poor old prune. You did bring an overcoat, didn't you? And that spiffing green and orange muffler Belinda knitted for you? It's cold out."

Amused by her fussing over him, Alec left her to her typing.

She read the statements typed by Piper. She had been present at the first interviews with Ben and Sebastian, of course, but the only notes had been a few facts scribbled down by Alec. He had gone over the same ground that morning with Piper taking shorthand, and then there were the changes and additions. No wonder Alec had been suspicious! She was glad she'd been instrumental in bringing out the truth.

With hindsight, she laughed at Ben's response to the accusation that he'd been chasing Grace. Naturally, unwilling women had never been a problem to him!

Moving her typewriter back from where Alec had set it aside, she started typing.

The second carefully edited statement was nearly done when Alec returned. "Nothing," he reported gloomily. "Sir Reginald greeted me as an old friend and remembered my name but not my job. Lady Valeria's not back yet. I'm going down to the Cheshire Cheese. Tom may have arrived by now, and I'm hoping going over it all with him will give me some ideas."

Daisy quickly finished the last paragraph and gave him her work, for which he was properly grateful. "My best to Sergeant Tring," she said as he turned to go. "Will you be back later?"

"I can't be sure. It depends on what I hear about George Brown. If I'm not off chasing him, do you think tomorrow morning would be a good time to catch Lady Valeria?"

"She won't go anywhere before church," she assured him, "and she's not the sort to get up only just in time for the service. Gregg told me breakfast is served at eight thirty on Sundays."

"Perhaps she'll be feeling pious and ready to confess," he said hopefully.

Alec left. Daisy returned to her article on Occles Hall. It was coming along nicely when Moody entered, still even stiffer than usual with outrage over her laughter, to call her to the telephone.

"What-ho, old thing." Phillip was on the line. "I say, I wondered if you'd care to go to the pictures tonight. They're showing *Robin Hood* in Whitbury. Douglas Fairbanks, don't you know. He's usually a pretty reliable chappie."

"I'd love to, Phil, but it would look awfully as if I'm abandoning a sinking ship."

"Come on, you're abandoning them on Monday anyway."

"True. And I am pretty keen on Douglas Fairbanks. I'll tell you what, it won't look so mouldy if I invite Sebastian to go with us. Ben's not well enough."

"And a bally good thing, too. I mean, I'm sorry he's ill and all that, but dash it, Daisy, you know how little space there is in the old bus."

"I don't mind squeezing into the dickey. It's not going to snow, is it?"

"Shouldn't think so. The clouds are just about gone. Fearfully cold later, I expect. We'll go to the early show, if you can be ready in time, old thing. Better borrow a few rugs."

"Then I'll definitely have to invite Sebastian. One simply can't just nab people's rugs like that."

He agreed, and they arranged the time. Daisy went to find Sebastian, who was delighted with the idea.

"Ben has taken a bromide and gone to bed," he said. "With any luck we'll get away before the mater comes home."

"I hope so. Will you warn Moody we shan't be in to dinner? And round up some rugs, or we'll freeze. I want to finish my article."

She enjoyed the evening thoroughly. It was fun having two handsome escorts, even though one was a childhood friend and the other preferred men to women. Douglas Fairbanks was at his swashbuckling best. They bought fish and chips afterwards and ate it out of the newspaper, Phillip and Daisy laughing at Sebastian's pleasure in the vulgar, forbidden treat.

It was nearly half past nine when the hardworking Swift carried them up the drive of Occles Hall. They rounded a bend to see red tail-lights ahead of them.

"By Jove," said Sebastian, "that's not the Daimler. It's a bit late for the Chief Inspector to call, isn't it? No, *by Jove,* it's the Morris! Bobbie's come home!"

The red lights disappeared towards the stables. Phillip drove on to the front door. Sebastian extricated his long legs from the front seat, helped Daisy scramble from the cramped dickey seat, and invited Phillip to come in for a drink.

"No," said Daisy firmly. "Your mother's probably already primed to explode because you went out, and on top of that Bobbie has returned. An outsider—another outsider—is the last thing Lady Valeria will want. You realize this means Bobbie didn't clear out because of Grace? Phillip, go and tell Mr. Fletcher at once."

"Righty-ho," said Phillip, obliging as always.

Their arms full of rugs, Daisy and Sebastian went into the house. "Do we tell the mater about Bobbie?" Sebastian asked anxiously, as they dumped the rugs on a chair in the Long Hall. "She'll be a few minutes putting the car away."

"It depends how noble you feel. Telling her at once will probably deflect her annoyance from you; or we could wait here until Bobbie joins us and beard the lioness together; or we can go in and let her expend some of her energy on your minor offence—and mine, I suppose—before Bobbie has to face her with a real shocker."

"All right, let's go in." Sebastian squared his shoulders

and strode towards the drawing room, spoiling the effect at the last moment by saying plaintively, "We don't have to tell her about the fish and chips, do we?"

He submitted to his scolding like a little boy. As Daisy might have expected, Lady Valeria's wrath was focussed not on the straying lamb but on the one who had led him astray. However, Sebastian deflected her vituperation by breaking in with an account of the film.

Sir Reginald said quietly and wistfully to Daisy, "Thank you, my dear Miss Dalrymple, for giving the boy a bit of fun."

Sebastian didn't have to enthuse over *Robin Hood* for long. Bobbie came in, square and solid in a motoring costume, looking tired but excited.

And behind her came the long-haired poet.

"Mummy, this is Ferdinand Wilkinson," she announced. "Dodo, old pippin, my mother, Lady Valeria, and that's Daddy, and my brother Sebastian, and Daisy Dalrymple. You remember, I told you about Daisy."

Mr. Wilkinson favoured the assembled company with a gentle smile and bowed slightly to Lady Valeria. "How do you do," he said. "I'm happy to meet Roberta's family, and any friend of hers is a friend of mine."

His sentiments were perfectly proper, his voice well bred, well modulated though not noticeably poetical. Lady Valeria only noticed his use of her daughter's Christian name.

"Roberta?" she said icily, looking him up and down from unkempt head to scuffed toe by way of maroon-patterned fawn Fair Isle pullover and shabby plus-fours. She turned to Bobbie. "Just *who* is Mr. Wilkinson?"

"His people have a place in Derbyshire. I met him last summer when I took the Guides hiking in the Peak District. We hit it off right . . ."

"And *what* is Mr. Wilkinson?" Lady Valeria's tone dripped contempt.

"Dodo's a poet, Mummy. Don't worry, not the soppy, sentimental kind, all drooping damsels. He's written a beautiful poem to me as Boadicea, the warrior queen!" Too starry-eyed to care for her mother's purpling face, she took Mr. Wilkinson's hand. "We're going to be married."

"And *how* do you propose to live?" Lady Valeria triumphantly played her ace. "You needn't look to me to support you."

"Bobo has found a job," said Mr. Wilkinson, gazing fondly at his fiancée, apparently oblivious of the bombshell about to burst over their heads.

For once, Lady Valeria was too flabbergasted to emit more than a squeak.

"That's why we went away," Bobbie hastened to explain. "It was a sudden chance I couldn't bear to miss. There was an advert in *Town and Country,* Daisy's magazine, for a games mistress at a girls' school near Cheltenham. Not Cheltenham Ladies' College, a smaller place. Waybrook, it's called."

"Never heard of it!"

Bobbie ploughed on. "The advert was in *The Times,* too, so I knew the job hadn't been taken. They needed someone urgently—the last games mistress dropped dead on the hockey field—and they offered a cottage on the school grounds, so I rang up. They asked me to go right away for an interview and they've hired me! Isn't it spiffing? To start as soon as possible. I couldn't tell anyone where I was going because I knew Mummy would have forty fits."

"Impertinence!" Lady Valeria's fuse went from fizzle to flare and detonated the delayed explosion. "A job! My daughter working like any shoddy shopgirl! Like a tawdry typist." She turned on Daisy and howled, "This is *all your fault.* Weaselling your way into a happy household with your monstrous modern manners, driving a daughter to disobey her mother and marry a penniless poet. . . ."

"Admirable alliteration," said Mr. Wilkinson, not quite *sotto voce.*

His mother-in-law to be glared at him, but Daisy intervened before Lady Valeria could begin to dissect his morals, his habits, his dress, his prospects, and his family tree.

"You flatter me, Lady Valeria," she said sweetly. "No daughter of so strong-minded a mother could possibly possess such a weak character as to let me drive her where she didn't want to go."

"Don't tell me you didn't encourage her to rebel with your independence piffle!"

"If I did, it was only by example." Daisy tried to recall just what she had said to Bobbie. More sympathy than encouragement, she thought, but she didn't want to explain that to Lady Valeria. "I hadn't the foggiest Bobbie was looking for a job. Actually, when I saw she'd been reading *Town and Country,* I rather hoped she was admiring my article. . . ."

"Your article! You don't imagine I shall let you publish whatever rubbish you have been scribbling about Occles Hall, I hope!"

"Occles Hall belongs to Daddy," Bobbie pointed out, speaking over her father's shoulder. Sir Reginald was simultaneously kissing her cheek and shaking Mr. Wilkinson's hand, after which Lady Valeria was going to find it difficult to complain that the poet hadn't asked his permission to marry his daughter.

"Good-night all," said Sir Reginald, looking round with a vague smile, and he drifted out of the room.

In the momentary hiatus while his deserted wife glowered after him, Sebastian asked casually, "I say, old girl, wish you happy and all that, and have you eaten?" A sparkle in his deep blue eyes, he seemed to find the situation frightfully amusing.

Bobbie grinned at him. "Yes, thanks, Bastie, we stopped on the way."

"Jolly good. Congratulations, my dear fellow," he said as, following his father's example, he shook Mr. Wilkinson's hand, "you've already learnt the importance of keeping my sister well fed. Care for a brandy, or a spot of Scotch? Or shall I send Moody down to the cellar for a bottle of the bubbly, old dear?"

"No, poor old Moody's feet will be killing him by this time of night. Since Daddy's already gone to bed, let's save the bubbly for tomorrow lunchtime."

"Champagne!" Lady Valeria snorted. "This is no time for celebration, Sebastian. Your sister has had a brain-storm."

"By Jove, Mater, that's a bit strong!"

"Brought on, I don't doubt, by the distress of finding her family under investigation by Miss Dalrymple's friend Ferret from Scotland Yard."

"Scotland Yard?" gasped Bobbie. "What on earth are you blethering about, Mummy?"

"I don't *blether,* Roberta. We shall discuss the matter in the morning, by which time I trust you will have come to your senses. Good-night, Sebastian."

Her son dutifully kissed her cheek and, ignoring the other three she swept out. Abandoning the fight, Daisy wondered, or retreating to regroup her forces? Either was uncharacteristic. Lady Valeria wasn't mellowing; were events beginning to overwhelm her?

Sebastian dropped into the nearest chair and burst out laughing. "Boadicea!" he crowed. "That's rich."

"Don't be silly, Bastie. Daisy, what's this about Scotland Yard?"

Before Daisy could answer, Mr. Wilkinson said pensively, "You're right, not Boadicea. That ode will have to go. Atalanta, she's the one. A sonnet, perhaps. Golden apples . . . sunlight dapples . . . Or free verse? Hush!"

"Isn't he top-hole, Daisy?" Bobbie whispered. "Who was Atalanta?"

"I think she was a beautiful girl who kept winning foot races. I must say he seems to be quite soppy and sentimental about you."

Bobbie blushed. "Usually he writes about steel mills and

coal mines and things. Frightfully modern. Men earning a living by the sweat of their brow and that sort of stuff."

"He doesn't mind living by the sweat of your brow?" Daisy asked, then hoped she didn't sound critical when she was only curious.

"Oh, he's had a book of poems published which brings in a few pounds. You wouldn't recognize his name; he writes as Fred Wilkes. They've asked him to teach an English Lit class at Waybrook, too. It looks good in the prospectus, having a published poet on the staff. So we'll do quite well. Daisy, what's this rot about a friend of yours from Scotland Yard?"

"You didn't know? He arrived the evening before you left, and Mr. Wilkinson actually breakfasted in the same room, though he did look as if he was in the throes of composition at the time."

"He wouldn't have noticed, then. This Ferret chap's here about Grace? But they arrested Owen Morgan."

"Fletcher," said Daisy severely. "Detective Chief Inspector Fletcher." She explained the situation. "So, you see, your clearing out like that looked frightfully fishy."

Bobbie roared with laughter. Sebastian, who had been teasing the oblivious Mr. Wilkinson with rhymes like *pies* for *prize, dinner* for *winner,* and *grapple* for *apple,* came over to join them. "What's the joke?" he asked.

"Daisy's Chief Inspector thinking I must have bashed poor Grace because I hopped it at the wrong moment."

"It's not really funny, Bobbie. I mean, I'm glad you've come back so he'll stop suspecting you, but now things look even grimmer for the mater."

"For Mummy?" said Bobbie, bewildered.

"She had the same motive as you, and then there's the way she loses her temper, and the worst of it is, she won't talk to Fletcher."

"Oh blast! It's no use trying to persuade her to be reasonable." An awful thought struck her. "Bastie, you don't think . . . ?"

Sebastian shrugged his shoulders helplessly. "I don't know. I just don't know."

"What can we *do?*"

"All you can do," said Daisy, "is tell Mr. Fletcher the truth and hope it was George Brown."

"George Brown is in Carlisle," Alec informed Tom Tring when the Yard at last telephoned with the news from the Clover Corset Company.

"Hundred and thirty, hundred and forty miles, Chief, if it's an inch," said the sergeant, who had come from London equipped with a map. "And you know what them Lake District roads'll be like, after the winter."

"Between your weight and the pot-holes, my springs wouldn't stand a chance. Fortunately, Brown's finished in the far north and he's driving down to Lancaster in the morning."

"Not more'n seventy or eighty." Tring's mustache quivered with satisfaction. "Nice and flat all the way."

"All the same, Tom, I'm going to leave you here to have a shot at the Occles Hall servants. Ernie's done a good job but he hasn't your experience nor your way of getting around people. We'll drive up to the Hall first thing in the morning, and see if we can shock her ladyship into cooperating. Then, unless she confesses on the spot, Ernie and I will go on up to Lancaster. Come on, I'll buy you a pint to console you."

"Ta, Chief, but later. I think I'll go have a natter with Mr. Chiver there. Landlords often see more'n they think they c'n remember, and likely he's the sort I c'n get around better nor you."

"Very likely." Laughing, Alec watched his vast sergeant cross the bar-parlour with his peculiarly soft tread and start a cosy chat with the innkeeper.

However, by the time they moved to the dining room for dinner, Tring was none the wiser. Afterwards he elected to join Piper in the public bar to try his luck there. Thus Alec, nursing a whisky in the bar-parlour, was surrounded by locals friendly and hostile when Phillip Petrie burst in.

"I say, Fletcher, have I got news for you!" Every head swung towards him. "Daisy asked me to tell you. . . ."

"Not here, old chap!" Forestalling the revelation in the nick of time, Alec took Petrie's arm and led him out to the lobby, followed by gazes burning with curiosity. He pulled the door to. "What's up?"

"Gosh, I nearly blurted it out in front of the plebs. Sorry to be such a chump. Brace up, Fletcher, Miss Parslow's back!"

"Miss Parslow? Dammit, there goes another perfectly good suspect."

Petrie turned out to know no more than that the Morris Oxford had returned to Occles Hall. Alec decided it was too late to do anything about it that night. Tomorrow he'd see Miss Parslow first and hope that, witting or unwitting, she'd give him further ammunition against Lady Valeria.

In the morning, frost flowers bloomed on the bedroom window, sparkling in the rays of the rising sun. After breakfast—Mrs. Chiver delighted with Tom Tring's appetite—the three men motored up to the Hall.

Alec sent his officers straight round to the servants' entrance. He'd have preferred to have Piper take notes and Tring add his massive presence to the weight of the law, but he had promised to keep Goodman and Parslow's relationship from them if possible.

When Moody opened the front door to him, he asked to see Daisy. He wanted to get what information she had about Miss Parslow's absence before he tackled the young lady.

Muttering dourly about Sunday being a day of rest, the butler showed Alec to the Red Saloon. Daisy came in a few minutes later, carrying a cup of tea.

"Did I interrupt your breakfast?" he asked. "Sorry."

"No, I'd just finished except for my second cup, unless it's my third, I'm not sure. You're not going to interview Lady Valeria in here, are you? Talk about showing a red flag to a

bull, and there's that picture, too, to put bloodthirsty notions
into her head!"

Alec looked around at the burgundy walls and the gory
battle scene. He grimaced. "I don't know that it'll make
much difference. If you ask me, the difficulty's going to be
getting her to see me at all."

16

"Daisy, do you mind taking notes for me this morning?"

"*Mind!* Don't be an ass. Are you actually asking me to?" She could hardly believe it, after all the rot he talked about her meddling. "You want me to protect you against Lady Valeria?"

"Don't *you* be an ass," Alec retorted. "Because of young Parslow and Goodman. I did say I'd try to keep it hushed up."

"Oh yes. But you won't need to break it to Bobbie, will you? She has no idea, and I told Sebastian that though confession might be good for his soul, she'd be happier kept in ignorance."

"I'll see what I can do. No promises, it depends on how cooperative she is. Don't you think she's bound to find out sooner or later, anyway?"

"No," said Daisy smugly. "For one thing, she won't be living here much longer."

Heaving a sigh, he asked resignedly, "All right, what have you done?"

"I can't really take the credit—or, from her mother's point of view, the blame—but my brilliant career convinced Bobbie that working for a living isn't the end of the world. She's already found a job, and what's more, she's getting married. You remember the rather Bohemian chap at the Cheshire Cheese?"

"I do indeed. I was just wondering whether to send out a police bulletin on him when Petrie told me Miss Parslow was back. Come on, give me the dope."

She told Bobbie's story, leaving the poet's inspiration till last. Alec laughed. "Boadicea or Atalanta, I can't wait to meet your friend," he said. "From what I've seen and heard of Wilkinson, the arrival of the Met may well have passed right over his head." He rang the bell.

While Moody came and went, Daisy seated herself at the desk with the notebook and pencils Alec had brought for her. Bobbie came in, rather more Boadicea than Atalanta despite her Sunday flowered blue silk. She marched up to Alec and shook his hand.

"Glad to meet you, Mr. Fletcher," she said gruffly. "Daisy's been telling me about you."

Daisy almost laughed at the look on Alec's face. This wasn't how a suspect was supposed to behave. Bobbie did utter a snort of laughter as she sat down in a chair facing the fire.

"Don't worry, only what a jolly good detective you are. I'm fearfully sorry about buzzing off like that but I thought the police had holed out. I didn't realize the local laddies had come a cropper. If I'd known the ball was in Scotland Yard's court, I'd have gone anyway, but I might have let you know the score first," she added candidly.

"Miss Dalrymple has explained your absence to me," Alec said dryly. "We need not go over that again. She'll be taking notes for me, incidentally."

"Jolly good. Daisy's frightfully clever, isn't she? All this writing stuff. I suppose you want to know what I was doing the night Grace disappeared."

"We'll start a bit earlier, Miss Parslow, with your brother's affair with Grace."

"I didn't know about it, not until he told me. I'm not aw-fully good at noticing that sort of thing," said Bobbie apologetically. "Besides, being five years older I tend to think of him as my little brother. I hadn't even realized he was interested in girls."

Daisy studiously avoided Alec's eye.

"I see. Go on."

"Well, it was pretty obvious poor Bastie was like a cat on hot bricks. Even I could see that. I asked him what was wrong, and he told me Grace was pregnant and insisted on marrying him. You could have knocked me down with a feather. I told him I'd take care of things and he wasn't to worry."

"You would get rid of Grace for him."

"If you mean murder her, I might have, for Bastie," said Bobbie aggressively, "but it didn't even cross my mind. The girl couldn't force him to the altar. He was scared to death of Mummy finding out, so I told him to use his own money to pay Grace off. I even offered to be go-between because he didn't want to see Grace. Then Mummy came in and accused me of ragging him. Well, I didn't care for that. Just let it wash over me. Bastie wouldn't stand for it, though. He told her everything, and after that I left it to her to sort things out, till. . . ." She hesitated.

Alec pounced. "Till?"

"Till that night. The night before she and Bastie left for Antibes. Bastie was still in a tizzy. Grace had told him Stan Moss was going to make her sue for breach of promise, and Mummy didn't seem to have done anything. When she announced they were leaving a week early, I thought she'd decided it would all blow over. With Moss involved, I knew it wouldn't. So I tackled her after dinner and we had a row."

"What time?"

"Tennish, I suppose. She'd been in the library with Ben. Daddy had just gone up to bed."

"What did she tell you?"

"She said she'd made arrangements, everything was settled, and I wasn't to stick my oar in."

"She didn't tell you what her arrangements were?"

"No. Mummy never explains anything."

"You didn't make a guess at what she had done—or intended to do?"

"I certainly didn't imagine she was going to hit Grace on the head! Mummy can be a pain in the neck but she's not a murderer."

"Yet you said you yourself might contemplate murder in defense of your brother." Alec was relentless. "You consider Lady Valeria less dedicated to his welfare?"

Glancing up, Daisy saw Bobbie's square, ruddy face pale. "No," she said uneasily, then burst out, "but murder! I mean, it's not playing the game, is it?"

She looked appealingly at Daisy, who hurriedly returned to her shorthand, afraid Alec might suspect her of interfering.

"All right, Miss Parslow," he said, "excluding murder, for the moment, weren't you surprised your mother didn't at least dismiss Grace?"

"Yes, I was rather. I suppose at least she controlled her to some degree while she was employed here. It upset Bastie, of course, her being here, but then they were going away anyway. I thought Stan Moss couldn't do much while Bastie was gone, so I'd leave things till he came back and see if it really was settled."

"How long did your argument with Lady Valeria last?"

Bobbie shrugged her shoulders. "A few minutes. Five or ten. It's pointless arguing with Mummy, I should have known better. She always knows best, and as I said, she never explains anything."

"What did you do after that?"

"Well, I was pretty fed up, so I went for a walk."

Daisy silently groaned. Not only had Bobbie no alibi, she actually admitted being out and about at the time when Grace had probably met her end.

"In which direction?" Alec asked with apparent casualness.

"Down past the dairy and across the fields towards Fox

Green. There are lots of footpaths and not too many trees, so it's easy to see your way at night. There was a bit of moon shining between the clouds now and then, and I took a pocket-torch, too."

"You didn't go anywhere near the village?"

"Fox Green?" Bobbie sounded puzzled. "No. It's a tiny place, just a few houses around a village green, and anyway I wanted exercise, not company."

"I meant Occleswich." He sighed. "I hoped you might have seen something useful. What time did you get home?"

"I heard the church clock strike midnight just as I reached the house."

"You didn't go anywhere near the Winter Garden?"

"No, I came up past the dairy, the way I went. Golly, is that when Grace was killed? Or buried?"

"We don't know, Miss Parslow. After two months it's difficult to be certain of anything."

"I suppose so. Jolly hard lines for you," Bobbie said sympathetically.

Alec asked her a few more questions, then said, "Thank you for your help, Miss Parslow. May I be permitted to congratulate you on your job and to wish you every happiness?"

She beamed at him. "Thank you, Mr. Fletcher, that's jolly decent of you. Do you want to see my fiancé next?"

"He wasn't in the area on December 13th?"

"No, he was at home in Derbyshire."

"We may have to check on that, but I doubt it. I must see Lady Valeria now. Do you know whereabouts in the house she is?"

"She's usually in the library between breakfast and church. She was brought up reading sermons on Sundays and the habit stuck. On the way down to church she tells us all about the absolute idiots who have managed to get their sermons published. Shall I tell her you want to see her?"

"Thank you, no. We'll go to her."

"Rather you than me," said Bobbie cheerfully, and departed.

"You don't think she did it," said Daisy, collecting up her notebook and pencils.

"No. Not that I'm sure she's incapable of it, but she's not devious enough to try to put me off the scent by freely admitting to rambling about the countryside at the relevant time."

"I don't think Bobbie rambles. She hikes. I suppose she's still on your list of suspects, even though you believe her."

" 'You know my methods, Watson.' " He followed her out of the room. "This is your last chance to back out of facing the dragon, Daisy."

"I'm not afraid of Lady Valeria. If she objects, which she will, will you let me explain why I'm there rather than another policeman? She'll think me impertinent, but you'd sound threatening, which would only set her back up."

"All right, though I expect her back will already be as high as it can go!" Alec opened the library door.

Lady Valeria sat in a Windsor chair by the window, a sombre figure in navy blue, frowning down at the book in her lap. She transferred the frown to Daisy and Alec as they entered. "Well, Miss Dalrymple?" she said coldly.

"You remember Detective Chief Inspector Fletcher, Lady Valeria. He has a few questions to ask you."

"I've heard that before and my answer is the same. I shan't dignify your iniquitous inquisition with a response, Fritter."

"That is, of course, your right, ma'am," said Alec, ignoring her massacre of his name, "but in view of what I have learned since we last spoke, I shall have to ask you to accompany me to a police station." It was sheer bluff. He had no more against her—motive and opportunity—than Dunnett had against Morgan.

"What you have learned! And just what have you learned with your underhanded enquiries?"

The bluff had worked, at least in part. She was no longer

trying to dismiss him out of hand. "I ask questions, Lady Valeria," he said. "I don't answer them."

Weakening, she turned on Daisy. "You may be a prying police person masquerading as a guest, Miss Dalrymple, or vice versa, but I have nothing to say which is any conceivable business of yours."

"At present, Lady Valeria, I'm masquerading as a police stenographer." Her voice was admirably calm. "Mr. *Fletcher* needs a record of the interview. His constable can easily be summoned, but we assumed you'd prefer someone who already knows all there is to know about Sebastian."

Her ladyship's brick red complexion faded. "All?" she croaked.

"All," said Daisy inexorably.

"I see no need to make anything public," said Alec, doing his best to sound conciliatory. He couldn't help feeling sorry for the woman and, more important, he hoped she'd stop regarding him as a demon. Caution made him add, "So far, that is. My officers are very discreet, but the fewer people who know. . . ."

"Sit down, sit down, my good man," she interrupted with forced impatience, neatly forestalling the words he hadn't been going to pronounce. "I can't be craning my neck at you. I don't know what you think you've discovered. I admit my son had an affair with the scheming slut and made her pregnant, but young men will sow their wild oats."

Already scribbling in shorthand, Daisy slipped away and sat down at the long library table. Lady Valeria ignored her.

Despite her denial, it was obvious she suspected her son's inclination and had hoped the girl's pregnancy disproved it. Alec decided nothing was to be gained by asking whether she had encouraged Grace to seduce Parslow. He'd try for essentials before she rebelled.

"Mr. Parslow told you he had promised, under threat, to marry Grace. You promised him—in his words—to 'deal with Grace.' What did you have in mind?"

"Naturally my first thought was to give her the sack. Unfortunately I was unable to force her to leave the district, besides which she made it clear her father would go to the Press if she was dismissed. I assume, since you spoke of threats, you are aware that Moss claimed he'd bring an action for breach of promise if Sebastian failed to marry his daughter."

"Claimed?"

"He wanted money, of course. That's all the lower classes care about."

"It has been suggested he was more interested in making trouble," Alec said dryly.

"Oh, I don't doubt he'd have been glad to see the heir to Occles Hall married to a promiscuous parlourmaid, or to drag the matter through the courts. The man's a spiteful savage. But I know these people. I knew I could buy him off."

Alec was fascinated by her apparently unconscious gift for alliterative invective. "You offered Grace money?" he asked.

"I offered to pay her a substantial sum to go away. The treacherous trollop accepted my offer and then came back and told me her father wasn't satisfied. That was when I decided to take Sebastian away without notice. Not only would a change of scene do him good; by the time we returned, Grace's condition would be showing and they'd be willing to settle for considerably less."

Her logic seemed questionable, but he let it go. "Grace didn't know you were leaving on December 14th?"

"She must have been listening at the door when I instructed Mr. Goodman to telephone Cook's to change the bookings. At least, so I imagined when I heard she had run away with a commercial traveller."

"When was that?"

"I can't give you a date. Roberta wrote to Sebastian when we were in Antibes. She wasn't yet lost to all family feeling."

"Yet you told Mr. Goodman before you left to dismiss Grace if she showed up again."

"Certainly. She had proved herself unreliable. One cannot have servants failing to return on time after an evening out. It's a bad example to the rest. Besides, I assumed news of our departure persuaded her she had wrecked her chances of getting anything out of me." Lady Valeria's tone of caustic satisfaction was convincing.

"You weren't surprised she hadn't made a last effort to wring money from you once she learnt you were off?"

"One can't expect logic of domestic servants. I was glad to have the problem solved so easily."

"By death," said Alec flatly.

"My good man, *I* didn't know she was dead," she snapped.

"Someone did."

"None of my family!"

"That remains to be seen." Perhaps the reminder would induce her to continue to cooperate. "Tell me what you were doing the evening of the 13th."

"How can I possibly remember at two months' remove!"

"Others have. It was the night before you left for France. You packed your bags?"

"My maid did. I will say this for Gregg, she knows what to pack without my standing over her every minute. I was in the library after dinner, giving Mr. Goodman his orders. Then I went to the drawing room. I suppose it was about ten o'clock as I was just in time to wish Sir Reginald good-night and that is the hour he generally retires. Yes, ten o'clock."

"Who else was in the drawing room?"

"My daughter, Roberta. Yes, I recall asking her where her brother was and she ripped out at me in the most extraordinary way. Roberta has an unfortunate tendency to belligerence, to feeling she knows best, which I have done my best to eradicate."

A muffled snort came from Daisy's direction. Alec pretended he hadn't heard, but Lady Valeria turned her head to freeze the offender with an arctic stare. Daisy, her head bent over her notebook, didn't even notice.

"How long did your . . . er . . . discussion with Miss Parslow last, Lady Valeria?" Alec said hastily.

"Discussion! I simply told her not to meddle as I had everything in hand. A minute or two, no more."

Whether she or Miss Parslow was more accurate as to timing, the quarrel gave neither an alibi. "And then?" he asked.

"I stayed in the drawing room, reading I believe, until I went up to bed, at what time I haven't the least idea."

"You saw no one?"

"No one, as far as I recall. Modern servants consider themselves put upon if one expects them to work after dinner. It's hard enough to find and keep them anyway. Oh, after I went up to my room, Sebastian came in to . . . to say good-night."

Alec saw no need to pursue the real reason for Parslow's visit to his mother's room. Both Lady Valeria and her daughter had had all the time in the world to lie in wait for Grace, to murder her with or without prior argument, and to bury her body in the soft earth of the flowerbed. Neither would be missed in this rabbit-warren of a house, with the servants in their quarters and the family going their own ways. Her ladyship might have had to go outside again to finish the job, after showing a presence in her bedroom at a suitable hour, but that was no hindrance to making a case.

Both had better motives than Owen Morgan, who was indisputably grief-stricken by Grace's death. However, a sizable hole Daisy had pointed out in the case against Morgan applied equally to the two women: surely either must have realized the body would be found when the garden bloomed, if not before.

"Well," snapped Lady Valeria, "are you finished, Flincher? I must go and get ready for church."

"I have no more questions for the present, ma'am, but I must warn you that tomorrow, if the case remains unsolved, I shall be turning it back to the local police. I shall strongly advise Superintendent Higginbotham to put a man in charge who is less easily intimidated than Inspector Dunnett. Whoever he appoints will receive the reports of *everything* I have discovered."

Lady Valeria quivered, an impressive sight whether caused by rage or dismay. "Everything?"

"Everything," Alec confirmed. "If you have anything further to say, you may tell me now or contact my sergeant either at the Cheshire Cheese or in your servants' quarters."

"Still pestering my servants!" she roared, face purpling as she surged to her feet. "Barbaric bully! I have nothing further to say." She cast a seething glance at Daisy as she stormed out of the library.

"She can't very well wring my neck in church," said Daisy hopefully. "Thank heaven Phillip's coming to lunch. I shall make him stay all afternoon. And I'll hide in my room this evening and type this up for you. Blast, I want to talk to you, but I must go and get ready for church too."

"It's time I was leaving for Lancaster." Alec briefly explained about George Brown's circumambulations. "We may not be back till late, but Tom's around if you need him. Be careful, Daisy. It's all very well joking, but I made a mistake letting Lady Valeria know you know about her son."

"I shan't accept an invitation to go for a nice walk in the country with her," Daisy promised.

With that he had to be satisfied. After a word with Tring, who had of course been invited to Sunday lunch in the kitchen, he and Piper set off in the Austin for Lancaster.

It was a beautiful day for the open road in an open car, crisp but sunny. The unlovely industrial stretch between Warrington and Preston at least had tarmac-surfaced roads to compensate. They stopped at a roadside pub for lunch, and drove into Lancaster at a quarter to three.

The Lancashire police had been notified by the Yard of their coming so no explanations were needed when they checked in at county headquarters. Alec asked the way to

Caton, the village where George Brown had said he would spend the night.

A few minutes later they pulled up before The Crook o' Lune Inn. The traveller had not yet arrived. Leaving Piper to hold the fort, Alec strolled along to view the actual Crook o' Lune, the bend in the river immortalized—according to the landlady—by Turner. No doubt it was lovely with leaves on the trees and the bluebells which, she informed him, carpeted the banks in May.

Brown at last turned up as the last light faded from the sky. In his mid-thirties, about Alec's age, he was good-looking in a rather smarmy way but with a pudginess which suggested coming corpulence. When the landlady pointed him out, Alec pulled in his stomach and vowed to get more exercise.

Piper in tow, Alec approached him as he reached the foot of the stairs. "George Brown? Of the Clover. . . ."

"Have a heart, old chap." His voice was Cockney overlaid with refinement. "No need to broadcast it to the world. What can I do you for?"

Alec flashed his identification. "Scotland Yard. We'd like a word with you, sir."

A hunted look entered Brown's face and for a moment he appeared to see a parade of past sins crossing before his eyes. Yet he sounded more puzzled than alarmed when he said, "You'd better come up to my room, Chief Inspector."

His driving coat tossed on the bed, Brown perched beside it. Alec sat on the room's only chair and Piper stood by the door, notebook and pencil at the ready.

"You stayed at the Cheshire Cheese in Occleswich on December 13th last, sir?" Alec asked.

"December? That'll be in last year's book. I don't—The Cheshire Cheese?" He paled. "Lumme Charlie, it's that girl. Is that what it is, guv'nor? The one the gardener killed?"

"Grace Moss. You were seen talking to her in the bar-parlour and she was thought to have run away with you."

"Grace, that's it. I remembered it was some religious name, not the Bible, Prudence or Patience or that." The Cockney underlay became more pronounced. "Read about it in the paper, didn't I, and I said to meself, that's the one that didn't come back, that is."

"Didn't come back?"

"Thought she'd run off with me, did they? That's a laugh. Not that I didn't try, mind. I'll be straight with you, guv'nor. I gave her the usual stuff, you know, friend in the moving picture business, she was just the type they wanted. Then she told me she 'ad a bun in the oven and. . . ." His voice trailed away.

"And you told her you knew a doctor who could help her."

"That's what I said, guv, but I don't, honest." His incipient double chin wobbled in panic. "It was just a come-on, see. She wasn't no spring chicken, twenty if she was a day, old enough to know the score. I thought we'd 'ave a bit of fun for a couple of days, then I'd pay 'er train 'ome to Mum if that's what she wanted. I'm not short a few bob. But she went off to get 'er things and she never came back. So I scarpered, didn't I. For all I knew, 'er Dad or 'er bruvver was out after me blood."

"You scarpered? At what time?"

"Closing time. She said she'd be gone ten minutes, so after 'alf an hour there wasn't much point sticking around. To tell the truth, I was 'aving second thoughts about 'er being knocked up, too. Picked up me bags and I was going to drive straight through to London. That's where I was 'eading, see. But I'd 'ad a couple, see, and I passed a place wiv lights still on so I stopped for the night."

"Where?"

"Cor lumme, guv'nor, I don't 'ave last year's book on me!"

"Think, man!"

Breathing heavily, Brown closed his eyes in thought, then opened them in inspiration. "I've got a map in the bus, guv."

Alec sent Piper down with him to find the map. His story rang true. Where women were concerned, the man was an unprincipled cad but not a murderer. He must have tried his "come-on" on countless discontented village maidens and weathered countless refusals. He'd have an alibi.

Something he'd said. . . .

Brown burst into the room waving his map. "I've remembered, Chief Inspector." The acquired accent was back in place. "Newport, the Royal Victoria Hotel. Not the kind of place that takes my fancy, but any port in a storm, what? I was just in time. They had some sort of do on so they didn't lock up till midnight. You'll find my signature in the register."

Piper unfolded the map and checked the distance from Occleswich to Newport. "Around thirty miles, Chief."

Thirty miles. Brown had left Occleswich at, say, twenty to eleven, and arrived in Newport shortly before midnight. Starting out along narrow, unfamiliar country lanes, once on the high road he'd drive with caution after the whisky he'd imbibed.

Even if he'd zipped along like the very devil, he'd not have had time to murder and bury Grace.

Frustrated, Alec said, "We'll check with the Royal Victoria, of course, Mr. Brown. What did Grace tell you that evening of her situation? What sort of spirits was she in?"

But the traveller recalled nothing more about Grace, not even the colour of her hair. As Alec suspected, she was one of dozens of pretty girls in dozens of country inns, pursued with varying degrees of success. All Alec could do was issue a warning about enticing minors away from home with false promises.

Brown was no more helpful in other directions. He hadn't particularly noted the other men in the bar-parlour. By the time he'd fetched his bags, started his motor, and driven out to the street, no one was about. "That's one of the things I like about putting up in small villages, Chief Inspector. Noth-

ing to keep a chap up late, barring a willing chambermaid."
He winked. "So I get an early start. That's the way to get
ahead in business."

Alec sighed, thanked him, and asked him to telephone his
whereabouts daily to the Chester police. The two detectives
took to the road again.

"If his alibi's good he's in the clear, isn't he, Chief?" Piper
asked.

"Yes," Alec grunted, peering ahead through the blurry
glass, "but now we know Grace actually did intend to
leave . . . Dammit, I can't see a thing. Our breath is freezing
on the windscreen. I'll have to open it." He pulled to the side
of the road.

With nightfall the temperature had plummeted and driving
conditions were atrocious. Alec had no attention to spare for
considering the significance of Grace's planned departure
from Occleswich. Slowed by icy patches on the roads, and
stopping for dinner halfway, they arrived back late and tired
at the Cheshire Cheese.

Alec told Tom Tring about the interview with George
Brown.

"Looks like he's out of it, then, Chief?" the sergeant rum-
bled. "Must admit I wondered where he'd've got ahold of
that windingsheet without the landlady kicking up a dust."

"The sheet! Great Scott, I'd forgotten it. The doctor's report mentioned it and the photographs showed it, but Dunnett's report ignored it, though that's no excuse for me."

Tom tactfully refrained from agreeing. "Mrs. Twitchell,
the housekeeper, swears none of her sheets is missing, and
she'd know. The head gardener, Bligh, showed me Morgan's,
all patches and darns, and swears they're all accounted for.
'Course, it don't knock anyone out for sure, and I don't 'spect
Dunnett kept the sheet but. . . ."

"But I bloody well shouldn't have missed it! So where . . .
Stan Moss! No one checking his sheets, and there's something else. . . . Hell, I'm too tired to think but I must see

him in the morning even if we have to chase him all over the county."

"Off to beddy-byes, Chief, and you too, young'un." Tom herded them upstairs.

"All right," said Alec, "but wake us early."

Sinking into bed, he was asleep within seconds. He woke in the small hours with two facts ringing in his brain.

First: Grace had kept only her parlourmaid's uniforms at the Hall. Second: she had promised Brown to return with her things in ten minutes. What a complete, fatuous fathead he was not to have realized she went from the inn to the smithy, not the Hall!

Stan Moss needed his daughter—as long as she turned over her pay, cooked and cleaned for him, and complied with his plot against Lady Valeria. But Grace had planned to run away. . . .

Even enlightenment failed to keep Alec awake, but a plan was ready in his head by morning. Over a hurried breakfast, he explained his reasoning to the others.

"So, although I'm not quite ready to let Brown or Lady Valeria off the hook," he finished, "everything points to Moss."

"Whew!" Piper heaved a sigh of relief, then blushed as Alec and Tom stared. "You see, Chief, the last thing you said last night was you got to see Moss, and I couldn't go to sleep for thinking of the way he's never there. So I got up and I went to Mr. Petrie's room and for all he weren't pleased to be woke up he listened. He's a real gent, he is. Anyways, he told me how to disable Moss's lorry without doing any real damage and so's it'd take a whiles to work out what's wrong, so off I went and done it."

"Against all the rules," Alec reproached him, grinning. "Well done, Ernie."

"How?" asked Tom.

"Mr. Petrie made me promise not to tell, Sergeant," Piper said virtuously.

"All right," said Alec, "since you're now a motor expert, Ernie, you'll take the Austin and check Brown's alibi. If it's no good, phone the Yard at once and have him stopped, then come back here. Tom, you and I will tackle Moss, but I'll have a go at him alone first. Routine enquiries—with luck he won't get the wind up and he may drop his guard. I want a confession, whether from him or from her ladyship. We still have no real evidence. You telephone Chester and ask them to have a police vehicle standing by. I don't want it coming yet, I may be wrong and I don't want to look a total chump. Oh, and while you're about it, tell 'em to let Morgan go. Phone from Rudge's station, and bring him along to the smithy about fifteen minutes after I go up there."

"Right, Chief," acknowledged Tring and the disappointed Piper.

Alec walked up the deserted street. Market day in Whitbury, the landlady had said. The shop was open, though, and unwisely he went in for tobacco. Mr. Taylor, his wife gone a-marketing like the rest, drew him into a chat from which he had great difficulty extricating himself without offence. He had to stop at the police station next door to tell Tom he'd been delayed.

As Alec approached the smithy, from the rear came a rumble of curses. He bit back a smile. Rounding the forge he saw the hefty blacksmith crouched by his battered lorry, siphoning petrol from the tank. The air was full of the stinking fumes.

Moss was an expert mechanic indeed to have worked out already what was wrong. Alec was only just in time.

"Fletcher, Scotland Yard. We've met. I have a few more routine questions to ask you about your daughter."

The man froze, not even looking round. "What?" he growled.

"How much money did you hope to extort from Lady Valeria by threatening a breach of promise suit?"

"Money!" He turned his head and spat. "All I wanted were a bit o' paper saying I c'd put in a petrol pump."

"Without Grace you hadn't a hope even of that, did you?"

Silence.

"You said you came home late the night she disappeared. What time, and where had you been?"

"What business is that o' yourn? It's a free country."

"Where were you, and what time did you get home?" Alec persisted.

"I were over to the Dog and Bone, in Whitbury," the blacksmith said sullenly. "Dunno the time. Don't have a watch, do I."

"Never mind what o'clock, then. You arrived just as your daughter. . . ."

With an inarticulate roar, Moss swung round, rising to his full height. Though not tall, he was built on the lines of a gorilla.

"Yes, I killed the little bitch!" he bellowed. "Going to leave me, she were, like her bitch of a mother. But you won't hang me!" He grabbed a rusty axle from the nearest heap of scrap metal and hurled himself at Alec, aiming a vicious swipe.

Alec sprang backwards. His foot hit a patch of oil and he staggered, arms flailing helplessly. The axle swept down.

17

"Good heavens," said Daisy, waving the letter that had arrived by the early post. "Mother's come through for once."

"Come through?" Bobbie asked. "I say, Dodo, don't hog
the toast, you brute. Bastie, is that the marmalade lurking
by your elbow?"

"No, plum jam."

Daisy passed the marmalade. "She says her gardener's
about ready to retire and she'll employ Owen Morgan. Isn't
it spiffing? Sir Reginald promised to give him a good reference. I'd better go and phone Mr. Fletcher to see when he'll
be released."

"Ask him when *we'll* be released," said Sebastian.

"I will," she promised.

As she went to the telephone she had a brilliant idea. She
and Phillip could take Owen to Worcestershire on their way
to London—well, not quite on their way, but with a bit of a
detour. Owen wasn't large and wouldn't mind squeezing into
the dickey. She could stay the night at the Dower House,
which would please Mother, and Phillip could go over to
Malvern to spend a night with his family.

Mrs. Chiver answered the Cheshire Cheese telephone.

"Chief Inspector Fletcher, please," Daisy requested.

"He's just this minute stepped out, miss," said the landlady.
"Going to the smithy, I heard him say. Shall I call him back?"

"No, thanks. I'll meet him there." Surely among all that

rubbish there must be a spot from which she could observe the interview with Stan Moss without being seen, if she hurried.

Luckily, she was wearing a warm tweed costume and country shoes. Not stopping for a coat, she sped from the house and down the path towards the village. As she passed the Winter Garden, she wondered for the hundredth time who could have been such an idiot as to hide a body where it would so certainly be discovered.

For the first time she found an answer: someone whose garden was paved over and grew nothing but rusty metal.

No—Stan Moss couldn't have killed his own daughter! It was unthinkable, unbearable. And even the blacksmith, a countryman however mechanically minded, must be aware that without careful replanting the excavated soil would grow no flowers.

Of course he knew, Daisy realized with horror. That was what he wanted. He loathed Lady Valeria, and what could cause his enemy more trouble than the discovery of a murdered servant buried in her garden?

She couldn't bear to believe the murder was premeditated. It was almost as bad, though, to cynically make use of his daughter's body after hitting out at her in a burst of violent anger. Sebastian had expressed surprise that Moss and his mother had never come to blows; Bobbie had said he had a filthy temper; Daisy herself had heard him threaten Owen.

And Alec was on his way to ask questions which could not help but arouse that temper.

Daisy ran. Even when she remembered he'd have Tom Tring with him, she went on running. Down the path, through the wicket, across the lane, panting round the end of the ramshackle cottage. . . .

As she reached the corner, she heard a wordless roar. A thick voice she recognized from the inquest shouted, "Yes, I killed the little bitch! Going to leave me, she were, like her bitch of a mother. But you won't hang me!"

Slowing just enough to seize a bent starting-handle, she dashed on. The blacksmith's bludgeon was already descending on Alec when she hit him over the head.

Moss toppled like a felled tree and lay still.

Alec was on his back, eyes closed, face white, groaning, clutching his left shoulder with his right hand.

Daisy dropped the starting-handle and fell to her knees beside him. "Alec," she whispered, "I think I've killed him."

"Better him than me, my avenging angel." He struggled to sit up, his arm dangling limply. She helped him. "I think I'm going to be sick," he said in a strangled voice.

"You can't!" she wailed, laying hands simultaneously on his clammy forehead and her own. "I am. Oh, Alec, does it hurt dreadfully?"

"As a matter of fact, no," he said, sounding surprised. "My arm's numb all the way from shoulder to fingertips. I just feel absolutely like death."

"Shock." At last she remembered what she'd learnt working in the hospital during the War. Pulling herself together, she cleared the bits of scrap he'd fallen on. Thank goodness his soft hat had stayed on and protected the back of his head. "You must lie down again, and try to keep that arm still, even if it doesn't hurt. I'm afraid it will soon."

He let her lower him onto the paving again, with his folded felt hat as a pillow. "Daisy, it would have been my head if you hadn't arrived." He gripped her hand.

"And *you* told *me* to take elementary precautions! We must keep you warm." Gently she disengaged herself, took off her jacket, and draped it over him, then restored her hand to his clasp. "I rang up the inn and Mrs. Chiver said you had come here. I just wanted to try to hear the interview, but on the way down everything suddenly came together. I realized how dangerous he was, so I ran to warn you. Alec, I ought to feel his pulse and try to stop the bleeding."

"If he's bleeding badly, he's not dead yet."

"I don't know. I haven't looked, but I hit him a terrific whack. I'd better. . . ."

To her profound relief, Phillip loped around the corner of the forge, followed by a sound like a galloping carthorse which turned out to be Tom Tring and Constable Rudge, both puffing.

Phillip stopped and stared at the scene, wild-eyed. He was unshaven, his blond hair stood up in tufts, his waistcoat was buttoned wrong, and he hadn't fastened his collar, let alone put on a tie. "Good gad, Daisy," he cried. "What's going on?"

Daisy burst into tears. "Stan Moss tried to kill Alec and I think I've killed him."

"Here, I say, old dear, no need for that." He felt in his pocket for a handkerchief which wasn't there. "Fletcher appears to be alive, if not well, and if you've bumped off the other chap, well, he's a rotter and deserves it."

"Hear, hear!" Alec agreed.

"He killed Grace," Daisy sobbed. "His own daughter. I heard him say so."

"Well, he'll dangle for it, miss," said Sergeant Tring, on his knees beside the blacksmith, "being as how you haven't saved the hangman the trouble. Coming round, he is, and going to start creating any minute. Good job I brought me bracelets. Here, Mr. Petrie, give miss me hankercher, and I'll trouble you for yours, Rudge, to bind up chummie's head. You're not going to kick the bucket, Chief?"

"Not yet, Tom." Alec raised his head but at once laid it down again, wincing. "Petrie, it's going to take two men to handle Moss, I expect. Would you mind going down to the police station and phoning Chester for me?" His voice faded.

As Daisy anxiously bent over him, Tring took charge. "Ask for Superintendent Higginbotham, sir. He's got a car standing by. Tell him we'll want an ambulance and a doctor, too."

"Righty-ho," said Phillip.

"And take Miss Dalrymple with you," said Alec weakly.

"No! I'm not leaving you till the doctor comes."

"Send the wife up, miss," said Rudge. "She's done a bit o' nursing. Tell her what's happened."

"Please, Daisy," Alec begged. "I don't want you here when Moss comes round. I promise I shan't shuffle off this mortal coil in your absence."

"All right, but I'll come back with Mrs. Rudge."

Alec and Phillip exchanged a look.

"No, you won't, Daisy," said Phillip with unwonted firmness. "Come on."

He helped her up and, with an equally firm grip on her arm, removed her from the battleground.

"Honestly, Daisy," he said reproachfully as they walked down the deserted street, "it's frightfully infra dig getting mixed up in a brawl like that."

"Infra dig be blowed! I suppose you think I should have let Moss kill Alec?"

"By George, no, but I could have stopped him if you'd just waited till I arrived."

She realized his pride was hurt. "You came too late," she pointed out, "but I was jolly glad to see you. What on earth brought you to the smithy?"

"Mrs. Chiver was worried when you told her you were going there, especially with the police on their way. I was drinking my tea in bed when she told me."

Daisy looked at him and grinned. "I bet you've never been out in public in such disarray in your life."

He glanced down at himself, raised a hand to his open collar. "I was in a hurry," he said self-consciously. "Come to that, you're not so spruce yourself. No coat, no hat, and your hair is all over the place."

"I'm cold." Shivering, she hugged herself, suddenly exhausted.

Daisy was glad to sit in the Rudges' cosy parlour with a cup of strong, hot, over-sweetened tea, while Phillip phoned and Mrs. Rudge bustled off with blankets, bandages, and a scarf for a sling. She didn't even protest much when Phillip insisted on driving her up to the Hall, though she made him promise he'd go straight back to the smithy to make sure nothing dreadful had happened.

"I'll pick you up at two," he said as he pulled up in the tunnel by the front door. "We won't get to town till late but you should be feeling better by then."

With a struggle, she dragged her mind from Alec's white face and Moss's still form. "Do you know, I'd forgotten we're leaving today. Phil, could we possibly go home for a night on the way?"

"Of course, my dear old thing." He regarded her anxiously. "You'll want to see your mater after such a fearful shock."

"It's nothing to do with Mother. Or, at least, only that she's going to hire Owen Morgan. We can take him in the dickey."

"Dash it, Daisy. . . ."

"Thank you, Phil dear." She stretched up to kiss his cheek and escaped into the house.

Moody met her in the Long Hall. "Miss Roberta's been asking after you, miss," he said sourly. "She's in the morning room."

Daisy's entrance into the morning room created a sensation. Bobbie rushed towards her. "Daisy, where on earth have you been? You went to make a telephone call and next thing we knew Moody said you'd rushed out of the house without a coat or hat or anything. And now you haven't even got your jacket!"

"I had to put it over Alec, to keep him warm." She started shaking and clapped a hand to her mouth as the ghastly nausea swept over her again.

"Oh blast! Come and sit down, you're white as a sheet." Bobbie's arm was around her, supporting her. "There, put your head between your knees. Thanks, Ben."

Ben had dumped an arrangement of honesty and Chinese lanterns and rushed the empty bowl to Daisy. For an awful moment she thought she was going to need it, to disgrace herself in public. Then her head stopped swimming. She took a couple of deep breaths and her pulse steadied beneath Bobbie's fingertips. The Girl Guides' first-aid course would come in handy for a games mistress, she thought irrelevantly.

"I'm all right now," she said, sitting up. Sebastian thrust a glass of brandy into her hand and she smiled shakily at him. "Thanks. Sorry to be such a drip."

"Oh bosh, don't be a chump," said Bobbie. "Golly, though, we're all simply dying to know what's happened, if you feel well enough to tell us."

She sipped the brandy and its fire drove away the last of the chill. "Yes, of course I'll tell you. I suppose it's quite exciting, really, but at the time it was perfectly beastly." Shuddering, she swallowed another sip.

They all sat down, Bobbie and Mr. Wilkinson on a sofa, holding hands, Sebastian and Ben circumspectly on widely separated chairs. Daisy felt a flash of pity for all the hiding they had done and all they had yet to do. At least Ben looked quite recovered after spending Sunday in bed.

"Go ahead," Bobbie urged eagerly.

She told them the story, from ringing up the Cheshire Cheese to Mrs. Rudge's departure with aid and comfort for the injured. The horror dissipated as she turned it into words, though she was sure frightful memories would return to haunt her sooner or later. "Phillip wouldn't let me go back to the smithy," she finished, "so I don't know what happened next."

"By Jove," Sebastian said admiringly, "you're a regular heroine."

"A thoroughly capable heroine," said Ben.

Daisy blushed. "Oh no, not really. There just wasn't anything else to do."

"You could have fainted before instead of afterwards," Bobbie pointed out, "or have been too squeamish to biff him hard enough. I can see Dodo's already composing a poem in your honour."

Her fiancé was indeed lost in a world of his own, though there was no way to be sure he was composing a paean to

Daisy. It would be rather fun, she thought, as long as it was the kind of poetry she could understand. Fortunately Bobbie didn't seem jealous.

"I hope you'll send me a copy," she said diplomatically.

"You must come and visit us. There's a spare room in the cottage." Bobbie's healthily pink face turned red with emotion. "If it wasn't for you, Daisy, I'd never have got up the nerve. . . ."

"Oh, that reminds me. I didn't have a chance to ask Mr. Fletcher what put him onto Moss, but since he confessed, I'm sure you're all free to leave. Though perhaps you'd better wait for official notification from Mr. Fletcher," she added, recalling disagreements as to who was suspect and who was not. Then she wondered whether Alec was too badly hurt to notify anyone of anything. "Or from Sergeant Tring," she said unhappily.

As if he'd read her mind, Ben said at once, "I'm sure someone will let you know as soon as a doctor has seen the Chief Inspector."

"Yes, of course, Tring will, or Phillip. Phillip's coming to fetch me at two so I'd better go and pack." Yes, she'd pack, but if Alec had to stay in hospital she'd have Phil take her to a hotel nearby. She did her best to smile. "I'm so very glad, for all of you, that it turned out to be Stan Moss."

Wearily Daisy went up to her room, to find that Gregg—on instructions from Lady Valeria—had already packed her bags. She took off her shoes and lay down on top of the counterpane. The next thing she knew was Bobbie gently shaking her shoulder.

"Daisy, it's lunchtime. Do you want it on a tray? I looked in earlier but you were out for the count. Mr. Petrie rang to say Mr. Fletcher's arm and shoulder are just badly bruised."

"Thank heaven!" Swinging her legs over the edge of the bed, Daisy leaned down to put on her shoes and hide the tears in her eyes. "Oh Bobbie, I was so afraid he might be crippled for life."

"Jolly good news, isn't it?" Bobbie moved on to her own concerns. "Mr. Petrie didn't know anything about official permission to leave, but he said he'd find out before he comes for you. We're all hoping to follow you down the drive. Bastie went down to the dairy to tell Daddy and he's going to tell Mummy at lunch. Rather short notice, but who can blame the poor pet? Are you all right? I'd better go and brush my hair."

Though almost all Daisy's hairpins had come out, she managed to find enough to make a reasonable job of her coiffure. Should she have accepted Bobbie's offer of a tray in her room? Lunch was bound to be an uncomfortable meal. Nonetheless, she hurried down, sharing as she did with Kipling's Elephant's Child the curse of " 'satiable curtiosity."

Or perhaps it was a gift, after all. Without it, Alec might be lying dead.

When she reached the dining room, Sebastian was just finishing telling his parents the tale of Stan Moss's confession. Lady Valeria's obvious relief changed to a look of malevolence as Daisy entered.

"So, Miss Dalrymple, it was all a storm in a teacup," she said, taking her place at the head of the table. "You and your Inspector Flincher making a mountain out of a molehill. I hope you're satisfied with all the distress you've caused for nothing."

"Hardly for nothing, Lady Valeria," Daisy retorted as Moody and the dithery parlourmaid served the soup. "Without the investigation, Chief Inspector Fletcher would not have come to suspect Moss and he might have got away with it. Besides, clearing Owen Morgan was as important as anything."

"Morgan! I trust he doesn't expect to return to Occles Hall after being incarcerated for murder."

"Now, my dear," Sir Reginald protested, "that's hardly fair to the poor lad."

"Don't worry, Sir Reginald," said Daisy blandly. "I've persuaded my mother to hire him."

"Maud Dalrymple always was a namby-pamby nonentity," snorted Lady Valeria.

"Oh, I say, Mater," Sebastian objected.

Smiling at him, Daisy shook her head. To Lady Valeria, most of the world consisted of easily steamrollered nonentities so it was pointless to be offended. Besides, Daisy was leaving Occles Hall in less than an hour and for Sebastian's sake she didn't want his mother to come to a boil before he even disclosed his plans.

Lady Valeria would blow her safety-valve then, without fail. Was Sebastian capable of standing firm and emerging uncrushed?

For the moment he held his tongue while her ladyship congratulated herself at length on being able to rid Occleswich of its eyesore at last. In passing, she squashed Mr. Wilkinson when he ventured to suggest that to ban a petrol station was to stand in the way of progress and to compromise England's industrial might. The poet's subsequent abstraction was accompanied by a gleam in his eye which made Daisy decide to beg for a copy of his forthcoming verse on his mother-in-law.

Sebastian waited until Lady Valeria was temporarily silenced by a mouthful of roly-poly pudding and custard. "Since Chief Inspector Fletcher's investigation is finished," he said, "we're all presumably free to go."

"Dodo and I are ready to leave the moment we get official word," said Bobbie in loyal support.

Lady Valeria swallowed her mouthful. *"I* have not considered myself bound by Fetter's preposterous demands. Did you want to go up to town for a day or two, Sebastian? I'll check my calendar. I expect I can fit it in."

"No, Mater," Sebastian said gently. "Ben and I are going to Greece."

Unfortunately, his mother's mouth was full again. She choked and turned purple, her eyes bulging—though actually, Daisy thought, she didn't look very different from when she was in a rage. However, her son thumped her on the back and pushed a glass of water into her hand. She gasped for breath.

"Don't be silly, Sebastian," she said, recovering. "I told you I'd take you to Corfu next winter. Perhaps we could manage it this spring since you're so keen."

"Sorry, Mater, it's not a holiday on Corfu I'm keen on. Ben and I are going to live in Greece. We'll go up to London as soon as the Chief Inspector gives the word. It will take a few days to see my solicitor and make arrangements, and then we're off, train to Marseilles, ship to Piraeus."

Lady Valeria forced a laugh. "What a child you are, dear boy, with your impractical daydreams. I suppose you imagine life will be one long holiday."

"That's what it is at home! I want to try some serious archaeology—and Ben will never have to survive another English winter. We can live cheaply there; I have enough for both of us."

She turned on Ben, spitting out the words. "You scheming sponger! Of course this is your idea, taking advantage of a naïve. . . ."

"Not at all," said Daisy sharply. "It was my suggestion. If you think about it, you'll see it solves a great many problems."

Lady Valeria gaped at her. Daisy was about to excuse herself to go and put on her coat when Moody came in and announced, "Detective Chief Inspector Fletcher is here, my lady."

Bobbie jumped up. "Good-oh! Come on, Dodo. Excuse us, Mummy."

She dashed out, followed by her fiancé, Sebastian, Daisy, and Ben. Alec, his arm in a sling, was in the Long Hall, sitting on one of the chairs with painfully knobby carved backs. To Daisy he looked awfully pale.

As Bobbie rushed up to him, he stood up with a slight smile. "Miss Parslow, Mr. Parslow, Mr. Goodman, I've no doubt you've heard the whole story. I came to tell you Moss has been arrested for his daughter's murder."

"Topping!" said Bobbie. "Daisy said he'd more or less confessed."

"Yes, and he's done a bit more ranting. Grace went home and told him she was going to London. The fury which made him strike her seems to have been chiefly because her departure would ruin his chances of forcing Lady Valeria to let him put up a petrol pump."

"How frightful!" said Daisy with a shudder. "He was obsessed."

"So was the mater," Sebastian said soberly.

"In its way, a classical tragedy," Ben observed.

Mr. Wilkinson was inspired. "I shall write a verse play!" he cried.

"Right-oh," said Bobbie with a fond glance. "I take it we may leave, Mr. Fletcher?"

"You're all at liberty to go where you will, with my apologies for intruding in your lives."

Bobbie promptly invited him to call in at the school cottage if he was in the neighborhood. Sebastian shook his good hand.

"You did rather put me through the wringer," he said, "but no hard feelings. Has Daisy told you Ben and I are following her advice and going to live in Greece?"

"So that's it! I knew she was up to something." Alec sighed and shook his head at Daisy, his lips twitching. "Miss Dalrymple has a finger in every pie."

"Fortunately for the rest of us," said Ben, grinning.

"I just try to help," she said with dignity. "Alec . . . Mr. Fletcher," she amended as Lady Valeria and Sir Reginald appeared, "are you all right? Will your arm be all right?"

"A week or two in a sling, then gradually decreasing agony for a few weeks. That's just from the weight of the axle. If he'd actually hit me on the head. . . . Well, they say he probably used something considerably lighter on poor Grace, yet she ended up dead."

"Don't!" Daisy shivered, suddenly very anxious to get away from Occles Hall. "Phillip didn't arrive with you?" she asked, reaching for the coat, hat, gloves, and scarf she'd left on a nearby chair.

Sebastian helped her into her coat as Alec said, "No, Petrie drove Morgan over to the gardener's cottage to fetch his belongings. They'll be here any moment."

Daisy embarked upon farewells and thanks and wishes for happiness, Lady Valeria responding to her coolly polite goodbye with a tight-lipped snort. Everyone accompanied her and Alec to the little room by the front door, which was piled high with luggage.

The doorbell pealed. Sebastian opened the door and there was Phillip. Moody appeared, looking almost cheerful, to help him carry out Daisy's traps. Daisy decided the butler was anticipating a life of ease for his aching feet with everyone gone.

A last round of goodbyes, then they were outside and the massive door began to close behind them. Daisy heard Bobbie say, "Come on, Dodo, time to pack our toothbrushes."

"Us, too, Ben," said Sebastian.

"Reginald, stop them!" Lady Valeria's voice was harsh, but Daisy, glancing back, saw her white, desperate face and for the first time pitied her.

"It's time I was getting back to the dairy, my dear," said Sir Reginald vaguely.

The door thudded shut. Daisy breathed a sigh of relief.

In the dim light under the tunnel, Owen huddled in the Swift's dickey, half submerged beneath tripod, camera, typewriter, and his own meagre possessions. The poor chap seemed to be in a bit of a daze. Outside, beyond the moat, Tring and Piper waited in Alec's Austin.

Phillip opened the passenger-side door of his motor-car. He was dashed relieved to be getting Daisy away from Occles Hall, even though, as it turned out, none of its inhabitants was a murderer:

Daisy pulled her hat down more securely and tied the scarf over it and beneath her chin. "I'm glad I'm going to see Mother one last time before I bob my hair," she said, climbing into the Swift.

"You're going to do it?" Phillip was horrified. "I wish you wouldn't."

"For heaven's sake, Phil, it was you who said. . . . Alec, what do you think? Don't you think it'll suit me?"

"I shouldn't dream of jumping to a conclusion without evidence," said the detective. "I'll wait till I see it."

"See it!" Phillip exclaimed in dismay. It was all very well palling around with a policeman here in the middle of nowhere, but never say the bally copper intended to pursue her in town!

"I shall be calling on Miss Dalrymple in London," said Fletcher smoothly, but Phillip had a nasty feeling he was amused. "To bring her news of the case, of course. She'll be a witness, I'm afraid."

"Oh, spiffing!" Daisy cried. "A real trial, not just. . . ."

The door opened and they all turned. Sir Reginald emerged, a large, round, paper-wrapped object in his arms. "I nearly forgot," he said apologetically, "I promised you a cheese, Miss Dalrymple. Good-bye, my dear, and thank you for all you've done."

Phillip reluctantly relieved him of his burden and he pottered off through the tunnel towards his dairy. Depositing the cheese on Morgan's lap, Phillip slithered in behind the wheel and reached for the self-starter.

Fletcher, his good hand holding on to the top of the windscreen, leaned down. "Petrie, you'll be getting a letter of thanks from the Met," he said. Well, he really wasn't such a bad chap, after all. "And you, Miss Dalrymple, will receive an official citation for bravery. And an unofficial warning against. . . ."

"I know," said Daisy, grinning up at him in a confoundedly intimate way. "Against meddling!"

Please turn the page
for an exciting sneak peek
of Carola Dunn's
next Daisy Dalrymple mystery
REQUIEM FOR A MEZZO

* * *

The sponge cake came out looking quite edible, success enough to satisfy Daisy considering it was her first attempt. The black bit round the edge of the bottom could easily be scraped off and she would fill the dip in the top with jam. Leaving it to cool on a rack, she took the *Requiem* tickets and went out to Lucy's photographic studio in the back garden.

Practically overnight, the forsythia had burst into bloom, a fountain of gold against the mellow red brick of the converted mews. Daisy wished some clever inventor would hurry up and invent a simple and satisfactory colour photography process.

The small studio was as usual cluttered with cameras, tripods, backdrops, and props. The desk in the corner was piled high with photos and bills, paid and unpaid, beneath which the appointment book undoubtedly lurked. Lucy was talking about having a telephone put in; she'd probably use it to hang up the black cloth she draped over her head when she shot portraits. How anyone who invariably emerged from beneath the black cloth without a hair out of place could stand the mess had puzzled Daisy for years.

"Lucy?"

"I'm in the darkroom, darling. I'll be out in a jiffy."

"Right-oh." Daisy sat down at the desk and began in a desultory way to sort out the jumble. She helped out in Lucy's business when things were particularly busy so she knew pretty much what was what.

Among the heaps, she came across a photo of Bettina and her husband. Roger Abernathy, standing behind his seated wife, gazed down upon her with a smile so fatuously adoring it made Daisy snort with disgust. Too sickening! Some men simply couldn't see past a head of golden curls, or perhaps, in this case, a golden voice. She buried the photo at the bottom of a pile.

The papers were all neatly stacked by the time Lucy emerged. She had already taken off her white darkroom coat and combed her dark bob. No chemical stains had been permitted to yellow her fingers to match her amber eyes. Tall and sleek, she wouldn't have been caught dead in last year's calf-length hems, though her budget was as limited as Daisy's; she made her own clothes and spent on materials and trimmings the equivalent of what Daisy put into books and gramophone records. Daisy's best hat, from Selfridge's Bargain Basement, always made her shudder.

"Angel!" she said as she caught sight of her tidy desk. "You shouldn't have."

"I jolly well couldn't bear looking at it while I waited."

"Then you know how I feel looking at your hair. The best birthday present you can give me is to have it bobbed."

"I'll think about it."

"Come on, Daisy, you've been havering for months."

Daisy sighed. "All right, I'll do it. Tomorrow morning. I've invited Muriel for tea—I hope you don't mind."

"Muriel? Oh, that poor prune next door. Why on earth . . . ?"

"I had to borrow some flour for your cake, and then she offered two concert tickets for your birthday."

"A concert!" Lucy groaned. "You didn't go and tell her I'd be thrilled?"

"No, darling, I said I didn't know about you but *I'd* be

thrilled, so she gave them to me. You needn't think I'll try to make you go with me."

"You'd better invite Phillip."

"Phillip! He'd accept because he thought I needed an escort, and like you he'd be bored to tears. There's nothing worse than going to a concert with someone who's bored. It's impossible to enjoy it. No, I'm going to ask Alec Fletcher."

"Oh Daisy, not your tame policeman! He'll be as bored as Phillip and not gentleman enough to hide it."

"A fat lot you know. You haven't even met him yet. Alec is a perfect gentleman, and what's more, he likes good music. He invited me to a concert at the Queen's Hall, but it was last week while I was in Suffolk doing the research for the third *Town and Country* article."

"But really, darling, a bobby! Too, too *déclassé,* even if he is a Detective Chief Inspector. A policeman simply cannot be quite . . . well, quite. And when Phillip's dying to marry you!"

"He's not dying to marry me, he simply feels duty-bound to take care of me because of Gervaise," Daisy said crossly. Her brother, Phillip Petrie's closest chum, had been killed in the Great War and she didn't appreciate the reminder every time she had this argument with Lucy. "Just because you think Binkie's blood-lines are reason enough to encourage him although he's a complete fathead . . ."

"Phillip's not the brightest star in the firmament," Lucy retorted.

"So why are you pushing me at him?"

Lucy sighed. "It's not so much pushing you at Phillip as trying to wean you from your 'tec. Lady Dalrymple would have forty fits if she knew you were seeing a common copper."

"Mother has forty fits whatever I do. She needs something to carp at. It's what keeps her going."

"True," Lucy said ruefully. "Well, I won't carp at you any

longer just now. I've got someone coming for a sitting—if you've unearthed my appointments book, you might look it up and tell me if they're due at quarter past or half past."

"Quarter past. I'll get out of your way. Don't despair, darling. Remember Alec's a widower who lives with his mother and daughter, both of whom may hate me on sight."

"No one ever hates you on sight, darling. They're more likely to pour their troubles into your ears as you step over the threshold."

Laughing, Daisy returned to the house. It was true people tended to confide in her, though she wasn't sure why. Alec, who had twice revealed to her more details of a current case than his superiors or he himself thought quite proper, muttered accusing reproaches about guileless blue eyes. She protested that her eyes were no more guileless—less guileful?—than anyone else's, and besides it made her sound like a halfwit.

Be that as it might, people told her things, and whatever Alec said, she had helped him solve both cases.

She was dying to ring him up about the concert, but she didn't want to disturb him at Scotland Yard. Didn't quite dare, actually. Detective Chief Inspector Fletcher could be quite formidable when annoyed.

It was a pity she and Lucy really couldn't afford to have a 'phone installed in the house. That evening, after an early supper of toasted cheese, Daisy nipped out to the telephone kiosk on the corner and asked the operator to put her through to Alec's home number.

A young girl's voice answered with a conscientious repetition of the number.

"This is Daisy Dalrymple. May I speak to Mr. Fletcher, please, if he's at home?"

"Gran, it's Miss Dalrymple!" The voice was muffled, as if the speaker had turned away from the mouthpiece. "You know, Daddy's friend. I can't remember, should I call her 'Honourable' or what?"

So Alec had talked about her at home. At least Belinda hadn't slammed the receiver into its hook on hearing her name.

"Miss Dalrymple." The girl sounded breathless now. "This is Belinda Fletcher speaking. Daddy . . . my father's just come home and gone upstairs. If you don't mind waiting just a minute, I'll run and fetch him."

Daisy contemplated the six minutes' worth of pennies lined up on the little shelf by the apparatus. "Could you ask him to ring me back right away, please? I'm in a public booth. If you have a pencil, here's the number."

"We always have a pencil and pad by the telephone in case there's an urgent message from Scotland Yard," Belinda said proudly. "Daddy says I'm very good at taking messages."

"I'm glad to hear it." Daisy read off the number. "Thank you, Miss Fletcher. I'm delighted to make your acquaintance, even if at a distance."

"Me too. I mean, I want awfully to meet you properly. I'll go and tell Daddy right away."

She rang off, leaving Daisy to wonder whether such enthusiasm wasn't worse than outright hostility. How on earth was she to live up to whatever exaggerated idea of her charms Belinda had got into her head?

Fortunately no one came to use the telephone booth before the bell shrilled. In fact, Alec rang back very quickly.

"Daisy! Don't tell me you've fallen over another dead body?"

"Certainly not. When I do, I'll 'phone up the Yard."

"I trust that won't be necessary. What's up?"

Daisy had sudden qualms. Among close friends in her set, it was perfectly acceptable for a girl to ask a man to escort her to an event if she was given free tickets, but perhaps middle-class mores were different. Could Lucy be right that it was a mistake for her to have made friends with Alec?

No, though he might laugh at her, he wouldn't think her

forward or pert or any of those ghastly Victorian notions. At least, not more forward or pert than he already considered her, and he seemed to like her anyway.

"I've got free tickets to the Albert Hall," she said tentatively. "On Sunday afternoon, three o'clock. Would you like to go with me?"

"What's on? A boxing match?" His grin came down the wire as clearly as if she could see it.

"Don't be a chump, it's a concert. Verdi's *Requiem*. My neighbour's singing the mezzo solo."

"I'd love to go, Daisy, and I'll do my utmost to keep the afternoon free, but though things are quietish at present you know I can't give you an absolute promise."

"I know, you might be called out to a murder in Northumberland. I'll keep the ticket for you. If you can't make it, I can always rope in Phillip at the last minute."

"I'll make it," Alec said grimly. He still wasn't convinced Phillip was no more to her than a childhood friend. "By hook or by crook."

"What an unsuitable phrase for a policeman!" Daisy teased. "Phillip'll be very relieved if you do. He'd hate it."

"I wouldn't want to be responsible for his agonies. May I take you out to dinner afterwards?"

"I'd like that, if you swear you won't leave for Northumberland between the soup and the fish."

"I swear. Even if it's John o' Groats I'm called to, I shan't desert you till after dessert. I'll pick you up at two."

"Spiffing." Daisy would have liked to go on chatting but if he had just come in from work he must be tired and hungry. Complimenting him on his daughter's telephone manners, she said cheerio.

On Sunday, Alec's small yellow Austin Seven, its hood raised against a wintry downpour, pulled up outside the house promptly at two. Daisy saw it from the window of the front parlour, where she was pretending to read *The Observer*. She dashed into the hall and jammed her emerald green cloche hat onto her head, tugging it down as far over her ears as she could, practically down to her nose. Then, in more leisurely fashion, she put on her green tweed coat.

The doorbell rang. She opened the door and Alec smiled at her from beneath a huge black, dripping umbrella.

"You're all ready to go?" he said, raising dark, impressive eyebrows. "No hurry, we've plenty of time."

"Yes. No." Flustered, she hoped he didn't think she wanted to avoid introducing him to Lucy, who was out anyway. "Come in a minute while I find my gloves. Shall I take an umbrella?"

"Mine is plenty big enough for two. And there's no wind, you don't need to pull your hat so low. I can scarcely see your face. Or is that the latest style?"

"No." In fact, now that he was close she couldn't see his face at all, nothing above the Royal Flying Corps tie in the open neck of his overcoat. She pushed the cloche up a bit. "Oh Alec, I had almost all my hair cut off—I promised Lucy—and it feels so peculiar and draughty. My ears feel positively *naked*. I don't know what you'll think. . . ."

"Nor do I, since I can't see a single lock. The hairdresser did leave you *some* hair, I trust?"

Bravely Daisy took off her hat and presented her shingled head for his examination.

"Hmm." Chin in hand he studied her, a twinkle in his eyes. "Just like Lady Caroline Lamb in the portrait by Phillips." Alec had studied history at university, specialising in the Georgian era.

"The one who chased Lord Byron? Didn't she go mad?" Daisy asked suspiciously.

"Yes, but she wrote a very successful book on the way, a scandalous *roman-à-clef*. On second thoughts, the chief similarity is the hair. Caro Lamb had short, honey brown curls like yours, but she had brown eyes, not blue, if I'm not mistaken. As for her expression of haughty wilfulness, only the wilful part applies to you."

"Mother would agree, but I'm not wilful, I'm independent."

"Same thing. No one could describe you as haughty, at least." He grinned. "And I don't suppose Caro Lamb ever had a single freckle on her nose, either."

"Blast, are they showing?" Whipping out her powder-puff, Daisy sped to the hall mirror and anxiously examined her roundish face. "No. You beast!" She dabbed a little extra powder on her nose anyway. "You haven't said if you like it, Alec."

He came up behind her and set his hands on her shoulders, gazing at her in the looking glass. "It's utterly enchanting," he said softly.

Daisy blushed, to her own extreme annoyance—too fearfully Victorian! "Here are my gloves, in my pocket," she said. "Let's go."

A few minutes later the massive rotunda of the Royal Albert Hall loomed before them through the rain. The huge auditorium had been planned by Prince Albert as the centrepiece of a corner of Kensington to be dedicated to the arts and sciences. Not completed until a decade after his death, it had for half a century been a major venue for everything from political and religious meetings to concerts and sports events. Colleges and museums clustered around it, and usually the streets were busy. However, it was a wet Sunday afternoon and they were early so Alec had no difficulty finding a place to leave the Austin quite close to the entrance.

In the lobby he bought a programme, and the usher directed them around the circular passage to the inner entrance nearest their seats.

The seats were perfect, neither too far from the stage nor too close, and a little above its level. Daisy could never understand why anyone would pay the premium prices to be in the front rows. All one could see was the conductor, the soloists, and the first ranks of violins and cellos, and just about all one could hear, too. That was where people sat who cared more for showing off their furs and hats than for the music. Not the place for her green tweed and the Selfridge's Bargain Basement cloche!

Behind her and Alec and to either side, and even behind the stage, the tiers of seats rose towards the distant glass dome, now a dingy grey. A full house was about eight thousand, someone had told her. At the moment the vast hall was thinly populated, but people were gradually filing in through the many doors around the circle.

"Good," said Alec, "there's a translation in the programme. My Latin isn't up to it, hasn't been for years."

Together they studied the words of the *Requiem*.

"Gosh, look at that," Daisy exclaimed, and read aloud, " '*Confutatis maledictis:* When the cursed all are banished, doomed to burn in bitter flames, summon me among the blessèd.' Talk about holier-than-thou!"

Alec laughed. "It is rather, isn't it? You have to consider it as opera. The story may be questionable but the music is divine. Listen to this. 'Day of wrath, day of terror, day of disaster and anguish, that great, hopeless, exceeding bitter day.' Just like one of those operas which ends with bodies strewn all over the stage."

"Ghastly! I'm not all that keen on opera."

"Nor am I."

They finished reading the programme as the orchestra players started to wander in. Odd notes, chords, and twiddles of melody arose in a tantalizing cacophony. A momentary silence fell as the leader came in and bowed to the audience, to a wave of applause. The first oboe sounded an A and the serious tuning of instruments began.

Daisy regarded the leader, Yakov Levich, with interest. A Russian Jew in exile, he was beginning to make a name for himself as a solo violinist—she had read a glowing review of his recent recital at the Wigmore Hall. Tall and almost painfully thin, he had curly black hair greying at the temples and a long, serious face with prominent cheekbones and a high-bridged nose.

An expectant hush fell as the choir filed in. Daisy turned her attention to picking out Muriel and pointing her out to Alec. She had more colour in her face than usual and the severe black of the choir uniform unexpectedly suited her. She opened her music score with a look of joyful anticipation. Obviously singing was one of the few pleasures in her life.

Eric Cochran appeared, baton in hand, his longish hair the only sign of Bohemian proclivity now he was clad in formal tails. He led in the soloists. First came the soprano, Consuela de la Costa, a voluptuous figure in crimson velvet cut dashingly low on the bosom.

"More appropriate to the opera than a requiem mass," Alec whispered.

"Perhaps she represents one of the temptations which lead the damned to Hell?" Daisy whispered back.

"Or the fiery furnace itself."

Behind Miss de la Costa, Bettina Westlea was a cool, slender beauty in blue satin with a more respectable neckline. Gilbert Gower, the tenor, came next. A handsome Welshman, he had been a staple of the English opera stage for years, never quite achieving the summit of the profession, but well respected. Next and last, the bass was another refugee from the Bolshevik Revolution. A Russian bear of a man with a full black beard, Dimitri Marchenko had as yet found only small rôles in England, chiefly in oratorio.

"I've heard him in the *Messiah,*" Daisy muttered to Alec. "His low notes have to be heard to be believed. 'Why do the nations . . .' " she hummed.

" '. . . so furiously rage together'? Most appropriate."

They settled back, clapping, as conductor and soloists bowed. Cochran raised his baton, brought it down with infinite delicacy. The pianissimo first notes of the *Requiem* murmured through the hall.

The music swept Daisy away. She forgot the grim words except to wonder at the brilliant way Verdi illustrated them. After the momentary annoyance of latecomers entering at the end of the *Kyrie,* the *Dies Irae* was gloriously terrifying. Marchenko's *Mors stupebit,* reaching down into the depths of the bass range, sent a shiver down Daisy's spine. Consuela de la Costa's voice was as vivid as her appearance. Mr. Abernathy had given Bettina whatever help she had needed and she sang the *Liber scriptus* with a thrilling intensity. Gower's clear tenor was a touch off-key in the *Quid sum miser,* but his *Ingemisco* was so beautiful it brought tears to Daisy's eyes.

The first half of the concert ended with a hushed "Amen" dying away into slow chords and silence. For a long moment Daisy, along with the rest of the audience, sat in a near trance before a roar of applause burst forth.

Soloists and conductor bowed and departed. The chorus began to file out.

"My hands hurt from clapping," Daisy said to Alec as they made their way out to the circular passage to stroll about during the interval.

"It was worthy of sore palms," Alec said, smiling. "Thank you once more for inviting me. I must write a note to your friend Miss Westlea, too."

"I'm glad you could come." She linked her arm through his, surely justifiable as the eddying crowd threatened to part them. "You do still mean to take me out to dinner, don't you?"

"Yes, I'm incommunicado as far as the Yard is concerned."

"Spiffing!" said Daisy.

"Hungry? There's the bar over there. Would you like a drink?" Alec asked. "I expect they have salted almonds or something else to nibble on."

"No, thanks, I'm not thirsty and I'll save my appetite."

"Did you notice Bettina Westlea had a glass under her chair she kept sipping at when she wasn't singing?"

"Her throat must get fearfully dry."

"The others managed without, not to mention the chorus. I wonder if that might annoy conductors enough to explain her lack of success. She has a lovely voice."

"I suspect she's just generally difficult to work with." Daisy decided not to describe Bettina's peevish self-importance in case it spoilt his pleasure in her singing.

They completed the circuit of the hall just as the bell sounded for the end of the interval. The second half began with a lengthy section for all four soloists. They sat down; the choir rose. Daisy glanced down at the programme: the *Sanctus* was next.

As she looked up again, she saw Bettina reach beneath her chair for her glass. Thirsty work, singing.

Bettina took a big gulp and choked. Her face turned bright red. With a strangled cry she sprang to her feet, the glass flying from her hand as she clutched her throat. Gasping, she doubled over, spun around in a grotesque parody of a ballerina's pirouette, and collapsed.

Her sprawling body writhed, jerked convulsively twice. For a moment heels drummed a desperate tattoo on the stage. Then the blue figure lay still.

ABOUT THE AUTHOR

Born and raised in England, Carola Dunn now lives in Eugene, Oregon. Her next Daisy Dalrymple mystery, THE BLOODY TOWER, will be published by Kensington Publishing in December 2008. You can visit her website at: www.geocities.com/Carola Dunn